I Wish.

A. L. Fox

GEMLALH

Contents

Content Warning

I wrote *I Wish.* as a way to get some feelings off of my chest without making the entire book about those feelings. The holiday season had been weighing heavily on my heart and my brain needed to vent without just... feeling like I was talking in circles to the same people (shoutout to my husband and mom). I wanted this book to feel fairly loaded—heavy. Not because I am a sadist, but also maybe I am? My beta readers would maybe agree with that labeling... I don't know. But I do know this:

This book, on page, talks about depression, anxiety and panic attacks, grief, death, cancer, alcoholism, parental abandonment, and therapy.

Briar is complex. This is not a "fun" or "light" read. This will not make you feel *good*... possibly at all. But it will more than likely make you *feel*.

And who doesn't love that?

I WISH.

If any of what I just mentioned is going to make you irreparably sad—make your brain unwell and your heart hurt beyond the standard "I like the pain" kind of thing, do not read this book, please. Your health is far more important.

I love you. You are good.

For anyone that has felt like maybe you're easy to leave...
I see you.

one

"AND HOW DOES THAT make you feel, Briar?"

"It doesn't. That's why I'm here twice a week."

I look up, finding Mark's eyes on me. His face is unreadable. I think that is probably a fairly standard characteristic of a therapist though. I'm not supposed to read him, he's paid to read me. We have a small staring contest. He's never very impressed with my lack of emotion, but then again, is he supposed to be?

It's not like it impresses me, either.

I sigh, giving him the win, and look around his office. On the fourth floor of a large building, the view out of his floor to ceiling window is pretty nice. Downtown Rapid City, South Dakota is busy this time of year. I watch a small white car sit in the same spot it's in every time I'm here, listening to the quiet tick of Mark's white faced clock that sits on his shiny black desk. The woodsy scent of whatever "calming" oil he has circulating through here fails at its job.

I run my thumb nail over the pad of my index finger, feeling the sharp pinch as I press harder than necessary.

Oh look, I can feel something.

I sigh again, really putting on the theatrics today.

"Briar, where did you go just now?"

Literally nowhere.

"I didn't go anywhere. That's the problem."

Mark sighs with me this time. "I can't help you here if you don't open up to me a bit." He shifts around, uncrossing his ankle from over his knee, on his large, brown leather chair. It squeaks as he sets his notepad on the round end table next to him, grabbing his bright white coffee mug that reads "#1 Shrink." I gave it to him for Christmas today when I got here.

He laughed. I faked mine.

None of my silence or sighing dramatics are in direct relation to Mark. He's great. He's kind and smart and gives great advice in the small moments that I *do* open up to him. But this year fucking sucked more than usual. So, after June I went from once a month with Mark, to twice a week. Now, for one hour eight times a month, I sit here in near silence and just feel... nothing. I give nothing. I think nothing.

"Can we discuss, perhaps, Aster?"

Well, that will certainly not help the whole "I need to feel something" situation. Any feelings associated with *that* topic have simply ceased to exist.

Flicking my eyes to his briefly I say a simple and flat, "No."

I turn my gaze to look back out the window. It's snowing now, large clusters of flakes filling the gray horizon. It wasn't when I got here so I really wish I would have put on more than my shitty, brown off brand Ugg boots. And I still need to go to *Fresh Family* for groceries.

I start to make a mental list of everything that I need when I see Mark get up and walk to his desk. He says nothing as he settles into the black swivel chair there. I watch as he clicks around on his laptop, listening to the printer *whir* to life and watch as he grabs a paper from it and walks towards me. He stops in front of me and drops to a squat.

At fifty-five, Mark's got this like, "cool guy" air to him. I don't think of him in any way outside of my therapist, that would be poor form, but I'm not numb enough to not notice that he is quite handsome. His dark brown hair sits cut close to his head, lots of little specks of bright white throughout. His thick eyebrows match and push towards each other above bright blue eyes. I watch the warm, dark skin on his face move as he takes a deep breath. He's roughly six feet when he's not looking at me from this viewpoint.

"Here is a list of recommendations for therapists in the area that I think you'll get along with."

I rear back, putting a hand over my chest. "You're breaking up with me?"

His face, already soft, gets even more so. "I don't know how else to try to get you to talk to me, Briar. I want you to get the help you need, the help you *deserve.* And maybe you're just too comfortable with me now. Too much so that we sit in silence. And if silence were what I thought you needed, I'd be more than content to charge you two hundred dollars to sit here and stare out the window. But Briar, the trauma you experienced this last year is something you need to discuss-"

"I don't know that I would classify," I swallow, "*that*... As a trauma. It didn't happen *to* me."

"And that's the problem, I think. You don't see that situation as something that happened *to* you. But it *is*. And it *did*. And as someone who has seen you for nearly a year now, who has heard about the inner workings of your brain and the things you went through thus far in life, I can confidently say that you need to discuss this entire thing with *someone,* Briar. Anyone. Literally at all. Because you're a talker when you find someone worthy of the words. And you haven't talked about Aster. Not to me at least. And you quite literally pay me for this. I'm here to listen. I can't do that if you don't talk though. So," Mark holds the paper out to me again, but I don't take it. "I think a new therapist might help."

"I don't want a new one," I say quietly.

"I don't really want you to have to go to a new one, but you need to work through this and you won't-"

"Okay," I almost yell. "I'll talk about," I swallow down this feeling of difficulty. "I'll talk about him. With you."

My brown eyes meet Mark's blue ones, and he gives me a small smile and nods. "I enjoy being your therapist, Briar. I do. I want to help you. Work with me here, okay?"

I nod. "Yes, okay."

He stands and folds the paper up before going to the garbage can by his desk and tossing it in.

"Was that you trying to play me into talking?" I stand from the couch.

Mark laughs and shakes his head. "No, Briar. Though I'm not surprised you'd ask that." His legs carry him to the thick brown door. "But today's time is up."

"I'll see you on Monday." I smile softly at him. "I like you as my shrink, Mark. I'll do the work."

"I know you will, kid. See you next week."

Four flights of stairs and one slippery sidewalk gets me to the driver side door of my gray Honda CR-V. I don't get in though, pausing by my car.

Aster.

I hear his voice. I see his smile. I feel his breath on the small part of my neck that he loved to press his nose to.

I close my eyes, squeezing them tightly and begging the feelings to stay away. I tilt my chin up, breathing deeply. The snow is cold on my face, and it makes my dark messy bun damp. Even so, I stay there. Face up to the light gray sky, pleading with my brain to stay quiet. Imploring the deep, nauseating pain to stay lost.

And even though I love the smell of winter—the icy, fresh air it breathes into me on any normal day during any other winter, I don't get lost in that today.

No, things are different now. *I'm* different now. The cold air only settles into the emptiness inside of me. Instead of filling it up though, it does nothing. It moves nothing. Makes me feel nothing.

I wish it made me feel.
Anything. Everything. Something.
I wish things were different.
I wish he was still here.
Hell, I wish *I* was still here.

two

"Sometimes it's okay if the only thing you did today was breathe." —*Yumi Sakugawa*

I CAN FAKE IT far better with my family and friends than I can with my shrink. And thank God for that. Because if my mom knew just how not-great I am handling things lately...

I shiver at the thought.

The Blue's, a restaurant we frequent, sits downtown, nestled between a candy shop and a bicycle repair shop. It's a hopping place on Thursday nights. Even in the dead of winter, with a brand new start of a year, when it's blowing snow and twelve degrees outside—she's busy. I unwrap my plaid scarf from my neck, the red bright even in this slightly-dimly lit building bright, folding it in half and resting it on the back of the chair my mom saved for me.

Right next to her. Where she always puts me.

I have one arm in my black jacket still when she stands up and tosses her arms around me.

"Ma," I breathe out after an incredibly long hug. "Can I finish taking my coat off?"

She steps away, never too far though, and gives me just enough room to hang my jacket over my scarf. I sit down and smile at my dad and sister.

The Davies are creatures of habit. Every Thursday we meet up at *The Blue's* for dinner, and every Thursday I paste on my smile and good attitude and make small talk until I can't feel my cheeks. Then, every Thursday I go home feeling more empty than I did before dinner. And it's no fault of theirs. My family are good people. They love me for me, and I love them for them.

But faking it is exhausting. To be real, to be honest, though... The questions and concerns and check-in's... So far, they don't notice anything is amiss with me. I can never decide if I'm grateful for that or resentful. Both, perhaps.

I look across the rectangular table to my dad, Brian. He's a soft man—inside and out. He's an inch or so over six feet. His hair is dark like mine and his eyes are green like my sister's. He holds a tan better than any of us. His weathered skin pulls and wrinkles from years as a construction worker, and his small round belly sits under his usual long-sleeved work shirt—today's is brown. I haven't seen them, but I'm sure his jeans are smudged with dirt and grease from whatever he was working on today. Contrary to popular belief—not all construction ceases during the winter. Especially not in the Midwest.

"How are ya, honey?"

"I'm good, dad. You?"

"Oh, just fine." Dad picks his menu back up.

"You look tired."

I look to my sister, my face blank. "Thanks, Quinn. Just what I love to hear."

She rolls her emerald eyes. I'm always envious of the color. I got shit-brown, and she got dad's bright green.

But that makes sense. Brian is *technically* my stepdad.

"Quinn," my mom scoffs. "Be nice."

"I am nice."

Now it's my turn to scoff.

I smile at my mom before focusing on the drops of water on the plastic cup in front of me. My mom is kind, albeit slightly... unhelpful? Maybe a bit emotionally unavailable on her good days, or on my bad days. I think I take after her in terms of loving. We love hard but reserve that for those we choose. We aren't necessarily picky, but we don't give our love freely, I suppose.

We fall into a normal quiet. Everyone looking over our menus, unnecessarily.

Quinn will get the chicken strip basket with a side of ranch and fries and eat a quarter of it. Dad will get the classic hamburger, everything on it, with fries, and a side of ranch and then also finish Quinn's food. Mom will get the same as dad, complain quietly about it being too pink in the middle of her burger, and then eat only half of her meal. I'll also get a hamburger, but with a salad and French dressing. I'll finish my whole meal, mindlessly and nearly without a word spoken. Quinn will comment on it, my silence or the fact that she hardly ate but I finished mine, and mom will scold her while dad gives her a glare. And I'll pretend it doesn't bother me when my size eight little sister comments on my size eighteen eating habits.

See? Creatures of habit.

Once all of that comes to pass as it always does, dad pays the bill and Quinn and I thank him and mom for supper. It's all very boring and standard. Mind numbing. Just the kind of shit I love these days.

"What are you doing this weekend?" Quinn asks me as we walk to our cars.

Quinn is everything I am not. She is thin and beautiful. Her hair is the same light brown as our moms, but she adds pops of bright blond every month. Where I wear mine up in a messy knot, hers is smooth and hangs down past her chest in mildly curled waves. Her green eyes pop off of her slightly tanned skin and she stands eye to eye with me, both of us roughly five-feet-eight. I've been jealous of her since she was thirteen and I was fifteen. Now, at twenty-seven and twenty-nine, the same jealousy stays rooted inside of me.

"I don't have plans. Just going to clean the house and relax. What about you?" I flip my key fob in my hand once, twice.

I don't look at her directly but more behind her. I hate that when I do look her in the eye, she's always giving me an "I see through you" look.

"Was going to see if I could come over and hang out."

My gaze drags to hers at that and I squint slightly. "Why?"

"Rude," she says, crossing her arms over her chest.

"Quinn, you never just come over to hang out. That's not what we do. We *could*, if you really want. But I don't think that's the case. So, why?"

She looks me up and down. Not unkindly, but not with a lot of warmth either. With more awareness than I'd like to see. "You're thinner. Your hair is messier than normal. You haven't worn more than mascara and blush the last five times I've seen you."

"Are you keeping track of that?" I ask, not believing this.

"Yes," she says matter of fact.

"Well, stop. It's creepy."

"You seem weird. Sad."

"I'm fine."

Fuck.

I feel my heart rate pick up slightly.

"You're not. And I see that. And I get why you're not. I wouldn't be. But are you doing anything about it?"

"I'm fine," I say again, more sternly. "I have to go. I'll see you next week."

I move to open my door but Quinn stops me by grabbing my wrist and turning me towards her.

"I'm coming over tomorrow for lunch. I'll bring it. Be home. Okay?" She doesn't give me time to respond before her arms are wrapped around my arms and she is hugging me.

This is probably pretty normal for most siblings—a hug. But not us. I don't remember the last time we hugged. Not because we hate each other. We don't. We just don't especially *like* each other, I guess. We never hung out a ton, always having different hobbies and friend groups.

She wears short skirts, I wear T-shirts—that whole thing.

"I'll see you tomorrow." And with that she is off and walking briskly towards her own car. The streetlights and signs from buildings cast a warm blue glow on her as she goes.

"What the fuck," I whisper to myself.

three

"You can avoid reality, but you cannot avoid the consequences of avoiding reality." —Ayn Rand

I PACE MY LIVING room for the eightieth time this morning. I'm glad Quinn at least warned me she would be coming over today. My house was a wreck.

I bought this place almost a year ago after moving back. It's on the west side of town and came up for sale at the perfect time. A beautiful ranch style home. It's got blue siding and a bright white door. I've got great neighbors that mind their own business and the whole block is pretty quiet.

The inside is all neutral colors, grays and browns and whites. I haven't gotten around to decorating the walls, it just hasn't been a priority with the last almost-year of my life being what it was. So the walls are bare and the windows have cheap white Target brand curtains. My couch is a hand-me-down from my parents, but it's comfy and brown and makes for a good place to sit, with a coffee table in front, so I can't ask for much more. I've got the standard side tables and a good bed and dresser and everything else you "need" for a home. The "wants" are a different story.

But I haven't wanted much lately.

Because I have been a depressed shell of my former self, things like cleaning have fallen to the wayside. I keep my dishes cleaned up and my laundry caught up but that's pretty much it. And barely. I eat out way too much now, so the first thing I did this morning was clean up the takeout containers that littered nearly every room. I cleaned out my fridge because I know Quinn will look in there. She seems to be in that mood. One I don't recognize, by the way. My bathroom has never looked better. My back hurts from how much time I spent in there.

I silently thank my nosy sister for the invasion and the motivation to get my house together. I just sit my ass down on my couch to relax when I hear Quinn enter through the garage door.

"I'm here," she hollers from behind me.

"And letting yourself in," I mumble.

"What was that?"

I get up and turn around, keeping the same empty expression I don't stray too far from. "Nothing. Hi."

I'm unsure of how to act. This is not our normal. It's weird and new. But I'll play along if it gets her out of my hair.

"I brought you a hamburger from *Blue's.*"

I internally swear. I am so beyond over those, but how would she know that and what else I would eat?

"Great, thank you."

We set up at my dark brown, round dining room table. The silence is loud but I long for it the second she opens her mouth.

"So, how have you been doing since Aster," she pauses and looks up from her chicken. "Since Aster left?"

I pause my chewing, reign in my anger, and swallow my truth. "Fine, Quinn. I've been fine." My tone is clipped, short.

She sets her chicken strip down and folds her arms across her chest. Her red hoodie stands out loudly in my dull dining room. "I think you're lying."

I suppress the urge to roll my eyes, barely, and shove another fry in my mouth.

"And I think you need to deal with this whole," she pauses, her hand coming and moving in a flurry of motion. "Thing."

"Thing."

This is the last *thing* I want to be discussing.

"Quinn, I'm fine. I don't think we need to discuss him and whatever else you think we need to discuss."

"I just think-"

"I don't want to talk about it."

"That you need to deal with it-"

"It's not any of your business."

"And if you would talk to me or-"

"*Quinn!*" I raise my voice. I slam my hands down flat on my table, causing her soda to almost fall over. Taking a big breath and reining it back in I whisper-hiss, "Enough."

"Briar," she matches my volume but her tone is soft. I look up and meet her tear-filled gaze. "I just want-"

"Enough," I say with a little more calm in my voice. "You can do this—come here for lunch and want to spend time together. But you do not get to insert yourself into shit that has nothing to do with you. Anything to do with him—*that* has nothing to do with you. So please, I am asking—no, I am telling you to be done." I look away before she can notice the lack of tears in my own eyes.

I'm exhausted. The acting like I'm *normal*—like I feel anything at all other than this gaping emotionless emptiness. Who knew feeling nothing would be so tiring? It's the faking the opposite that does it, though. The placating smiles and positive attitude. I do it all day at work. The whole "fake it until you make it" phrase flits through my brain four days a week for ten hours each day while I'm in that nursing home.

"I just love you," Quinn says quietly.

I look up and meet her eyes again. "Quinn," I match her volume and tone now. "I really love you too. I'm fine. Okay? Please."

She takes a minute before squaring her shoulders and nodding. "Okay."

We smile at one another as best we can.

"So, how is Hot Shrink Mark?"

I roll my eyes and laugh, thankful for the switch in topics. "You're insane."

"Oh! Do you think you could tell him that and then he'd take me on as a patient?"

"No," I say while giggling, shaking my head. "You're incorrigible."

She shrugs, her laughter mixing with mine, and I find myself feeling *something*. Small and almost barely there, but something.

Happy? Content? Fine? I'm not sure but I don't get to analyze it for long before it's gone.

The rest of my weekend is spent relaxing alone but with random texts every now and then popping up from my sister. Some of them are random gifs—Jess Day from New Girl giving her period spiel because apparently that's the boat Quinn's in this weekend. Others are silly TikToks—mostly really bad line dancing. We talk more over the weekend, meaningless and mindless things, than we have in years.

It's nice. And a little weird.

But a nice weird.

four

"It takes courage to bloom." —*Dhiman*

MARK LAUGHS AT MY retelling of my sister and I's conversation.

"I'm old enough to be her father," he says.

"I know. She's crazy."

We both settle in, the mood taking a bit of a dive. Well, my mood at least.

"You ready to talk today, Briar?"

I look out the window, choosing the same spot on the top of the parking garage to watch. The same white car is there again. I take a deep breath and close my eyes, gripping my clear plastic Starbucks cup tighter.

"No," I whisper. "But I'll try."

He nods his head a few times, encouraging me. "That's all any of us can do. *Try.*"

I look to Mark and find him watching me closely, patiently. I take a drink of my iced latte and try to steady myself, only to find myself rolling my eyes.

"You know I can't even say his name? How stupid is that? I've had to have said his name hundreds of times over the last almost fifteen years of knowing him. In various situations. In anger and sorrow. In pride and passion. And now I can't speak it? Like it's a bad word or something? What is that? Why can't I say it?" The last question sounds rhetorical but I would love for Mark to have any actual answer.

"I'm not sure the exact reason but I think a part of it is you have yet to acknowledge what happened fully."

Mark is so gentle with the truth. But yet, I find myself cringing.

"If I can't say his name, how can I verbalize *that?*"

"I think you just do, Briar. Like we said earlier, you try."

I take a few minutes. Checking the clock I note that longer than seems possible has gone by. But minutes pass and when I look back to Mark, his patience not wavering, I square my shoulders.

"Okay," I say, bobbing my head up and down. "Okay."

Mark squares his own and says back, "Okay."

I swallow, closing my eyes and bracing myself. "As-" I shake my head and then lean forward, setting my coffee on the table in front of me and shaking out my hands. "Lord-Okay-Aster."

I said it so fast, the words becoming one, that it didn't even sound like his name. But I said it. And that matters. It counts.

Mark smiles proudly and I give him a small one back.

"Go on, Briar. Give it a bit more *try.*"

I nod. "Aster," I say slower this time. "Aster-"
Deep breath, Briar. Come on.
"Is gone."

"I miss summer already," I say to Catt as she walks towards me.

I look next to me, her strawberry blonde hair swishing by as she takes her seat. She just got it cut over the weekend. A "back to school bob" she said. It hangs straight and hits just below her chin, curving inwards just the slightest. Her green eyes pop brightly on her sun kissed, freckled skin. It's still warm enough for summer clothes at the beginning of September in South Dakota and her fitted black V-neck shirt and white jean shorts make me envious of her small frame.

"Ugh!" she moans, arching to pop her back on the blue desk chair she is in. "I do too."

Catt and I are sitting in third period—science. Summer flew by and now we are sophomores. Almost top dogs... almost. At least, that's what I have to tell myself to keep from hating the idea of three more years... I flip open my yellow notebook to start doodling, like I do at the beginning of every class. It's not that I don't enjoy school...

It's just that I don't enjoy school. It's boring and the teachers I have are fine but that's just it—they are fine. Science is one of my least favorites. It just doesn't click in my brain. English? Sure. History? Some days. The rest of them? Absolutely not.

As I put the finishing touches on my doodle, a cute little swirly flower, I feel Catt hit my arm and hiss "look" at me. I look at her, setting my pen down to rub my arm.

"Ouch," I say. "Look at what?"

Her focus is on the door to the classroom, and I follow her gaze.

"Who," she breathes out, "is that?"

Whoever he is, he's beautiful. He stands by the teacher's desk with one hand on the strap of his backpack, handing Mr. Cloyer a piece of paper with the other. The attention of everyone in this room is solely on him. He's new, that is for certain. His hair is this honey blond that makes me think of, well, honey. He is all tan and tall and handsome, and I swipe my hand over my mouth to check for drool. I'm broken out of my trance as he turns around and starts walking towards the seat Mr. Cloyer pointed him to. Catt makes a choking sound next to me and I dart my eyes to her and find her staring almost straight through me.

"What is your-"

"SHH!" She points behind me like a maniac.

I turn and make a choking sound of my own. My cheeks warm and I think I die a little bit.

"Hi."

I look around me, positive he can't be saying that to me. When I see no one else paying attention, aside from a very wide-eyed Catt, I look back and point to myself. He laughs and nods his head.

He laughs and I take a moment to feel if my heart is still beating because I'm sure he just coaxed it from where it lives inside my chest with that sound.

"Hey," I cough out after Catt hits me on the back of my head.

"Hi," he says again, his smile wide and showing off nearly every single one of his shiny teeth. His voice is deep. Deeper than the average, I'm assuming, sixteen-year-old. "I'm Aster."

I take his extended right hand and shake it, praying to God that my palms aren't sweaty and showing how nervous I am.

"Her name is Briar," I hear from behind me. Catt pokes her head over my shoulder. "Briar, speak, babe."

I drop Aster's hand and mentally tell myself to get it together. What the heck is the matter with me? I've talked to boys before. Cute boys! Kissed a couple even just this last summer!

"And I'm Catt, Briar's best friend." Catt shakes Aster's hand, his eyes only staying on her for a second. "New here?"

I thank God for my outgoing best friend taking over while I have an internal malfunction.

"Yeah," he says and runs his hand through his shaggy hair.

This close I can see his eyes are a dark, blue gray. Not blue, no. They are actually gray. They're beautiful and I have to force myself to look away before I make an even bigger fool of myself.

"Moved here from North Carolina. My dad is in the Air Force and got stationed here."

"Oh wow, North Carolina. You ever been there, Bri?"

When I don't answer because I hardly heard anything other than the soft, light accent Aster has, Catt kicks the side of my leg from where she's sitting.

"What?" I snap, whipping my gaze to her.

Shooting me a glare before looking back at Aster, Catt says, "She's a little tired today. Don't mind her."

I kick her back and force myself to get it together.

Clearing my throat I ask, "Air Force? That's cool. Are you upset about moving?"

Aster smiles at me and I have to rein in the uncontrollable nerves he's giving me.

"Nah, North Carolina was fine but nothing beyond that. I'm excited to be up here."

"I bet you're the only sixteen-year-old to think that," I laugh.

"Sixteen next month," he says proudly.

We share another small moment of quiet, just watching each other from where we sit, before Mr. Cloyer calls the class to attention.

I focus on absolutely nothing aside from the way Aster holds his pencil in between his index finger and thumb. I watch the way he bounces his left foot up and down through the entire hour. And how every now and then his gaze slides to me, not from the side. Fully onto me. And I know he sees the way my cheeks blush each time. I can't hide that, and my pale skin makes it obvious.

I try to ignore the incessant flutter in my stomach and the erratic beat of my heart but none of it ends. Not even when the class does. And especially not as Aster smiles at me while he gathers his things and leaves, shooting me a small wave and a "see you tomorrow."

"Oh my gosh, Briar. Are you mental? What was that?"

"Catt..." My voice is barely a whisper. I look at her as we pull our backpacks over our shoulders. "I have no idea what happened with me,

but I don't think I can handle sitting next to him for the rest of the semester. I'm so embarrassed."

"I don't think you have to worry too much about that, spazz. I've never seen you so weird like that." Her scoff makes me laugh and brings my fogged mind back to reality.

I run my hands over my face, groaning. "Could have handled that better."

five

"Give yourself grace as you grow through grief. Be patient with your pain." —Alex Elle

AFTER MY SESSION WITH Mark, discussing Aster and being able to even think his name now, I feel sad. I thought that maybe I would have felt empowered, but nope. No such luck. I feel bummed and upset and mad, and I wish I could feel differently but here we are.

At least I'm feeling, I suppose.

I'm upset with myself. And I'm upset with Aster. He left and I'm here just dealing with the repercussions of the whole thing. On top of it all, I got my yearly "Happy Holidays" card from my deadbeat father and his family.

I feel as though the standard situation when it comes to having a bum of a parent is that they aren't in your life. Period, that's it. They just aren't there. It's typically a thing where they're just absent.

Mine is different.

My father is absent but only in the most fatherly ways. I know his family—*our* family. My siblings... sort of. My aunts and uncles and grandparents and cousins. I go to holiday gatherings and weddings and funerals. I see him at all of those things.

It's always been a weird sort of thing—our relationship. Or rather, lack thereof. He's never put in much effort, if any at all, and I *used* to put in a ton. He has other kids, my siblings. I have some semblance of a friendship with them but not much more than that. His wife is fine, but nothing too noteworthy. That may just be a me thing, though. How any woman can love a man who openly doesn't care about a child he fathered is beyond me, but I'm basing my opinions on what and who I know.

What I know is that discarding a child you hadn't planned on simply because you just can't be bothered to care is wildly unimpressive. It's also crazy when, as the abandoning parental figure, you act as though everything is as normal as can be in public settings. A kiss on the cheek and a "hey sweetheart" don't excuse years of not being around in the ways that count.

And *who* I know is my dad, Brian, the man that raised me. How he didn't *have* to love me, but he *chose* to anyway.

They look so perfect—this family. The perfect color palette, jewel toned shirts and dresses and dark pants. Everyone's hair is expertly coiffed. My brother and his wife are picturesque, her slight baby bump on display. My sisters stand side by side and look happy and elegant as can be in near matching sweaters and skirts. My stepmother is resplendent in her teal, flowy dress and ivory cardigan. And sitting in the middle of it all is my father. His dark hairline has receded over the years and his skin has wrinkled with time. But all in all, he is just as he was when I was ten. He is a handsome man, charming and charismatic. An absolute narcissist. He's got a good job that he has held for decades. His wife plays the role of duty perfectly. His three "real" children are the picture of happiness and success.

I scoff and throw the Christmas card onto my white kitchen counter.

No one talks about his alcohol problem. Or the fact that he's a deadbeat with zero remorse for it. No, of course not. We don't speak of such frivolity.

I'm often looked at as a "*drama queen*" because I don't reciprocate the bull shit. I don't hug him back anymore. I don't even say hello now when I see him. I don't kiss his ass or accept Christmas or birthday gifts that his wife picks out. I refuse to play the part of the abandoned daughter who isn't upset about being discarded— because that's just it.

I *am* upset.

I'm pissed. I'm sad. I'm bitter. I'm jaded.

I am not even thirty years old and my heart feels the weight of a hundred years of hurt.

And then, throw on Aster's *abandonment...*

It's no wonder why I don't think I will ever love someone again. Let alone ever be good enough to *be* loved again. Not when nearly everyone seems to leave me, one way or another.

Mark is going to eat this shit up at the end of the week.

I felt the need to clear my head a bit after the reeling I did upon receiving my father's family portrait... sans me. An aimless drive usually does the trick. Somehow, tonight, I ended up where I had least expected.

The air is fresh tonight out here. The kind of winter air that just feels and smells clean—*new*. The sky is an inky dark blue and because I'm sitting just outside of town, the stars are more prominent than from in the city. I watch as a plane takes off from the tarmac in front of me, remembering a night that feels like another life entirely.

"Where do you think they're going?"

"Florida."

"No way. It's got to be somewhere cooler than Florida."

"Okay..."

I take a bite of my Slim Jim, turning my head to look at Aster. He's so handsome. I don't think you're supposed to be in love with your best friend like this. But I am, and I don't know what to do with that.

So, I do nothing.

"Ireland." Aster looks at me with a smile that sets my soul alight.

"Ireland?" I ask.

He chuckles and looks forward again. "Yeah, Ireland. What do you think they'll do there?"

It's winter break for us. Catt's at work tonight so instead of a trio, it's a duo. Just Aster and I...

Me and Aster.

Us.

Lord, do I wish there was an "us".

Being freshly sixteen is messing with me in ways I had not expected. It's like I can't control the longing, needing feeling I have for this boy. I have never, and I mean never, wanted someone or something as fiercely as I want Aster Marcus Levi Briggs.

Being in love with your best friend is insane.

"Briar?"

I blink a few times and nearly choke on the bite of greasy jerky I haven't done anything with.

"What was the question?" I look back towards the airport.

Aster laughs and asks again, the right corner of his mouth lifting up, "What do you think they'll do in Ireland?"

We do this often now. We come to this dead-end little road right outside of town after stopping at the gas station and getting snacks. We park facing the airport. We sit back, turn the music to a soft lull, and we make up these wonderfully crazy stories of the travelers we can't see.

"Okay," I say. "Well, first... Who's going? What's the relationship? A couple of best friends on a girl's trip? A bachelor party? What are we dealing with here?"

Aster cups his jaw, thinking it over, and I force myself to focus on the landscape and not the way his muscles flex as he does that.

"*Best friends, like us. A guy and a girl. Going to Ireland.*"

My stomach does that weird flutter thing that it's so accustomed to doing these days around Aster and we share a smile.

"*Alright. They get to Ireland and find a cab to their hotel.*"

"*But it's a B&B kind of hotel. Nothing fancy. Old and a little sad.*"

"*But charming!*" *I say, mock offended for the nonexistent B&B he's describing.*

He laughs and shakes his head, his honey hair brushing across his forehead. "*Yes, okay, charming. And they only booked one room. They are best, best friends. They can share a room with a couple beds, and it isn't weird.*"

"*Right, not weird.*" *The butterflies turn into feral bats inside my belly.* "*They get to their room and unpack and take naps because I bet flying all the way over there was exhausting.*"

"*Sure, naps. And then when they wake up, they go for an adventure.*"

"*They climb all these hills, going on a hike! I hear it is a beautiful country. And once they get up top...*"

"*He takes her hand,*" *Aster says, his voice softer now.*

I slowly look at him. The atmosphere has shifted. Somewhere between "*charming*" *and* "*exhausting*" *we shifted. His body is closer now, turned towards me and leaning on the center console of his Jeep. I've pulled a knee up towards me and my entire being has drawn itself towards him. I swallow and don't take my eyes off of his.*

"*He takes her hand,*" *I repeat back to him.*

Slowly, like ice melting at ten in the morning on the first sunny day after a blizzard, Aster moves his hand to where mine sits on my knee. His eyes don't leave mine.

"And he tells her, in front of the cliffs of whatever they're called-"

"Moher," I choke out. "Cliffs of Moher."

I don't have any idea what is happening right now. I think I might puke. Or melt right into his black pleather seat.

Aster chuckles at me and takes my hand in his, turning it so it's facing up. He leaves it on my knee, tracing the lines on my palm slowly.

"Cliffs of Moher." He swallows hard and looks to where his hand now rests on mine before bringing his eyes back to mine. "He tells her, his best friend and favorite person in the world, his other half... that he doesn't want to be just her best friend anymore."

I feel time stop. Like this moment will be suspended, frozen, put on paper and forever remembered.

"He doesn't?"

"No, he doesn't. He can't. Not anymore. Not after he realized just how special she is."

"And what caused that realization?"

"Her laugh." He says it so simply. So factually.

"Her laugh?" I ask with a giggle of my own.

I have zero idea of where this is going at this point. All I do know is that if his hand leaves mine any time soon, I might very well die. Right here, in this Jeep.

"A kid in class told a joke that wasn't at all funny. This kid is bad at jokes, he doesn't tell them well. But he tries and he's nice. A little weird, and the other kids make fun of him. But she doesn't. She smiles

at him and talks to him and asks about his bearded dragon and she laughs at his bad jokes every day. She sees him and notices him. And when she laughed at this particularly poorly executed joke..." His eyes go wide like he just realized what he did. What he said.

Henry... He is talking about Henry. And me. Aster is talking about my odd, little pal Henry and how bad his jokes are and how I like him anyways because he's a goober and he's nice and the kids in our school aren't.

"So, what does he do after he tells her how special he thinks she is?" I whisper.

I don't know how I am still breathing but here I am, inhaling his words and everything that he is.

"I don't want to just be your friend anymore." Aster's voice is soft but sure, this hypothetical vacationing couple no longer existing. "I like you. A lot. I like your laugh and how you give it freely to those that you love, those that have earned that part of you. I like your smile and how it's constant but also not. I like how smart you are and how you always help me figure shit out without making me feel stupid. I like you, Briar. A lot. And I'll stay just your friend, if you want. But I... I'd like to be way more than that. If you want."

"I want." It comes out immediately, on the very last letter of his declaration.

His whole face lights up at my rushed admission.
"You do?"

"Badly, Aster. I love being your friend. But more *sounds like it could be really fun too."*

He laces his fingers with mine and laughs, running his other hand through his already messy hair.

"Catt is going to give you so much shit about this," I laugh.

She will. She's going to fake-mock us relentlessly.

He lets that comment roll off his shoulders like it's nothing and we sit there, quietly soaking in this new normal.

"Dance with me?"

I pull back and laugh. "What?"

Aster rushes to grab his phone that's plugged into his stereo and finds a song with a satisfied smirk. He doesn't start it yet, rolling all four windows down and turning the volume up to what will be way too loud. Without a word, only a brief glance and a large smile, he gets out and runs to my door. I laugh as he opens it quickly and grabs my hand, pulling me out and into him.

"Dance with me."

I say nothing as he reaches in and presses play, closing my door. He leads me to the front of his car and spins me in a circle before bringing me to him. I'm aware of every atom of mine that is touching every atom of his. The headlights illuminate the space we are in and the music is softer than I thought it would be but loud enough to hear.

"Clay Walker?" I ask.

"Hypnotize the Moon," he says. "It's one of my parent's favorites to dance to, too."

I smile at that, at him and this and us. Leaning my head on his chest, I breathe him in. His voice is smooth as he sings softly with the music.

After a few moments, his chin resting atop my head, he says, "So, just to clarify... Will you be my girlfriend, Briar Renee Davies?"

I don't hesitate or play it cool at all. "Yes!" I nearly yell.

His smile widens and his eyes flick down to my smile, to my lips. I suck in a breath and he holds my gaze for a just a moment before gravity seems to take over. Our lips meet for the first time in a warm greeting. It's soft and slow, smooth and easy. Right and perfect.

I giggle and then flush with embarrassment as we pull apart.

But it doesn't matter, Aster just smiles at me even more. He knows me. He knows I'm a bit rough and loud. He knows I have no filter and can be crabby or abrasive, honest and kind too. A bit embarrassing at times.

He knows me. And yet...

He just chose me.

I don't brush away the fresh tears falling down my face, landing on my bright orange hoodie. *His* bright orange hoodie. The feeling is foreign—crying. It's been nine months since I've had a single tear fall.

I lean my head back, watching a plane take off and whisper, "Ireland, maybe."

I watch a couple more planes take off in the late, cool night. I remember us at the beginning. I recall the moment two sixteen-year-olds started to become something special—the beginning of Aster and Briar.

six

"The ones that love us never really leave us." —*Sirius Black*

THE WORK WEEK GOES by like any other does. A lot of filing paperwork and discussing random administrative things with those that I need to talk with. By Thursday I am crabby and tired, and I desperately would like to skip family dinner at *The Blue's.* But skipping would raise questions and I already have Quinn trying to be in my business. The last thing I need is for my mom and dad to join in on the watching and prying.

"I don't think she's as good as you might think she-"

"Hey, fam," I interrupt my sister's sentence and glare at the back of her head, wishing for her perfect ponytail to be... less perfect. "What are you talking about?"

"Oh, um-"

"Sweety-"

"You."

Quinn, mom, and dad all speak in unison. But I catch dad's "you" and turn my glare to the front of my sister's head now.

"Why?"

Mom looks around nervously, dad takes a drink of his beer, and Quinn squares her shoulders.

"I think you're unwell."

I laugh out loud. It's a harsh, brash sound. "Unwell, Quinn?"

"Yes, Briar. Unwell. You seem depressed and sad and even after seeing you over the weekend, I'm not convinced that you're not taking this whole Ast-"

"That's enough, Quinn."

I sigh in relief at my dad's interruption.

"If your sister wanted to discuss that, then she would. She's fine." Dad turns his head to face me next to him. "You're alright, right kiddo?"

I hate lying. I opt for a really honest approach in life. Whether it be about something serious or not. Lying and scheming and being fake is just something that always makes my chest heavy and my brain foggy. But here are my options right now: I lie to my dad and say I am fine. Orrrrr... I tell him the truth and admit that I am incredibly depressed and concerned that I may not ever feel loved by anyone or feel love towards anyone ever again, and that just having someone other than me, and Mark, say *his* name aloud is too much for my heart to handle.

"I'm fine dad."

The fog rolls in and my chest immediately feels heavier with the lie.

"Let's just eat."

"Briar!"

I ignore the urge to whip around and scream "what" like a psychopath at my sister while I rush to my car.

"Briar, please!"

Nope, ignore her. That's what works for everyone else in the world—ignoring people. It can work for me too.

"Briar, come on. I wasn't trying to upset you."

I wish I sounded half as put together after sprinting down half a block. I'd be so out of breath from a quarter of that.

"Briar," Quinn grabs my elbow. "Please. I'm sorry."

I laugh, angrily, and turn to my sister. "Sorry? For what? For talking about me behind my back? For faking it last weekend just to see-"

"I didn't fake it!"

"What was going on so you could gossip to mom? What are you sorry for, Quinn? Don't pretend you care."

I want to take it all back the second I say it. I watch in real time as her face goes from empathy to anger.

I am a bitch. The meanest, rudest, saddest bitch.

Some might even call me prickly.

"Did you know that your name means prickly?"

I slowly look up from my desk, trying to hide my smile that, regardless of what we are doing or where we are at, does not stay away when I am near my boyfriend.

Boyfriend...

Aster and I have been a steady couple now for four months. School is slowly arriving to an end for the year, our sophomore year coming to a close. For only being my first boyfriend ever, my experience incredibly minimal, I have never been happier.

Aster is the perfect boyfriend. He is attentive and kind. He and Catt get along better than Catt and myself some days. My family loves him. His family loves me.

I love him.

And he loves me back.

"Excuse me?" I ask with faux annoyance.

He smirks his stupidly perfect smirk and rolls his eyes as he takes a seat at his desk next to me. Catt on the left sticks her head around me and laughs.

"You're in trouble now, Asteroid."

Her silly nickname makes us laugh.

"Briar," he begins. "Any of a number of prickly scrambling shrubs, especially sweetbrier and other wild roses."

Catt and I just stare at Mr. Dictionary.

"It makes sense though," he begins again. "You are a little prickly sometimes."

"Okay, ouch. Right?" I look to my best friend.

She's hiding a laugh, poorly, behind her hand. "I mean, I don't know, Briar. It's kind of sweet."

"Sweet?! Aster just called me prickly!"

"Like a rose bush!" They say it in unison, and we all break out in laughter.

I cross my arms over my chest and pout. "I don't think I'm prickly. Just... picky maybe. About who I like and who I'm like more genuinely nice to, or whatever. Like, my standards might be a bit high, I guess."

Aster scoots his desk closer to mine and I wait for Mr. Cloyer to reprimand him like he does every other day. He takes my hand in his and kisses my knuckles.

"I think you're like a sweetbrier, Briar. Beautiful and giving, but people might have to work for it a little bit. Risk the pricks, sometimes. The thorns. You're great."

I huff and squeeze his hand back. "Fine, I am maybe a little prickly. I don't see anything wrong with being selective about who I let in though."

"Nothing wrong with it at all, babe."

Catt gags from the other side of me and Aster rolls his eyes.

"Mr. Briggs. Desk. Now."

Aster doesn't take his eyes off of mine while he moves his desk to its place. I roll my eyes and shake my head, my focus returning back to my doodling—the heart I'm shading in with "B + A" in the center.

"Briar? Where did you just go? Prickly? What does that mean?"

I shake my head, my focus coming back to the dimly lit street I'm on. My sister's concerned face and voice filtering back in.

"What?"

"What just happened? You like, zoned out."

Quinn's face is the picture of concern. Pinched eyebrows, scanning eyes, pressed together lips.

"I'm fine." I take my arm out of her grip. "I'm fine and I need you to worry about me less and about you more. I'm sorry for what I said but don't talk about me to mom and dad again and don't bring up Aster again. Ever, Quinn. Butt out."

"You're not fine."

"You just don't give up, gosh." My hands drop to my sides and I tilt my head back to look up at the night sky.

"No." She crosses her arms over her black coat covered chest, bringing my eyes back to hers. "I don't. And you wouldn't either if roles were reversed. If I were heartbroken and sad and alone and drowning, you'd fight for me. So, this is me fighting for you. Take your time, be mean and mad and harsh, lie and hide and whatever. Fine. But I'm not going anywhere. Our relationship is weird already so it's not like it can get that much stranger if I don't heed your warning and cower away. You don't scare me. Your hurt doesn't scare me. I love you. I'm here for you. Deal with it."

I WISH.

I swallow my venom that I reflexively want to spew. Instead, I opt for nothing. I turn away and get in my car and leave my strong willed, brave little sister on the curb. I don't leave her words there though. No, those stick with me through the night.

"You don't scare me. Your hurt doesn't scare me. I love you."

seven

"Sometimes we are just the collateral damage in someone else's war against themselves." —*Lauren Eden*

It's a sunny January day. That doesn't mean it isn't cold. Oh no, it's a balmy twenty-four-degrees outside. But a sunny twenty-four is like a cloudy sixty-one here. I'll take it. The weekend went by in a blur. I cooked half of the meals I ate and ordered in the rest, or just didn't eat, which I call progress. I don't remember the last time I had used my stove. I texted Quinn an apology Friday evening and she responded back with a simple "I love you anyways."

"Do you think your relationship with Quinn is fractured or strained for a specific reason?"

I'm brought back to the room and to Mark. It's our Monday session and I explained to him how horrible of a sister I am. I gave him a breakdown of our argument from Thursday and explained that while I don't appreciate the hovering Quinn is doing, I also don't *not* appreciate it. So now, I'm sad *and* confused, and over feeling both of those things.

"I think it's a me problem."

I like to think that I am fairly realistic. I'm acutely self-aware and with that comes the cold truth of the fact that sometimes I know exactly what my issue is and yet I choose to continue to be a problem. Which is all, well, a problem.

"I think that as we grew up and I saw how perfect and pretty and smart and good at everything Quinn is, it ate at me a bit. I was, or I guess am," I pick at the seam of my black leggings. "I am not an openly nice person, I guess? I don't just smile at anyone and everyone. I don't laugh at everything for the sake of laughing. I don't go out of my way to make kind small talk or make someone feel extra comfortable. I don't think I'm mean. I just don't think I am nice *first*." I shrug my shoulders.

"There is nothing wrong with saving your big kindness for those that you let in all of the way."

Mark leans forward, pulling the sleeves of his dark brown sweater up to his elbows before placing them on his knees and folding his hands together in front of him. His black framed glasses give off a small green tinted reflection and his khaki slacks rise with the movement, showing off his neutral toned plaid socks.

"Do you think you're mean or unkind, Briar?"

"No," I say. "I actually think I'm quite nice... Just, selectively. Like, I don't pick and choose who I am nice to. I just also don't pull niceties out of my ass at the drop of a hat, I guess. I don't know, Mark. I don't *think* I'm mean."

"I don't think you're mean either. You noticed my new glasses today and complimented them. Not a lot of people notice small things like that, and then not a lot will even say something. I think you may underestimate how good you are."

"Aster," I swallow my nerves and focus on the toe of my black sock, having taken my shoes off the second I entered this room like I always do. "He used to tell me that my heart is good and kind and that it stays that way because I reserve all of that goodness and kindness for the people that I let into it."

"Sounds very wise. I don't think I could argue with that assessment."

I smile softly. "He'd also call me prickly, like a rose bush, and then make some silly compliment about the blush that would come to my cheeks matching the color of the roses on the bushes."

My smile fades.

"It's okay to still be sad, Briar. It's also okay to not maybe be as sad as you were yesterday, or last week."

When I don't say anything, Mark relaxes back into his chair and scribbles something in his notebook.

"Let's change topics, yes?"

I nod, chewing on my bottom lip.

"Have you hung out with any friends recently?"

Friends? I don't really have those. I haven't ever been a big circle kind of gal. I kept it small. Catt and Aster. A couple people entered that circle when I lived in Omaha for college. But they slowly faded from the circle when I moved back home. Or I suppose I was the one that faded.

"No, I haven't."

"Have you reached out to Catt lately?"

I shake my head. Shame forms in my gut at the mention of my once-upon-a-time best friend.

"I don't know what to say to her anymore. After the last time..." I sigh, shaking out my hands and turning my gaze to the window. "She was so mad, Mark. I said some really shitty things to her."

"You don't think she'd forgive you?"

"I don't honestly know. She was there for the whole Aster *thing*. I don't feel like I was wrong for being upset for her part of things. I was out of line in what I said but I wasn't completely insane for being pissed. I don't know if she'd even answer if I called."

"Try."

I look at my bossy therapist, tilting my head in doubt. "Try?"

He laughs at me. "Yes, Briar. *Try.*"

Try I did. Which is why I now sit at *The Blue's* on a barstool waiting for Catt to show up. I look around, waiting for her to arrive, taking in the scene. Friday's are a bit busier than the Thursday's I'm used to.

"Hi, I'm sorry I'm late! There was so much traffic on the interstate and then I tried to cut through town by going by the high school but there was so much traffic there too and then I hit every red light down here and now-"

She stops abruptly after taking her coat and scarf off, hanging them off of the back of her stool. Her smile falters and her eyes widen.

"Do I look that bad?" I joke.

I look sad.

"You look sad."

See?

"I'm fine, Catt." I get up to hug her. "No worries about being late."

She hugs me tightly and I almost start to feel something. An inkling of hope or sorrow, I don't know. But she squeezes me once more before grabbing me by my arms and stepping back to look at me.

"You've lost weight. Are you eating? You look great but you always looked great so that's not a surprise. It's your eyes though. They aren't bright and they used to be. And I know what you look like when you're healthy. This doesn't look healthy." Her eyes roam my whole being and I want to curl up and die. "I didn't think I needed to be super worried, I kept track of you and knew you were still working and doing the Thursday nights with the fam still. I assumed you were doing fine. Now I think that was a mistake. You're not fine and it's clear to me so I don't know why your mom hasn't called me yet because it should be clear to her too. Talk to me."

"You make it tough to get a word in when you ramble like that," I attempt to joke.

Catt looks at me through unamused eyes but doesn't move to sit down or let go of me. "Don't make jokes. You're not okay. Are you?"

I could lie to her. I could. And I should. Because if I tell her I am so far from okay... Catt doesn't let her friends, me, suffer in silence. She'd see right through it.

"No," I say quietly. "I'm not okay."

Aster and I had our first big fight today. It was horrible. So, here I sit. Catt's room is bright and light and pretty, just like she is. Posters of Viggo Mortensen as Aragorn adorn her yellow walls. Her queen daybed has the whitest sheets and comforter, they look like fresh snow. Fresh pink daisies sit in a purple vase on her sky-blue painted desk.

Her whole life is exactly as you would think it is from one look at her room—colorful and light. Her parents are good and she's an only child so she's their sole focus. They've got one fuzzy gray cat named "Smiles" and if that doesn't tell you how happy her life usually is, I don't know what would.

Right now, I'm like a storm cloud in her perfect world though. I'm so upset over the things Aster and I argued about. It's the summer after our sophomore year and both of us got jobs at different places. So, we haven't seen a ton of each other but when we do it's been wonderful.

"Tell me again what happened. I think I need to hear it one more time before I best friend the shit out of this situation and fix all of your problems." Catt smiles at me from where she sits on her floor. She's painting her toenails a bright green while I lay on her bed.

I run my hands over my face and sigh. "He asked to hang out tonight and I said I couldn't because I picked up another shift at Chili's. He complained that I keep doing that and then we don't see each other. But how is it my fault that he doesn't ask to make plans until the day of and then I've already made plans to work because I refuse to just sit at home doing nothing? And I don't know, Catt. He just got all upset and told me that he misses me, but he said it in like, a really mean way and then stormed out of my garage. It was ridiculous."

Catt screws the top of her nail polish bottle back on, fanning her toes with her hands. "Okay, so basically, he just isn't seeing you enough? In his opinion."

"Yeah, I guess. I mean, we haven't hung out a ton since school got out but he works at the oil changing place a lot too so it's not just me that is the issue. He won't plan ahead, Catt."

"So why don't you plan ahead?"

I sit up and look at my friend, squinting my eyes at her. "Well," I start. "I don't know. I guess I could make the plans. Or some of them. Or maybe ask him what he has going on when I have the chance to pick up a shift." I think on it.

"He just loves you, babe. I'd miss you too if I never saw you." Catt winks at me.

I laugh and toss one of her frilly pillows at her. "I should probably go talk to him. You know, work on the whole communication thing."

I roll my eyes at the thought of this even being a thing at sixteen. But, when you meet the love of your life this young, things like communication and other mature issues become relevant I suppose.

Twenty minutes later I am standing on the Briggs' white front porch, knocking on their bright yellow door.

"Briar!" Aster's mom has the sweetest, vaguely southern voice. She's tall like Aster and thin. Very tan and very pretty, with bright blonde, straight hair. Big bangs and bright blue eyes. Her smile is kind and so is she. "Sweetheart'" she hollers as she lets me in. "Briar is here for you." Turning her eyes back to me she says, "He's in his room, baby. Go on up."

"Thanks Mrs. Briggs."

With that, I head up the dark wooden stairs. Their house is beautiful. It's one of the older ones in this city so it's all Victorian and fancy. My hand grazes the brass doorknob to Aster's room as it swings open. I don't even get a breath out before I'm wrapped up into Aster's strong arms and pulled into his room.

"I'm sorry, I'm sorry, I'm sorry." He keeps repeating his apology as he holds me to him, kissing random spots around my head and face.

I wrap my arms around him just as tightly, soaking in his freshly showered smell and Old Spice deodorant.

"I'm sorry too. I shouldn't have let you walk away like that-"

"No," he pulls back and looks me in the eyes. "No. It wasn't you. It was me. I woke up in a mood and then I just wanted you and to spend time with you and then I overreacted, and it wasn't fair to act like an ass when I'm the one choosing to not make plans ahead of time. But that changes now. I'm going to become a planner, baby. We're going

to make so many plans. All the plans. Ever." Aster punctuates each declaration with a kiss. My nose, my cheeks, my forehead, my neck.

"I could also be making the plans. You don't have to do it alone."

"Never alone. Not with you, sweet Briar."

I hum at his cute nickname.

"I'm sorry I got mad. I love you."

"I'm sorry I got mad too. I love you back, Aster."

"Look at us, surviving our first big fight. I'm so proud of us." He laughs at himself as he tugs me to his bed.

"Yes, we are quite mature."

"I'd fight with you for the rest of my life if it meant I got to hug you after."

Aster nuzzles his nose into my neck as we hold each other on his bed. His door is open and his parents are trusting so neither of us really worry too much as we fall asleep for a midafternoon summertime nap. I fall asleep in blissful happiness.

Never alone, not with him.

eight

"May the petals teach me the art of letting go." —Xan Oku

I LET IT ALL out last night with Catt at the bar. And fuck, it felt good. It felt good to talk to my best friend after months of nothing. It felt good to say Aster's name to someone who knew him and loved him in a similar way to how I knew and loved him. It felt good to just talk about how sad I am and have someone look at me—*see* me. Catt sat and listened to it all. She didn't interrupt. She didn't interject or add to my feelings. She cried with me, and she laughed with me, and she sat with me. She held me while I fell apart and then she let me see her crumble a little bit too. She allowed me to apologize to her for the horribly mean things I said to her last year. She apologized for her role in the situation. We forgave each other.

And now, a new day, we are getting tacos and margaritas for lunch.

"Listen," Catt begins as she dips a chip in the salsa. "I was thinking..."

"That is never something that ends up being fun for me," I joke, taking a sip of my strawberry blended marg.

"Hardy har. Anyways, I was thinking. Let's go out tonight. Like, out-out. To a bar that you aren't at every week with your dad. We can dance and drink a little bit and just..."

Go back to that part of us, is what she doesn't say. But I feel every word.

Catt shakes her head, her dirty blonde hair that hits the middle of her back in a straight sheet, moving with her. "It's stupid. Too soon or whatever. It's okay-"

"No," I interrupt her. "I mean, yes. Let's go out tonight."

Her green eyes go wide and I laugh at the excitement there. "Really?!"

"Yes, really."

"Okay! Let's get ready together? Your place?"

"That's perfect."

It's crazy how easy it was to fall back into it with Catt. Not surprising, no. But wild, nonetheless. Last year our fight was big. It was bad and horrible and explosive, and I thought for sure that was the end of us. But last night... Everything fell into place with us. I think the time apart was necessary, but it doesn't make any of it easier to live with. We lost out on precious time together.

"Let's not do the whole time apart thing again." My request is out of nowhere and in a moment of comfortable silence. "It sucked. And like, not to get all morbid but we both know life isn't never-ending. I don't want to miss out on you. On your life. On lunch dates and late-night talks. I don't want us to miss out on each other again. Let's not do that again. No matter what, okay?"

Catt's eyes are lined with tears as she nods and agrees. "I missed you," she says softly. "A lot."

"I missed you a lot too."

We dry our eyes and laugh at our emotional selves before finishing our lunch date and grabbing supplies from Catt's apartment.

We decided to be crazy and wait until after eight to head downtown. We are done up and ready to take Rapid City by the throat. Lizzo was screamed as we put ourselves together. Hair was curled. Copious amounts of deodorant and antiperspirant were applied. Aleve was taken because while we may not be twenty-one anymore, we are very realistic. Laughing, we climb into our Uber and meet Craig the driver and take a short ride to the bar.

We go straight to the bathroom once inside *Phresh*. This bar is the typical go-to for a night out. Rapid City isn't exactly a "clubbing" kind of town. But *Phresh* has cheap drinks, a big dance floor, a good DJ, and clean bathrooms.

"We look hot!" Catt yells unnecessarily from beside me at the triple sink in the quiet bathroom.

I laugh and shake my head. She looks hot, no doubt. Her long legs and fit frame are showing off in her less-than-knee-length dark blue dress. The sleeves are long and there is no shortage of cleavage. She dressed it down with a bedazzled jean jacket and the whole outfit is giving Taylor Swift vibes. Her hair is curled loosely, and her makeup is perfect.

"No, no! Don't you dare start to doubt how good you look now!" Like she can read my mind, Catt scowls at me.

I look cute. Kind of hot, I suppose. I don't do dresses, and Catt didn't even try to push one on me when we were picking out outfits. I went with a cute pair of heeled booties and loose-fitting, light blue ripped jeans. My shirt is a slightly fitted, maroon V-neck long-sleeve shirt and I am out of my comfort zone by not wearing a sweater over top of it. But I would physically perish due to heatstroke if I had worn one. I guess I'd rather be self-conscious about how my stomach looks instead of dripping sweat. My dark hair is curled and half up. It's longer than usual, what with being depressed and all that jazz. I typically go light on makeup because I am a sweaty gal and there's no point in layering it on when it will inevitably just wick right off. Still, I look good tonight. Better than I have in a while. Which isn't saying much seeing as I haven't gone out in about a year.

"We do look good," I say to Catt as we exit the bathroom.

Once we each have drinks and find a place to sit down for a bit, we don't talk much. Both of us are people watchers and so we do just that while sipping our fruity rum.

"Don't look now-"

I totally look to where her eyes just were.

"I said don't-"

"When you say that, people look Catt!"

We both laugh.

"Okay, well. Now it doesn't matter because they're coming over here."

I did not think this through. The whole "men might find us cute and talk to us" thing. If I had, I probably would have feigned illness and skipped this entire thing. I don't know how to talk to guys anymore. I had one guy. For like, a long time. And then I had a couple guys that I... *talked* to... but then I had the same one guy again for a second practically, and then Aster left and now here I am. I am not ready for this.

"I'm not ready-"

"Ladies."

Fuck.

Catt doesn't even bat an eye before she scoots over and motions for them to sit with us.

Listen, I'm not a total nun now. I can acknowledge how attractive these men are. McTall has the height going for him, sitting next to Catt. He has curly blond hair, and it looks like hazel eyes, though it is dark in here. His face is clean shaven, and his smile is wide and bright.

The man that sits next to me after I slowly and silently move over is also in the tall category. McMan, we will call him. Because he seems to be just that—all man. He's broad and stacked. His arms are probably the size of my calves, and I've got some big ol' calves. They both have on dark jeans and work boots. My gaze travels up my new booth-partner. A light gray hoodie sits under a dark red flannel. He's got a dusting of dark scruff on his jaw and above his smiling lips. His nose is a little crooked in one spot, like it's been broken once and didn't get set properly. Dark, thick eyebrows sit heavy above bright blue eyes that are startling for two reasons.

One, they are the prettiest eyes I have ever seen.

Two, they are looking directly into my brown ones.

I feel my eyes go wide and my cheeks blush, immediately turning my gaze to Catt who is trying to hide her laughter as she looks between me and McMan. McTall is doing a less than stellar job at stifling his laughter, his chest shaking under his white T-shirt and green flannel.

"You okay, babe?" Catt asks after getting it together.

I nod and take a big drink, finishing what was left in my cup.

"Empty," I say, shaking my cup like a spazz. I don't look to Mc-Man as I ask as quietly as I can in here, "Can I get out please?"

He chuckles and it takes everything in me to not beg him to laugh again, the sound so beautiful. I follow him out of the booth, scooting around him, and say nothing as I briskly walk to the bar to order another drink. My hands are shaking, and my heart is racing, and my head is buzzing and none of it is from the singular shot of Malibu that was mixed in with my pineapple juice. After I order a new one, I try to calm myself by taking deep breaths. I internally cringe at how insane I am acting.

He's just a guy. In a bar. On a Saturday night. It's fine.

"Busch, please. I've got hers on my tab, Lane."

I turn to look at him then and say, "You don't have to."

McMan just smiles and takes his beer from Lane, the bartender, before grabbing my drink as well and nodding towards his friend and Catt.

Who are already *very* cozy together.

Without another word McMan is stalking towards the booth. And I, with next to no other choice, follow after him. I try to resist the urge to look at his butt, to watch the way his shoulders stay steady as he walks to our table. I fail.

Wow.

He gets in first, giving me the outer seat. I internally thank him for not putting me on the inside. I hate sitting in a spot that makes me feel stuck. And being between a literal wall and a wall of a guy—I would have felt very stuck.

Again, I am not a small woman. And he is not a small man. The booth is not a large booth and so our thighs are snuggled up nice and close, our shoulders near touching, as we sit next to each other. We aren't talking. Every now and then I'll try to glance at him in secret but he'll already be looking at me and then I'll practically choke on my drink and he'll smirk and I'll die for a second and then act like none of it happened. Until the next time.

"Let's dance!" Catt yells as *Love Me Like You Do* by Ellie Goulding bumps over the speakers at an almost intolerable volume.

I don't know who she was talking to, but McTall doesn't protest as he gets up and takes her hand.

My best friend being *the* best friend though, leans in to whisper in my ear. "What are we doing? You want to dance? You want to ditch? You want to stay with him or go with just me? You say the word, babe."

I love this woman. If I hadn't met my soulmate at fifteen, she'd be it. I suppose Aster can be my romantic soulmate. Catt is my platonic soulmate.

I smile and whisper back, "I'm fine. You go dance with McTall and I'll stay put with McMan. Maybe I'll meet you out there." I pull back and wink.

"McMan and McTall, I love it. Come dance in a song or two please!" Catt places a swift kiss on my cheek and then off she goes with her new friend.

The lights are flashing and bright, green and purple and blue. The building thuds with the bass from the music and the laughter and yelling filters through the air from the patrons. I get lost in people watching. The scantily clad women, my bestie included, grinding and swinging and dancing with the very Midwesterny dressed men, and each other, all look to be having a blast. A few pairings are in various spots near tables and walls, close and kissing. Laughing—so much laughing.

I don't remember the last time I laughed with a stranger. Or an almost-stranger.

"McMan and McTall, huh?" I suck in a breath. "Which am I?"

I hadn't forgotten about this warm, hot body next to mine. I just had been biding my time, waiting for him to get bored enough to leave or something.

Jokes on me.

I sip on my drink and try to rein it in and act cool. Things I have never excelled at.

"Oh, uh," I take a big drink, swirling my black straw around. "McMan." My voice is quiet so he leans in closer.

"What was that?" His deep voice is full of amusement, and I finally look over at him, our eyes locking.

He's close now. Having moved in to hear me. I can smell the mint of the gum he's chewing and the cologne that he must have sprayed on himself. It isn't overwhelming, I note. It's nice, actually. And I've always been an Old Spice or bust kind of gal. His dark lashes flutter a couple times before I answer him.

"McMan."

His smile grows and my desire to smile back does as well. I haven't smiled at a man in months. Like, so many months that I honestly can't tell you the last time I even thought about another man.

But here I am, thigh to thigh, damn near nose to nose, with a man that isn't Aster and I'm *not* hating every second of it. I'm nervous, sure. But that's kind of my M.O.

"McMan..." he sits back, turning his torso slightly so that one arm rests on the table, his hand circling his beer bottle. The other sits on the back of the booth.

Fucking hell, this guy is just... lengthy. Top to bottom.

And now I'm thinking about his...

What the fuck is going on and why is it happening right now?!

Silence coats this booth, my skin, my lungs. We sit there, still touching but neither of us moving.

"I think I should-"

"Do you want to-"

We stop speaking at the same time and look at each other, laughter falling from our mouths. His eyes go to my lips and mine to his.

I do something that shocks me. And surprises him.

"Dance. Do you-"

His reply is instant and enthusiastic.

"Absolutely."

<h1 style="text-align:center">nine</h1>

"You can only move on if you accept that it's gone." —*The Goddess Rebellion*

PHRESH IS CLOSING IN thirty minutes which means I have been here for three hours longer than I had anticipated. But, time flies when you're flush with a man that dances like he probably-

Enough of the dirty thoughts, Briar.

I feel his hands on my hips, his grip firm but loose. His breath on my ear sends a shiver through my body, making the hair at the nape of my sweat-slick neck stand upright. My ass is nestled up nice and cozy with his crotch and either it's the seam of his jeans... or I'm not the only one feeling *something* from this dancing we've been doing for the last couple hours.

Any man would get a semi with anyone rubbing their ass on them like this. Don't think you're special.

I talk myself out of the possibility of him finding me attractive. He's being a good wingman, that's what I've decided.

His friend, McTall, is impossibly close to Catt. Their mouths have found their way to each other on multiple occasions. I'm nowhere near upset with Catt for doing her damn thing though. I applaud that shit. I'll do my part, keeping his friend busy, so they can do whatever it is they need to. Such a sacrifice to have this incredibly handsome stranger to dance with.

"Miles."

I startle at his voice and the feeling of it at my neck, below my ear now. His laugh vibrates against my back and I find myself leaning into him more than I probably should.

But I just can't help it.

After a moment of silence, he leans in again and says, "My name. It's Miles. And yours?"

I turn around, his hands never leaving my hips. "Why?"

His face stays in an amused state, his eyes roaming over me. "Why what?"

"Why do you want my name?"

If I don't give him my name, then we can simply stay as we are—strangers dancing in a crowded bar so our friends can get it on. But if I do give him my name... If I give him that vital first piece of knowing someone...

"Well, it feels a bit odd to ask someone on a date without using their name." He smiles and I freeze. His face turns a bit concerned but not mad or annoyed. "Unless you don't have any interest in that which is completely fine. I can stay McMan and you can stay Nameless and I don't have to ask you on a date. No hard feelings."

He sounds so sincere and as he starts to sway with the music again, my body following suit, I believe him.

"Briar."

His smile grows and his eyes light up. His hold tightens and mine does the same around his neck.

"Briar." My name on his lips sounds like something out of an audiobook, all practiced and perfected. "Briar." He says it again like he's testing out the feel of it around his tongue, through his teeth, in the air.

I feel a tap on my shoulder and then I'm pulled out of Mc-Man's—Miles's arms, and into Catt's.

"Would you hate me if I Uber back to McTall's place with him?"

I laugh and kiss her on the cheek. "Absolutely not mad. Do your thing, girlfriend. Love that for you." I wink at her, and she kisses me back.

Her eyes grow serious as she says, "I'm so glad you're back in my life, Briar. I missed you. I love you. I'll call you in the morning."

"Never again, Catt. I love you back. Have fun, be safe. Keep your phone on so I can track you."

I'm pulled backwards back into the strong arms of Miles as he leans in and asks me how I'm getting home tonight. I don't get the feeling that he's trying to invite himself over. It feels like he's just checking.

"An Uber," I say, leaning my head back onto his chest.

"I'm sober, haven't had another beer since we got out here. I drove. I could take you home. Zero strings. It'll give me the chance to ask you out in a more quiet environment."

His smile is soft, and his eyes are kind. Which is why I say yes and how I end up in the passenger seat of his big white pickup.

"Plug your address into here and I'll get you home."

I take his offered phone and do as he asked.

"Oh, you live near where my grandparents used to live. Small world."

I clam up a bit once we head down the road. It's different in here. His pickup is personal and quiet and calm. There are no other bodies bouncing and swaying here. The music, one of the country XM radio stations, is quiet and soothing.

"So," Miles starts. "Zero obligation, obviously. But I would really love to take you out. On a date." He looks over at me and smiles. "Would you go on a date with me, Briar?"

My stomach flutters with something akin to butterflies. It's a feeling I haven't felt in far too long. My heart feels a small squeeze, guilt taking a hold of it.

But Aster left so I shouldn't be feeling guilt over this nice man asking me out.

So, I choose to do what last-week-Briar wouldn't.

"I'd love that, Miles. Yes."

His smile grows and mine does the same. We pull up to my house a minute later and he puts his pickup in park but doesn't shut the engine off before getting out and meeting me at the hood.

"I'll walk you to your door," he says as we step up towards my house. "Makes me feel like a gentleman."

"It's very nice of you. Thank you."

I am awkward and weird and why the fuck did this handsome stranger ask me out?

Not to be self-deprecating, but if the shoe fits... There were plenty of other women at the bar tonight. Zero shortage of hot, available, willing ladies. And he chose to ask me out? Why? He could have just left it at the dancing if it were for the sake of his friend getting with Catt. And because I am filter-less and also nearly unfeeling... I ask him.

"Why me?"

He pauses halfway up the small stoop to my front door. I stand eye level with him now, my back to my door and his to the street. My porch light illuminates his face and I take in how cute he is.

"Why what?" His face is genuine confusion.

"Why me?" *Fuck it.* "Why did you ask me out? We danced, sure. It was nice-"

He laughs a cute laugh, his eyebrows raising slightly. "Nice?"

"And I know we were wingman-ing for our friends so that's fine. I didn't mind being that for them. Or that being why you danced with me in the first place. But you didn't have to ask me out. Unless you felt like it was some sort of chivalrous thing to do? Like it made you the good guy to do so after dancing with me? Was it a pity thing? I'm not trying to sound crazy." *I clearly don't have to try.* "I just don't want you to have felt obligated to ask me out."

As I finish, I take in his expression. It isn't annoyed. He's not mad or bothered by my brand of crazy. In fact, he almost looks happier than he did a moment ago? Not even amused. Simply happy.

Miles takes one more step up, bringing him to tower over me but not by his normal height.

"How tall are you?" I can't even stop myself from asking.

Without missing a beat and with a smirk I think I'll have memorized by the end of tonight he says, "Six-three."

Swoon.

"And to answer your question," Miles grabs a hold of my hand, lacing his fingers through mine and putting his other hand on my hip, bringing me closer to him. "I will have you know that *I* was the one that told Garrett to check out your friend because I had already checked you out. So technically, he did the—what did you call it? The *wingman-ing*? He did that for me. I wanted to talk to *you,* Briar."

My breath hitches as his smile stays firmly in place.

"Why?" My voice is quiet and I hate how insecure I sound.

"Because I heard your laugh."

"I like your laugh and how you give it freely to those that you love, those that have earned that part of you."

I shake away Aster's voice.

"I heard you laugh at something. I turned to look around, searching for the source of that incredible sound. It was like my brain couldn't move on from it after that. I had to hear it again. I had to see it happen in real time. So, that's why. I heard you laugh, and that was it."

"Huh." It's all I can come up with and now I feel like a moron.

But Miles isn't deterred. "Are you free tomorrow?"

"Tomorrow?"

He laughs and runs his thumb over my knuckles. "For our date. A lunch date? Tomorrow? I can come here to pick you up at noon?"

I nod in agreement and Miles leans in. My throat closes, along with my eyes. But my lips stay untouched.

He presses the lightest, most tender kiss on my forehead. Then he pulls away, kisses the hand he's holding before releasing it, takes a step down the set of stairs, and proceeds to watch me unlock my front door. Once inside, I turn around and smile at Miles, waving.

"See you tomorrow, Briar." And with that, he's gone. He's in his pickup before I close my door, both of us having waited for the other to be safely tucked away in our respective places.

"Your laugh."

ten

"Wait, I'm sorry." Catt gasps on the other line. "You have a *date* today?"

"Well, don't sound so surprised. I can date."

I only feel mildly offended by her shock. It's fair, though. *I* didn't even expect this.

"Oh, babe. No. I know you can date. I just don't remember the last time you did date."

Me neither, honestly. It was with Aster, whenever it was.

"Well! This is very exciting!"

Catt called twenty minutes ago, waking me up. I was surprised to see it was already ten. She regaled her "incredible sex" from the night before with Garrett, Miles's friend. Then she asked about Miles and how my night went. She was mildly bummed when I told her it was less intimate than her night.

"I don't know where we are going. I have no idea what to wear, and what if last night was a fluke and he is actually a total weirdo or he sees me in the light of day and realizes I'm like, not that cute and stuff and then-"

"Okay, that's enough of that." I can practically see Catt waving her manicured hand in the air. "You're incredible. You're hot. You're smart. You're funny. I can't wait to hear about the whole thing later today when you call me because that's what I am demanding you do."

I take a deep breath. Fuck, I *am* nervous.

"Wear your Dude's, the cheetah print ones. With your cute, mildly ripped jeans. That dark green sweater that's long and then do like," she thinks for a minute. "Oh! The white V-neck. That's it. Casual. Cute. Comfy."

She's not wrong, that outfit is all of those things. After telling her that and saying our 'I love you's, we hang up and I get dressed and ready. My hair goes into a clip, not needing to be re-curled. And my makeup stays light.

I'm pacing my kitchen, shaking out my hands and trying to talk myself into chilling out, when I hear a knock on the front door. The stove clock says eleven-fifty-two and I find myself not at all surprised that he's a little early. I take a deep breath, preparing for him to potentially be disappointed when I open the door. His smile only grows, though, and I find mine doing the same.

"Hey, Briar. How's your morning been?"

I step outside after grabbing my purse, locking my door, as I tell Miles, "It's been good. Slow. Talked with Catt, my friend from last night. She said her night was good."

Miles laughs as he leads me to the passenger side of his pickup, his hand lightly touching my lower back. "Oh, yes. I know all about their night."

We both laugh as we get in his pickup.

"You're gorgeous," he says as he looks over at me, buckled up and a hand on his gearshift.

I feel my cheeks warm and smile softly. "Back at you."

He shifts into gear and asks, "I was thinking we could go to that new pizza place that opened up by the mall? Any aversions to pizza?"

"Pro pizza. I haven't been there yet."

"Great!" His excitement seems genuine and calms my nerves a bit. "I haven't either. I hear it's good."

The rest of the drive is filled with mindless chatter and simple conversation. It's nice. Relaxed and easy.

He is nice.

I was afraid I would be filled with thoughts of Aster and everything to do with him. And, it turns out, I am. I think of him often while talking with Miles. But I find that it's not as much as I had anticipated, and I also don't feel guilty for it like I thought I would.

I can't explain what that does to me—not feeling guilty for being on this date or enjoying Miles' company. Aster left me. And even if I had left him, it *has* been almost a year.

That thought jars me out of my own head and brings me crashing back to this pickup and the handsome man next to me.

Focus on the now, Briar.

We get inside the restaurant and sit down, separate sides of the table this time. He orders an iced tea and I order a water. Neither of us had more than a couple drinks last night, it feels nice to not have alcohol as a buffer then and now.

"What kind of pizza do you like, Briar?"

"I like almost anything. As long as there isn't fish on it and it isn't the weirdest combination, I'll probably eat it."

Miles smirks and I spin the Claddagh ring that sits on my right pinky. I got it as a gift when I was seventeen. From Aster. Thoughts briefly turn to him again until Miles continues our conversation.

"Well, good to know. But what kind do you *like*?"

I laugh and accept the fact that Miles seems to want actual facts and not placation. "I like pepperoni and pineapple on thin crust. That is my fave."

I straighten my shoulders and lift my chin and wait for the *"What?! That is insane!"* comment. It doesn't come, though.

"That sounds fire. Let's do that."

My eyes widen and I stutter out, "Oh, we don't have to!"

His smirk gets even smirkier somehow. "I know we don't *have* to. I want to though because it sounds good, and I like to try different things." With a wink, he turns to the waitress as she walks up in the next second and orders my favorite pizza.

When he's done ordering, alone again at our little table, we take a moment to look at each other. His face is all soft and kind, warm. And I only hope that I'm giving back what he's giving me right now.

Miles breaks the quiet by asking, "Where do you work?"

"I work in the administrative office at the nursing home on the east side of town. What about you?"

"That's badass. I work for the department of roads. I do mainly highway maintenance. That's how I met Garrett. We've worked together for the last five years. Did you go to college here? Or at all I guess?"

"I went to school in Omaha." I smile at the memories I made there a lifetime ago. "How old are you?"

"Thirty. You?"

"Twenty-nine. I'll turn thirty in November."

Miles' eyes grow wide. "No way! I turned thirty in November. What day?"

"The twelfth," I say happily.

"I'm the thirteenth!"

We both smile at each other broadly, and I bask in the normal feeling of this whole thing. I'm just a girl, on a date with a handsome man—and I'm actually enjoying it.

"Crazy. And you have family here, yeah?"

I nod my head and take a drink of my water. The waitress drops our pizza off as I answer him. "Yep, I've got my mom and dad and my little sister. Quinn's got her own apartment, and my parents live in the Valley. My dad works construction for Stealy and Son. And my mom is the secretary at the elementary school by their house. Quinn, my sister, is a couple years younger than me. She's a teacher at one of the middle schools in town. They're all good people. What about you? You have family here?"

Miles nods as he takes a bite of his pizza. "Holy shit!" His eyes get big as he looks at me. "This is better than I had expected!"

I laugh at his enthusiasm and dig into my own slice.

It really is good.

"Anyways, yes. Yeah, my family is here. My mom doesn't work, she stayed home with us kids and then just kept up the home front as we got older. My dad is a surgeon at the same-day place in town. I've got two older brothers and a younger sister. They all live out of state, one in Seattle and two in Boston. They do fancy shit, lawyers and doctors. We all get along so that's cool."

I bob my head up and down as he speaks, listening closely. He sounds super fond of his incredibly successful family. It's for sure too early to disclose the fact that I have a deadbeat father in another state and half-siblings through him that I don't really speak with. That's more like fortieth or fiftieth date information. Day before marriage, maybe? I don't know, but I do know I am not ready to have *that* conversation.

We talk about family pets and if we have any—neither of us do. By the end of the date, I feel like I know Miles far better than I had anticipated. It feels very cool to have gone on a successful date like this.

"What's your last name?"

Miles laughs softly and wipes his fingers with his napkin. "O'Brien."

"Oh, you're Irish then?"

"You bet. My grandparents came straight from Ireland when they were twenty. Then they had my dad and uncle."

"That's very cool." I nod my head.

I try to shake off the faint familiar voice whispering *"Ireland"* over and over again.

"What about you, what's your last name?"

"Davies. We're mutts. A little bit of everything. A melting pot of random places." I laugh and he follows with his own.

Miles pays the bill and I thank him as we head to his pickup. He stops at the passenger door, waiting with his hand on the handle. I look up at him, and I mean *up* because he's fucking tall.

"I'd love a second date. Thoughts?"

I pretend to mull it over and decide to just go for it as the idea pops into my head. "Do you have plans this evening? I've got a really nice surround sound system at my house. I'm sure we could find something cool to watch." I rush to add, eyes big and voice a couple octaves higher, "But you can totally say no! No big deal!"

My bold-for-me invite leaves me feeling a bit embarrassed as I wait for his reply.

Which is a resounding "hell yes" and a megawatt smile that makes my breath catch.

I shoot a few texts to Catt on the way to my house.

I WISH.

eleven

"You carry so much love in your heart. Give some to yourself."
—R.Z.

I WALK UP THE stairs to Mark's office, my steps feeling and sounding lighter than usual.

I feel lighter than usual.

This past weekend was incredible. Between bouncing back with Catt, and meeting Miles, my whole soul feels like it's been able to take its first breath since-

And there's that missing weight.

"Hey, kid. How was your weekend?"

I step into Mark's bright room, making my way to the same couch and slipping off my shoes. We both get settled and I let the silence surround us.

"Briar?"

I meet Mark's gaze and feel the tears well up in my eyes.

"Hey, what happened?"

His voice is soft, and kind and I feel like a traitorous bitch filled with guilt and sorrow.

"I felt happy."

I take a moment to pull my shit together before elaborating. Mark lets me. He gets me by now and knows sometimes I need just a minute to figure out how I'm feeling.

"I went on a date this weekend."

I don't miss the surprise that flicks across his face.

"And I enjoyed it."

Mark smiles softly. "And now you feel like you shouldn't have?"

I nod.

"Oh, Briar. You can be happy. Heck, you *should* be happy."

I swallow my scoff and blink up at the ceiling, preparing to talk this out because this is new territory.

"I remember the first time Aster and I talked about what would happen if we ever broke up. We were so nervous about it because we were more than in love—we were best friends."

Movie night at the Briggs house is always an entire event. Aster's mom, Fiona, makes it this huge thing. She loves an excuse to host, and I love that for her.

I'm snuggled up with Aster on the couch in their living room. His parents are on a date, but that didn't stop Fiona from going all out on the snacks and stack of DVDs she rented. Aster and I settled on "How

To Lose A Guy In Ten Days". We both laugh at something funny before turning our faces towards each other for a quick kiss.

Their couch is a deep one, wide enough for us to lie comfortably together. I'm on the inside, snuggled nice and close between the back of the couch and Aster's warm body. His arm is slung behind me, holding me tight, while his other hand rubs small lines on the top of my hand that rests on his chest.

Our quick kiss turns into a much longer make out session. We've hit second and third base in the last few months. We aren't in any rush to go beyond that, only being juniors in high school.

My seventeenth birthday came and went last month and now Christmas is next week. The house is decorated in the most sophisticated way. Nutcrackers and antique ornaments, warm strings of light and crimson berries, the smell of cinnamon and orange. It's becoming my favorite place to be this holiday season. I'm surrounded by those things and the feel of Aster's hands on my arms, running up and down, pulling me closer to him. I didn't think I could be any closer—he proves me wrong.

Against my forehead, taking a break from the kissing, he whispers, "Junior year is already halfway over."

I look into Aster's eyes and nod my head.

"Then it's our senior year."

I nod again, not sure where he's going with this.

"What happens after that?" His question is quiet, serious.

I rest the side of head back onto his chest. "Well, Omaha is where my dad went to college. I've always wanted to do that, go there like he did."

"Omaha."

I nod again.

"I think I want to stay here and do the firefighter academy."

I put my chin on my hand, looking at Aster. "Okay."

"But then we would do long distance, right?"

"Aster, what brought this up? That's forever away."

"I've just been thinking about our future I guess. My dad requested to not have to move again until after my senior year. He got approved for that. I guess no one ever asks to stay at Ellsworth Air Force Base."

We both laugh.

"And since he told me that, I've just been thinking a lot about life. About what I want and what we might want. I want to stay here. I like it here. I want to be with you."

I smile at that.

"I want to marry you someday, sweet Briar."

My smile grows. "You do?"

He nods and kisses my forehead. "I want to stay here and go to school. I want to become a firefighter. I want to buy a house with you on the west side. I want to marry you, and then have some babies with you. Raise them here, where our parents and Catt and Quinn are. Spend the rest of my life here. With you and the life we build."

I kiss the tip of his nose. "I'm in."

He moves to face me fully, his eyes wide. "Yeah?"

"I'm so in, Aster. I think I still might want to do college in Omaha but that doesn't mean that plan has to change. Not much, anyways."

His smile falters slightly. "But what if that does change something? What if you get there and find someone else? Or you just realize you like it there more than here? What if that causes us to like," he swallows and whispers, "break up?"

"Oh, Aster, no. I don't think that will happen at all. Have faith in us."

I run my fingers through his already messy hair.

"You're my best friend, Briar. You're the love of my life. I can't stand the thought of something happening and us ending. You're more than just my girlfriend."

"Aster," I say slowly, smiling. "I'm going to love you for the rest of my life. And maybe knowing that at seventeen should make me sad, I don't know. But it doesn't. It's a fucking relief, honestly. To feel that. To love you. It's an honor, really. To know that isn't one sided—to be loved the same by you. How lucky are we to have found the one we belong with at such a young age? I don't foresee that changing."

I take a breath after rehashing that conversation, living that memory again. That one hurts. Knowing what I know now, having experienced what I did with him. It's like a punch to the gut. Seventeen-year-old me was naïve and happy.

I miss her.

"Briar," Mark says softly. "It's okay to have felt joy this weekend. That doesn't take away from what you had with Aster. That doesn't mean you didn't love him, that you don't still, like you think you did and do. Enjoying your life is good, it's healthy. It's *normal* to eventually feel okay."

"It doesn't feel good…"

"Why?"

"I don't know how to explain it." I shrug, feeling confused and sad. "It feels like I don't deserve it, I guess. Like, I got my one shot and then I lost it and now I'm just, alone and sad and that's my destiny?"

"Why would you think that's something you deserve? To be sad and alone forever?"

"Because I left him. I left him first. I went to college and shit didn't go like it was supposed to and now here we are. I broke us before he did. It's my fault."

twelve

"Just keep swimming." —*Dory*

THE THING I HAVE found about grief, over any heartbreaking situation that I have lived through, is that it isn't routine. It isn't predictable. They, nearly everyone I have spoken to, say there are these five stages of grief; denial, anger, bargaining, depression and acceptance.

I say bullshit.

I don't know about stages. All I know is that for months, nine to be exact, I have felt next to nothing. In the beginning... I was enraged, I admit. That stage of grief seems to be one that is often met with open arms. People love to be mad, right? I seemed to have skipped denial, having witnessed Aster leaving myself. Living in a state of delusion wasn't exactly an option in my sometimes-too-realistic brain. So, I had gone straight to anger. For a few days I recall just being so...

Furious.

At him. At Catt for her part in things. At myself. At the entire world and every deity and God and ruler known and unknown. I cried the first day—wallowed. I screamed the second day until my throat was raw and my head was pounding from dehydration. I hid on the third day, not answering calls or texts or the door. By the fourth day, a Tuesday just like today, I was numb. I no longer felt anger. I had never denied his absence. I didn't try to bargain my way out of this hole that I had found myself in. I paused at depression and never moved in the direction of acceptance.

My biological father is a high-functioning alcoholic.

I am a high-functioning shell of depression.

How far does the apple fall?

Last night's session with Mark left me feeling hollow. More so than usual. It is no fault of his. I walked into his room feeling light and alive for the first time in nine months and then I remembered everything that happened last April and was quickly brought back to the reality that I live in.

Well, that I walk in, I suppose. *Living* feels a little too kind of a term for what I do on a daily basis.

I didn't call Catt like I had said I would. I didn't blow her off entirely, sending a text that said I had a long day and was going to bed early. Which wasn't a lie. I was in bed by eight-thirty and reading *Heir Of Sun and Moon* by Jenessa Ren on my Kindle. A little romantasy to take my mind out of my own reality was what I needed before sleep fought me off all night.

The joy I had felt up until last night has faded entirely and the numbness that I have been content to live with for almost a year has settled itself back into my bones. Work gave me the opportunity to become reacquainted with my "I'm fine and there's no need to worry about me" smile, though it didn't take long. One weekend without it didn't completely screw up the muscle memory I had going.

It's perfect timing now, though. As I pull the take-and-bake pizza out of the oven and wait for Catt to let herself into my house, I give myself a little "hey, keep your shit together" chat.

Fake it until you make it.

Especially with her. Our relationship is just now kick starting back up again. I don't need to go and make her feel guilty for things she has no control over now.

So, I will smile and nod and try to fake those little crinkles in the corners of my eyes. I can do it. I've been doing it this whole time.

"Honey! I'm home!"

I don't have to fake the giggle that escapes me at my best friend's arrival. It's been the same greeting since we were twelve.

"Smells great! Pizza?"

"Yep," I say as she rounds the corner of the kitchen and pulls me in for a hug.

"I want to hear about every detail of your Sunday and anything in between then and now, immediately."

I sigh, getting ready to tell her it is already over and that I haven't heard from Miles since Sunday night when he left. Aside from the text or two, that we are most definitely going to pretend don't exist on my phone right now, from him telling me how much fun he had and how he'd love to get supper this week sometime.

That was all before I remembered how atrocious I'm meant to feel.

"No, don't tell me it's over already! McMan fizzled out?" Her pout is genuine.

"He didn't, no. I did."

Catt sits down at the table, bringing a can of seltzer that she snagged from my fridge to her lips. Her blonde hair is in a massive bun, little wisps sticking out all around and out of her black scrunchy. While she appreciates a good reason to get all dolled up, her normal state is far more relaxed. We're both in black leggings and fuzzy socks, oversized T-shirts. She's got a white puffer vest over the top of her shirt. Neither of us have a speck of makeup on. Comfy and cozy and back at it together again. My heart warms at the thought.

"What happened, Bri?"

I swallow, thinking. How honest do I want to be? I don't want to make her sad. I don't want to lie. But isn't that all I've been doing this whole time?

"I just don't think I'm ready to see anyone."

Catt sets her pizza down, wiping her hands on her napkin and pulling a knee up to her chest.

"I know we just got back to each other," she starts, twisting her lips to the side. "And I really, *really* don't want to do anything that potentially fucks that up..."

"Okay?"

I set my own slice of pizza down and sit back in my chair, keeping my hands in my lap and not over my chest so that I give off the vibe of *"please, be honest with me."* Even though I don't think I want to hear her honesty.

"It's almost been a year, Briar..."

I stiffen. "I know how long it's been."

She nods slowly, biting her lip. "And at what point do you think you'll let yourself feel again?"

I don't answer. Mainly because I don't have one. But also, because the one I do have would just elicit a whole other conversation.

"I just think that if you wanted to—if you really wanted to..." She looks away and pauses. "He wouldn't want you to be like this for forever, Bri." Her voice is almost too quiet to hear.

But I sure did.

I get up and take a walk to the sink, washing my hands to give me something to do.

"I don't want to fight. I don't want to upset you. I just want-"

"It's not about what you want, Catt." I try to rein in my anger. I don't want a repeat of April.

Like she's reading my mind she says, "I don't want to lose you again. I also don't want to watch you stay in this weird, numb state of life though. That's not living."

"I don't want to talk about this. About me. I'm fine."

"I don't believe you though... And I like to think I know you better than most."

"I don't need you to believe me. I just need you to respect me when I tell you I don't want to discuss this again."

She nods and gives me a small smile. "Please talk to me if you ever want to... Okay?"

I smile back, my very practiced and rehearsed one, and nod. Her smile falters only for half a second before she fakes her own and we eat in an uncomfortable silence.

I break the quiet eventually, having muted my brain enough to converse. "So, McTall?"

We both break out into laughter at his nickname and Catt tells me all about how Garrett and her hit it off and are hopefully going to casually see each other.

I don't bring up Miles, and neither does she.

I do find myself feeling... *something* about the lack of him in this conversation, however. Even though it's my doing, I can't help but *feel* some type of way about it.

Almost like I miss him... But that can't be.

I don't miss people anymore.

thirteen

"I learned a long time ago the wisest thing I can do is be on my own side." —Dr. Maya Angelou

THE BOOKS I READ describe wraiths as these zombie-adjacent creatures. Numb, mindless almost, not alive but just existing. I wonder if time flies for them in the books like it does for me in reality...

It's the end of March and life now is exactly as it was two months ago. And nearly identical to those few before then as well. My sessions with Mark are always filled with talking about how I deserve to feel anything at all and I leave feeling nothing at all. And while I can say Aster's name aloud, and hear Mark say his name, that's about the only amount of progress I've made there. Quinn has been so busy with teaching and coaching volleyball that she's been less on my case than I had anticipated. My mom and dad are both still oblivious to my deep dark depression. And Catt hasn't brought up my lack of happiness since our pizza night in February, so we've been on the up and up.

Life is fine. Which is really all I can expect from it at this point. Taking what I can get.

I hadn't heard from my father since after the new year, in the form of his picture-perfect holiday card. That lovely stretch of not having thought of him ended today when I got a text from my cousin on his side reminding me of her upcoming wedding and that she, and I quote, "expects my fine ass to be dancing the night away in celebration of her love." It's taking place here in Rapid City. My father lives in Nebraska so he'll have to travel if they come up for it. Our whole family is spread through the few states around here—South Dakota, Nebraska, Iowa.

I laughed and said I would be there. I immediately regretted accepting the invitation in general because...

Now I have to see my father and his picturesque family that should be my family too.

And...

I don't have a date—a buffer. Catt can't go because her family is having a wedding of their own that weekend. I hate going to this shit alone.

"Alone with your own family? How?"

Easy. I don't fit.

When you go to a family event, be it a funeral or a wedding, who do you usually sit with? At the big, eight person, round table—who's next to or across from you? Probably a parent or a sibling, maybe both.

I don't have that. I don't have a spot at *their* table—not with *their* dad.

I sit with an aunt. I stand in line at the buffet with my cousin and use the excuse of helping her with her four kids' plates as the front for being with them. I don't wait for my sisters or brother in the parking lot and walk in with them. I don't call them before to see if they'll even be there. It just isn't what we do. I stand near a group I'm not "in" for large family photos, not near my father or his family.

As a child it wasn't by choice. I was just placed where I was, and he never argued or moved me. As I grew, I chose where I placed myself and by then it was just the norm.

The "norm" is fucking bull shit.

I sigh and sit on my couch, turning on *Jurassic Park* after scrolling through Netflix.

I love my cousins on my father's side. They're all great. My aunts and uncles are really awesome too. I've never had any issues bonding with them or having relationships with them. They all have their own relationships with my father and siblings and then I have my own with them. It's always been something that has felt odd to me, the double sided-ness of it. But it's not like I'd ask any of them to choose me over him or something. In the same breath though...

It gets harder and harder every year to be fake. To fake the hugs. To fake the smiles. To fake the small talk. To fake being fine with being the abandoned one, "the other daughter".

And lately, in the last few years, I have found myself feeling a bit... bitter. My family has always just ignored the lack of relationship their son or brother or uncle has had with me my whole life. I didn't go to family events with him—I got dropped off by my parents after arranging it with an aunt, or that aunt just brought me along with her family. As I got older, I just showed up to shit.

I've grown to feel tired of the placating. From everyone. I watch at events. I see everyone acting as though he's a standup guy who doesn't drink too much. A guy who didn't used to react, objectively speaking, a bit aggressively to his son when he didn't score or play right in a game. I know he doesn't help with my grandparents. I know he doesn't "pull his weight". And yet no one bats an eye. It's all fine. Because "that's how he is."

Well, how he is is not good enough for me.

I can't go to this wedding alone or I might drown in feelings that have no business being at such a celebration.

"Sweet Briar," Aster whispers as he grips my chin and tilts my face to his. "What's going on in that busy brain of yours?"

I give him a small smile as we stand by his black new-to-him Subaru Outback. We're in the dark parking lot of a Super 8 in the middle of nowhere-Iowa. My uncle is getting married tomorrow and we came a day early because of the eight hour drive. It was a good trip over here. A lot of Taylor Swift was sung. Slim Jims and Mountain Dew were ingested. Laughs were shared. After we dropped off our bags and relaxed, waiting on everyone else to arrive, we decided to go for a drive and see what Iowa in November is like.

Cold. It's Cold.

We also decided to make use of his new hatchback style trunk on a very empty, calm dirt road. So, that was fun.

Now, standing in front of the hotel, my family congregated in the lobby area around all of the tables and in some of the brown cushioned chairs... I feel nervous. I hate feeling nervous around my family. But seeing my father and the kids he chose... It never sits quite right with me. And after he missed my birthday last week, for the eighteenth time, I'm feeling angry and annoyed and bitter towards the man.

More so than usual.

"I just don't want to deal with Jack tonight. Or tomorrow really. Or ever again."

Aster runs his cold hands up and down my coat covered arms, pulling me closer to him. I rest the side of my head on his chest, gripping the front pocket of his way-too-big orange hoodie. His chin settles on the top of my head and I feel his breath move the dark strands of my ponytail.

"I hate him for being so awful to you."

"He could be worse. I know. It just sucks that he sucks the way he does."

"What kind of father forgets to wish his oldest, or any of his children, a happy birthday every single year? It's sick."

I love how much Aster is always on my side with Jack. Sometimes I think he might dislike the man more than I do.

Not making my own bitter comment, I say, "Let's get inside. It's cold."

We make our way to the automatic doors, unable to hide our arrival with the squeaking it causes.

"Look who's back!" My aunt gets up, excited to see us. "Kristy said you guys went for a drive."

She says it loud enough and winks auspiciously enough that my cousins all hoot and holler at the intended meaning behind her words. I laugh, only slightly uncomfortable. Aster laughs and holds my hand as we walk to an open spot near the middle of the lobby.

"They better not have been out doing anything like that."

Jack's gruff, smoker's voice grates on my nerves immediately.

"Oh, she's eighteen! Who cares," my aunt says as she sits back down, rolling her eyes at her brother.

"Not yet she's not."

I feel Aster stiffen, my own shoulders sagging at the fact that the man whose blood runs through my veins—He doesn't even know how old I am.

"Actually," Aster says with far more bite than I have heard him hold before. "Briar turned eighteen last weekend, Jack."

My father's name does not sound kind coming out of Aster's mouth. My entire family goes quiet then, everyone's attention going entirely to this conversation. We're all witnesses to this incredibly uncomfortable and on-brand moment.

"You'd know that if you'd ever bother to wish her a happy birthday."

I squeeze Aster's hand and bring my mouth to his ear. "It's fine, honey. Relax. Let's go upstairs."

He gets up with me, not breaking Jack's eye contact. But Jack says nothing, looking only mildly caught. Which surprises no one.

"Goodnight, kids." My other aunt, the more reserved one, is quiet as she stands and hugs us both. "See you tomorrow."

She looks at me like she knows it isn't "right" or "normal". Like, she understands and sees that this is all odd and shouldn't be "okay". But she says nothing else as we get ready to go upstairs, no longer wanting to fake it with everyone else.

"Goodnight," is all I say as we walk towards the stairs.

Once we reach them is when the conversation in the lobby picks back up—football and other emotion-free topics being discussed.

"I love you," I say to Aster as we make our way to the room.

"I fucking hate that guy," he says at the same time. "But I fucking love you, Briar Renee."

I swallow the lump in the throat, gripping my chest as the memories fade. And on impulse, something I almost never act with, I grab my phone and text someone I definitely shouldn't be texting.

> It's been a while, but I've got a wedding that I genuinely can't go to alone. Got any plans next weekend?

McMan

> I've never been freer than I am next weekend, funny enough. What time should I pick you up? :)

fourteen

I RUN MY HANDS through my loose waves one more time as I check out my reflection in the new mirror by my front door. I'm not sure what had me getting this the other day at Hobby Lobby with Catt but I silently thank myself for the cute addition.

Miles will be here any minute and while I don't necessarily regret basically booty calling him for a wedding date... I kind of regret it.

Ignoring the nerves, I swipe on some deep burgundy lip stain, telling myself to remember to blot at it in five minutes when there's a knock on the door. My stomach goes to my throat and my pulse kicks up to about a million. But he's here and there's no going back now.

I'm momentarily stunned when I open the door at how handsome Miles looks tonight. He looked good the other two times I have seen him, yes. But tonight...

His dark hair is longer, probably covering his ears and getting into his eyes when it isn't combed back like it is now. His scruff is trimmed to perfection, almost in a sheer sort of way that you can see his skin peaking through a skosh. And his lips are tipped up into an impressive smirk. His smirk... Wow, I missed that.

I missed that?

I missed that.

"Hey, stranger."

His voice is exactly how I remember it, and even though it's not yet been two months since I saw him last, I can't help but feel like it's been years.

"McMan," I smile and step back, letting him into the house. "How are you?" I ask, trying to keep it light and breezy.

That's me—light and breezy Briar.

"Good, good." He pauses halfway through the door, leaning in and placing a kiss on my cheek. "How have you been, Briar?"

I swallow down the squeak from his quick kiss that about escaped me and say, "I've been fine, thanks. Listen..." I twist my hands together after closing the door. Looking into his sky-blue eyes, I tell him, "I want to apologize for just kind of, um-"

"Ghosting me?" His voice is light, but his gaze is more honest, a bit heavy, even with a smile.

"Yeah," I concede, my shoulders sagging. "Ghosting you. I hate that I did that. I am really sorry."

"It's all good. I'm glad you reached out last weekend. I'd be lying if I said I hadn't thought about reaching out before then. But I can respect boundaries and didn't want to push yours. You had your reasons, I'm sure."

Yeah, reasons...

I'm depressed and sad and also numb all at the same time which is basically just a melting pot of "messy".

But I can't tell Miles that. Instead, I smile and tell him, "I'm really glad you said yes to this. It would also be a lie if I said I hadn't thought about you too." And that's true. I had been thinking about him.

His smirk turns into a full-blown smile, and I return one in kind.

"So, whose wedding are we crashing?"

"It's my cousin, Kristy." I smile as I grab my little purse and phone from the coffee table in front of my couch. "Ready?"

"You look incredible. I don't think I've said that yet. Beautiful, Briar."

I feel my cheeks warm, my already blushed face turning a more natural shade of pink.

I do look good... Not to toot my own horn or anything. It's hard to find really chic, beautiful outfits when you are a certain size and shape. But this one, I am proud of. Nude heels, a dark purple skirt that swishes around my ankles as I move, with a black V-neck shirt, the sleeves hitting just below my elbows—shoutout to Amazon for this winning ensemble. My hair is half down and wavy, my makeup is smoked out and smooth, and with it being March, there is no humidity to ruin a damn thing.

Without even telling Miles what I had been planning on wearing, we somehow complement each other flawlessly. His light gray shirt is tucked into dark gray slacks, and it's buttoned up just high enough on his chest that there is a small amount of tanned skin showing, a small smattering of chest hair peeking out. His arms are covered, the sleeves buttoned at his wrists. Both items of clothing are fitted to absolute perfection on his body. He sits somewhere in the middle of "I work out" and "I don't do that at all" and I find it incredibly attractive at how just normal he feels—relaxed. A pair of black dress shoes that look freshly shined and a beautiful silver watch top off his outfit.

He's honestly a little intimidating with how good he looks.

"You look great too," I say after a far too long pause. "I'm ready."

Once we are seated and buckled, Miles knowing the way to the church where the wedding ceremony is being held, I take a deep breath and ready myself to explain Jack to Miles.

"You okay there, Briar?"

I turn my gaze to his and swallow. "Huh?"

"You're holding on pretty tight to your purse there." He smiles, nodding his chin to my white knuckles.

"Oh." I try to lighten my hold, succeeding very little.

"Are you alright?" His voice is softer now.

"I'm fine. I just, I think I need to tell you something and it is going to be weird for the both of us but I need you to just understand that I'm not a total crazy person and wow I just need to spit it out."

I take a breath and feel his hand grab mine, pulling it onto the little console between us. And the craziest part of that? I let him. I don't even flinch. He grabs my hand like he's been doing it for years and I don't even think to react in a way that shows he hasn't been.

I release a loud sigh. "Okay. So, this wedding is for my cousin. On my father's side. My dad, Brian, who raised me?" Miles nods. "Well, that's not the same person. My biological father is kind of not great and that's who's side of the family this is for. And so, when I invited you it was kind of as a way to have like, um-"

"A buffer?" Miles sounds calm and not at all offended that I'm basically using him.

"Yeah, yes. A buffer. I'm so sorry. This is so stupid. We can turn around. This is insane. I should have never put you in this sort of pos-"

"Whoa, slow down, Briar. It's fine."

I look over at Miles, my eyes narrowed. "It's fine?"

"Hell yeah," he says, squeezing my hand that he is still holding. "It's fine. I'll buffer for you any day, honey."

I blink at him, not sure if he's being serious. Well, that's a lie. I know he's serious. I don't know how I know but I know.

"So, your father. Do we hate him or just dislike him? Do I shake his hand or knock him out? Kick him out at the knees so you can take him out on your own? Where are we at here with that?"

I laugh. I laugh so hard I feel tears threatening to ruin my perfect makeup. I cackle, if I'm being fully honest. Once I've gained some semblance of control over myself, I look over at Miles and find his eyes wide and on me. His lips are slightly parted and his hand is still in mine, resting between us.

"What?" I ask, smiling and catching my breath.

"This isn't a line, please know that," he says. "I *really* love to watch you laugh, Briar."

I sigh and rest my head back on the seat. "It's not something I feel like I do very often anymore," I say almost accidentally.

Miles lets my quiet admission go without saying anything more about it.

"No, don't knock Jack out," I say after a few minutes. "But you also don't have to fake it with him either. I sure as fuck don't anymore."

"Deal," he says as we pull into the packed parking lot of the church. I spot Jack's black GMC pickup right away, parked next to my brother's almost matching one.

"Oh," I say as we unbuckle. "I also have two sisters and a brother. But it's weird between us for reasons that are probably my fault. So, like, do with that what you will."

I almost recoil at my own nonchalant-ness making that statement. But the truth is the truth. We're all adults now. If we wanted to talk more, we probably would.

"Noted. I also definitely want a more in-depth story at some point if you're ever down for that. Knowing why I hate this guy would be beneficial to the inner punches I'll be throwing at him."

I laugh and meet Miles at the front of his pickup. He smiles down at me, tucking a stray strand of hair behind my ear.

"Beautiful," he whispers.

We never kissed all those weeks ago. Our two days together, though close, we never quite got there. And we don't now, either.

Miles grabs my hand and loops it through his arm before walking us both into the church. I square my shoulders and raise my chin, pulling on my mask of indifference that I wear whenever I'm near Jack and his chosen family.

Being the one that chooses to not fake it with someone is exhausting, though. I am reminded of that fact every time I see my father, thirty minutes in.

Now, over two hours in, I'm damn near empty emotionally. I didn't have much in that regard to begin with today, but it's nearly all gone now.

I look to Miles, his one arm slung behind me on my chair and his other resting on his crossed knee.

The ceremony was beautiful and Catholic and *long*. The reception started almost an hour ago and it's in a rustic, gorgeous barn just outside of town. When we arrived, we each got a drink and some snacks. We found a couple of seats at a table near the center of the room, my cousins having arrived right before us flagging us down and saving me from the awkward job of evading Jack. The bridal party will arrive shortly, thus beginning the meal portion of the night and then hopefully things will kick off from there and I'll be able to Irish-goodbye-it after Kristy's first dance.

Exhausted, remember?

"Need anything?"

My eyes meet Miles' and I smile at him.

"I'm okay, thanks though. Do you need anything?"

"Maybe some fresh air. Come outside with me?"

I nod and we stand, his hand going to mine and our fingers intertwining. My cousins and their dates all smile around their own conversations and tell us they'll save our seats.

"I have to say..."

I brace for literally anything and everything. Judgment or questions or comments about how weird the air is when I'm in a family setting like this one.

"It's kind of wild to me that he doesn't even *try* to talk to you."

I don't have to ask who he's talking about.

"Like, I know you avoid him. But to not even *try*? He's just..." Miles runs a hand through his hair, messing up his combed look.

"He's just what?"

See, I get it. I get why Miles thinks it's insane. I know it's weird and it's not normal. I understand that he probably thinks it's a me thing and that I pushed Jack to this point—the point where we don't even look at each other. I think that most people just assume I'm dramatic and rude and that's why he walks North and I walk East. But I faked it for so long. I couldn't do it anymore. I would leave events and feel so gross about the bull shit smiles and hugs. So now, instead of feeling gross, I just feel tired after ignoring him for however long I'm around him. I don't know which is worse, honestly. Depends on the day, I suppose.

But that isn't something someone can understand unless they live it.

"He's missing out."

Miles's comment is surprising and not what I had expected. My face must reflect my thoughts. He steps closer to me. We're by the railing of a balcony that overlooks some hills and a small little part of town. There are a couple round fire pits that are currently housing small fires. Miles takes both of my hands in his, pulling me into him and holding me there, our fingers linking and hanging at our sides.

"He's missing out on how incredible you are. I know I don't know you much. Though I hope to change that." He winks at me, and I roll my eyes playfully. "But from what I do know... You're great. And the fact that a man who *should* be your dad in life—that he *chooses* to let you ignore him... He doesn't deserve you."

I swallow hard, willing myself to not jump into his arms and beg him to say it all again.

"He chooses to let you ignore him."

"Thank you. That-," I chew on the inside of my cheek. "No one really gets it. Gets *that*. Not like you just did, anyway. Thank you."

He smiles softly, watching me intently for a moment. "Don't ghost me tomorrow, yeah?"

His request catches me off guard, the vulnerability and honesty there shaking me. I look into his eyes, searching for some sort of tell or lie or trick.

"Why?" My voice is nothing more than a whisper.

Why would he care? Why did he agree to come? Why does he want to talk to me at all?

All of these questions circle my brain, and he must see them because without any hesitation he brings his lips to mine.

This kiss is soft. It's light and warm and quick. It's like my voice a moment ago—a whisper.

We pull away from each other, eyes roaming over every centimeter of the other's face. And then I'm letting go of his hands and I'm gripping his arms, right above his elbows. His hands go to my waist, gathering the fabric of my shirt in his fists. And our lips meet again.

But this kiss is not soft. This kiss is anything but. This kiss is...

Fuck.

This kiss is hungry and hot. It's melting and crushing. It's consuming and it's overdue.

And it's over far more quickly than I would have preferred.

Our breaths are labored, and our chests are touching with each one taken. One kiss did that. *One.* Well, two. But it was that second one...

"Don't ghost me tomorrow, please." Miles makes his request again, softer and gentler.

I nod my head and hold his gaze. "Okay."

I don't think I could even if I wanted to now.

fifteen

"Never allow someone to be your priority while allowing yourself to be their option." —Mark Twain

"Briar, honey."

I bristle at the voice from beside me at the restroom sink.

"Marnie, hi," I say to my stepmother.

I have no real qualms with Marnie. I also don't have any real respect for her either but that's not necessarily her doing. She loves a man who chose to not give a shit about me. It is what it is. My beef isn't with her. It's just like, kind of around her.

"How are you? How have you been?"

I think she means well. I've always *hoped* she means well.

"I've been fine."

"I heard about Aster-"

"Oh, you know what," I interrupt her. "I told my date I wouldn't be long, and I've already been gone beyond that. I'm a woman of my word, so I'll chat with you another time Marnie. Bye." I try to sound pleasant as I rush through my parting words, but it feels inauthentic.

I exit the bathroom in a rush and run right into my sister-in-law and her baby bump.

Can't catch a break now.

"Briar!"

"Nicole!" I attempt to match her enthusiasm, hoping it doesn't sound too forced.

I resist the urge to smother her precious bump with love. Having a sibling, or an in-law, who carries your niece or nephew and not feeling like you have the emotional right to love on that child is actual torture and if the FBI isn't already using that as a method, they should really think about it. They can give me a call for the details if need be.

"How are you?" both of us ask at the same time, causing a little laughter to flow between us.

I like Nicole. I even like Nicole's husband—my brother. I wish things were different. But when you grow up being kicked out of family portraits so that your stepmom can hang the "real" one in their house... Well, sometimes things don't have to happen on site to form wedges between people.

"I've been good," Nicole answers first. "A few of months left before this little one arrives and then we'll be even more exhausted and busy." Her smile tells me how genuinely excited she is about the whole thing.

"I'm so happy for you." And I mean it. I am.

I'm also so sad for me that I am missing out on it all. I don't know how to repair things that are so far beyond broken.

"Can I text you when she arrives?" Her question jars me out of my thoughts and my face must show it. "So that you can come to the hospital to meet her? Kyle and I talked about it," she says slowly, cautiously, as though to not scare me off or upset me. But if she only knew just how elated I would be to be involved in literally anything... "And we both would love to have you-"

Yes," I say almost too loudly. "Please. Yes."

We both smile and if I weren't so numb on the inside then I'm sure my eyes would be just as glassy as Nicole's are.

"Come say hi to my date and I later? After things get going?" I extend the branch back.

Trying.

She nods excitedly. "Yes, we definitely will."

Nicole squeezes my arm before turning and walking away.

"What are you all smiley about?"

I look at Miles as I sit down next to him, his arm immediately going to the back of my chair and his hand pulling lightly at a piece of my hair by my shoulder.

"My sister-in-law, Nicole. She met me as I was coming back, and we had a really nice talk. I think she and my brother will come say hi later." I feel proud at how steady my voice is. My nerves are going crazy.

"Briar, that's incredible. She's the pregnant one, right?"

I smile and nod before taking a sip of my water.

"I can't wait to meet them."

"Thank you," I say softly, leaning in so I can be less loud. "For not being totally put off by my family drama and craziness today. For coming with me to this. Making me feel less alone."

Miles just smiles and leans in, closing the distance between us. His lips touch mine for a small kiss and I can't hold in the hum of contentment that leaves my throat. His smile turns into a smirk and my face gets warm with embarrassment. But all he does is kiss me again.

Usually at a wedding I get fresh air during the father daughter dance. Unless it's a wedding that I'm attending with my mom, dad, and Quinn. This wedding is not an exception to my Jack-Family rule. But I don't even have to make the first move. Miles somehow can sense how anxious I'm getting while we wait for the DJ to announce that the time has come for Kristy to dance with my uncle. Before he can even finish saying it, Miles whisks me to the patio with the fire pits and fresh air.

"I feel like I am thanking you for saving me an awful lot tonight."

He pulls me close as we sit down on a cushioned loveseat. "No need to thank me, I just wanted you to myself for a few minutes before the dancing begins." He kisses the top of my head. "You smell so good. Like," he takes a big inhale, his nose pressing softly to my hair. "Strawberries and oranges?"

I nod and laugh quietly. "Literally. That's the scent of my shampoo and conditioner."

"I've got the nose of a bloodhound, baby."

We sit there, eyes on the fire, in quiet comfort for what feels like only seconds. I hear the door open, the music loud for a second before quiet again as it closes, and see Kyle and Nicole walking our way and taking the chairs across from us.

"Hey, Briar."

I nod at Kyle and smile, trying to rein in my excitement but also show that I'm happy to see him. "Hey. This is Miles. Miles, this is Kyle and Nicole."

"Hey, Miles. Nice to meet you."

"Hey, man." Miles stands up and meets Kyle halfway for a handshake. "Nice to finally meet Briar's brother. Congratulations on the baby. Nice to meet you too, Nicole."

Kyle smiles at me at the "brother" comment and my heart warms. Nicole smiles at Miles and says hi back.

Kyle and Nicole are beautiful. Apart and together. Her skin is so richly dark. Her hair is always, and I mean *always*, in its curly perfection. She gets it highlighted so it's this gorgeous, dimensional, textural hair that I find myself envious of every time I see her. Her eyes are a deep brown and always bright. She's curvy and petite, the top of her head reaching Kyle's shoulder when they stand toe to toe. Kyle is six feet tall, and I would describe him as... lanky. He's handsome—all of Jack's kids are good looking. His hair is a light blonde like his moms and his eyes are the same blue as our fathers. I missed the gene that allows me to carry a solid tan on my skin, but Kyle did not. Their baby is going to be insanely beautiful.

"So, how long have you two been dating?"

"Oh, we aren't."

"A day."

I look at Miles and he looks at me, our answers overlapping. We laugh and look at my brother who looks confused and concerned. Nicole hides her laughter behind her hand as she looks between the three of us.

"I asked him to come as my buffer tonight, so I didn't have to deal with your dad by myself."

That's one way to not fake it, I guess.

Nicole's laughter, no longer being contained by her hand, fills the patio. Kyle's follows soon after and before I know it, all four of us are laughing and talking and catching up.

For the first time in my life, in Kyle's life, I am sitting here and feeling like I really have a brother. Only a few months separates us in age, Marnie getting pregnant nearly right after my mom got pregnant.

Go Jack.

I find myself wanting to tell Aster all about it. Because he was there for a lot of the mishaps and heartache that really began to be prevalent around the time when we met.

I can feel my face fall, feel the guilt start to creep back out into the open hole from where I must have hidden it away for the day. And then I can feel Miles' fingers gripping my chin and turning my face to his.

"What just happened?" He asks it so quietly, discreetly. Nicole and Kyle are now talking amongst themselves, giving us privacy. "Are you okay? Where did you just go?"

I shake my head, not trying to get out of his grasp but also trying to maybe pull away. I feel like I should *want* to pull away. But he doesn't relent, his grip firm but soft.

"I'm fine."

He gives me a long look and kisses the bridge of my nose gently. So gently that it makes my heart squeeze.

"When you're ready to tell me your secrets, Briar, I'm ready to hear them. Okay?"

I say nothing, unsure of how to respond to that. Instead, I just nod. And when I let myself think about it, just for a second, I find that I *want* to tell this man my secrets. I want to show him how unfeeling I have been on the inside. I want to see him understand me in such a deep, visceral way. Want to show him that until he entered my life, I didn't think I'd ever *feel* again. Not that I even know what I am feeling with him right now, but the fact that I'm even questioning it... It all means something.

Because I know he will try to help me. I know he will try to make me *feel* more.

And I'm terrified of where that will lead.

Because I think he just might succeed.

We go back inside and find that open dancing has begun.

"Dance with me, Briar?"

I find myself unable to say no, and simply not wanting to. Miles leads me to the dance floor, pulling me close to him. He rests one hand on my lower back, his thumb gently moving. His other is holding one of my hands to his chest, right above his heart. I grip behind his bicep with my free hand. We sway together, the song playing slowly. Garth Brooks' version of *Make You Feel My Love* is giving all of the slow dance vibes.

My brown eyes meet Miles' blue ones, and his smile brings mine out.

"I can feel your heart beating," I say as I look at where our hands lie on his chest.

"And how does it feel?" His voice is deeper than it was a minute ago—rougher.

I swallow. "It's fast."

He nods and smiles. Then he leans in and kisses my forehead. "It is."

"Why?" It's all I can think to ask, my insecurities needing to know if I'm part of the reason.

"You."

He says it so simply, so factually.

"You."

sixteen

"Talk to yourself like someone you love." —*Brene Brown*

"So, Briar. How was it seeing your dad over the weekend?"

I sigh and rotate my iced latte in my hands. "I didn't even really see him. I only spoke with Marnie for a second and then talked with Kyle and Nicole which was really nice."

"Your brother and his wife, right?"

I nod.

"You didn't speak with your sisters?"

"They both left after the ceremony, so I didn't have the chance or anything. I don't know if we would have talked anyways, I guess."

"Have we really dove into everything pertaining to Jack and your siblings? I think that may be a nice change of pace for us today. If you're up for it?"

I take a deep breath and nod, preparing myself for the very Lifetime Network-worthy tale of how I came to be.

"Okay, so. My mom and Jack had been casually seeing each other for a few months, having met at a bar one night. They were both twenty-one and from surrounding towns, I think. She had met his family, my grandparents, at least. They'd gone to a couple family dinners together, I guess. A couple months in, my mom found out she was pregnant with me. She called Jack and let him know. She told me that she had made it clear that she didn't expect anything from him, she just would have hated herself if she had kept it from him. She said he sounded fine, told her to meet him for lunch at his apartment at the end of that week or something."

I brace myself for the look of shock this next part always coaxes out of people. "She showed up however many days later that was, and his roommate had answered the door and told her, like she should have known or something, that Jack had moved out that week and was gone. So, my mom just kind of moved on. Didn't reach out again until I was born. She sent a mail announcement, apparently that was a thing?"

Mark smiles softly and nods, finding my question a little bit funny.

"So, she sent that to his parents' home. I think it was to be a little *petty*, maybe? Kind of like a 'hey you can't keep her a secret' move. My grandparents told my aunts, and my aunts called my mom asking if they could all meet me and be a part of my life. My mom said absolutely."

Mark shows no sign of shock though. "And then Jack got your stepmom pregnant?"

Nodding I say, "Right, so. Like, three months after my mom got knocked up with me, Jack got Marnie pregnant. And Marnie was just barely nineteen or something. Her parents were super religious. Like, beyond my grandparents Catholicism. So, they essentially made Marnie and Jack get married. They obviously have stayed together, good for them or whatever. Kyle is a few months younger than me. And then Madeline and Christine are two years younger than us, twins. My mom met Brian when I was a little over a year old and then they got married when I was two and had Quinn the next year."

"And have you ever tried to speak with Jack about your feelings of abandonment?"

I sigh as I tell him, "I have. I remember when I was like, fourteen maybe? I was all up in my hormonal feelings about how much I wished he'd paid attention to me. Like, maybe if I were good at sports like Kyle or skinny like Madeline and Christine... maybe then he would care about me? Show up for me? So, I sat down with my purple spiral notebook and wrote him a letter. Bright orange ink, even. I remember crying and then my tears hit the paper and I just let them—left them there. Thinking that it would make a difference if he saw how sad I was." I laugh, though it's humorless. "I never got a reply after I mailed it. I saw him later that year at my aunt's wedding and he asked me to dance. Save face and all that. I was elated, though. Halfway through, I got the courage to ask him if he ever received a letter from me." I swallow the embarrassment. "He nodded and said yes, that he got it and read it and that he just didn't know what to say back."

"So, he said nothing?" Mark's voice is soft.

"So, he said nothing. And that was it. We haven't discussed it since."

He nods and then shakes his head. "I am not sure why we haven't ever discussed this, honestly. And this may not be the right *therapist* thing to say but I would like to commend you. I wouldn't have been surprised if after that start to life you were sitting before me as an alcoholic with a few different baby-daddies."

I snort at his "compliment". I chose Mark, and continue to stick with Mark, because when I do open up to him... The way he "therapy-s" me—it just works for my brain. He makes it all relatable and easy to digest. Or as easy as can be, I suppose.

"And while there would be nothing wrong with you had that been your case, it's admirable that it isn't. You're somewhat of an anomaly."

The statement makes me a little uncomfortable, the truth in my head tugging at me.

"I feel like I could wreck it all if I wanted to," I whisper.

"What do you mean?"

I sit back and look out the window. The sky is blue and open today, though the air is still cold.

"I mean... I could be that. I feel it—inside of me. I feel the narcissism. I feel the option to be dependent on something like alcohol. I feel the loneliness and I feel the choice there, inside, that I could change it all. That if I wanted to sleep around and marry someone bad for me, I could. It's like this weird self-awareness. That like, if I wanted to be Jack, or be like Jack, I could do it in a heartbeat. I could choose that for myself."

"And how does that make you feel?"

I look at Mark. "It's scary. To feel that piece of him inside of me. To know that I could fuck it all up if I wanted to. Or if I simply didn't care enough not to anymore, I could change everything. And..." I stop, unsure of how to voice this.

"And?"

"And I feel like I'm nearly there, Mark. Like this gnawing emptiness inside of me would welcome that narcissism and the addiction and the unhealthy relationships with open arms if only to just fucking feel *something*. To feel anything at this point. I'm tired of feeling nothing. And then there was this boy-" I cut myself off, remembering that I haven't told Mark specifically about Miles.

"A boy?"

I sigh dramatically, feeling my cheeks blush. "I met Miles a couple of months ago, I told you about that date. The night I went out with Catt. After fixing our friendship?"

He nods.

"He was there with a friend and at first when they came over, I thought he was just being a good wingman for his buddy but then at the end of the night, Catt going home with Garrett, Miles took me to my house. He was really nice and respectful. He asked me on that date, and I said yes and the next day we spent pretty much the entire day together."

"But?"

"That Monday I was feeling great but then, I don't know if you remember... I felt guilty. For being happy and not devastated to the full extent over Aster. You told me it's okay to be happy, but I didn't text Miles again after that. But then the wedding last weekend came up and I got freaked out and acted on impulse and asked Miles to go with me and he said yes. After months of not talking, me blowing him off like that, he said yes? Why would he do that?" I shake my head at the thought. "So, we went to the wedding, and we had the best time and he kissed me a thousand times and my chest started to feel all... warm and alive again and my head only had this like, faint echo of Aster and when I realized *that* I felt horrible. How dare I feel such happiness with someone else? But that's insane because Aster is fucking gone, and I don't know what to do with Miles because I told him I wouldn't ghost him again and here I am debating doing just that. My heart and my head are both telling me to let myself like this guy but then my head and my heart are both whispering Aster's name to me in the deep, quiet moments and I don't know what to do with any of that."

I breathe a full breath for the first time after verbally throwing all of that up.

"Have you told Miles about Aster?"

I pull back like I've been struck. "Why would I do that?"

Mark laughs at my sudden offense. "Well, if you continue to see him, I think you might want to try to tell him. Aster is a big part of your life, Briar. A big part of your story."

I say nothing. I can't tell Miles about Aster. Right? That would be crazy. And we aren't even really dating.

Except I guess he said we are, and I didn't argue.

"Let's table this, and switch back to Jack. What do you think about some homework?"

I groan and Mark laughs.

"I think you should write him a letter," he holds his hands up at my terrified expression. "You don't ever have to send it. But you could if you wanted to. And I think for you, it might make you feel something to get it all out on paper."

I nod and think it over. It's not like I would send it. But I guess I could if I wanted to?

It wouldn't make a difference—he'd ignore me either way.

"Okay," I agree.

"And if you continue to see Miles, I think you should tell him about Aster. It's been almost a year. It would be okay to let someone else in on that part of you, Briar."

I nod, thinking it over.

Let someone else in on that part of my life? Tell Miles about Aster? Open that door for the questions and pity and thoughts and feelings?

I don't know about any of that.

But I do know this—I definitely don't want to ghost McMan again.

I called Miles after work today because I needed to go grocery shopping, and this morning when we were texting he mentioned also needing to do the same. He said he'd meet me at *Fresh Family* and that's how I ended up here, in the toilet paper aisle with him at seven on a Wednesday night.

He's got one cart and I've got my own. I've followed him so far, mainly so I could check out his butt in those dirty old jeans, but he made me swap the last aisle over.

"Hey, Kleenex brand or generic?"

I look over at him holding up a four pack of each and turn back around before saying, "Kleenex every time."

"No way. Really? They're hardly different."

I pause my step and face him. He's all smirk and dirt and whatever kind of highway dust he's been in all day. His hair is a mess and he doesn't wear hats which I love. His eyes are extra bright against the work-worn face of his. A bright yellow long sleeve shirt hangs loose on him, his jeans and boots leaving dust as we go.

"The Kleenex with the lotion in them saves my nose every winter and I will hear no slander about them," I say as I slowly step towards him, bringing my cart with me.

He makes his way to me, the toes of his work boots hitting the toes of my sneakers as we get to the middle.

"Generic brands are just as good, ma'am."

"On some stuff, yeah. But no way on this one, *sir*."

"You're nuts."

"You can keep those at your place. I'll keep the good ones at mine."

"I'm replacing every box of tissues at your house with these from now on. And when you change it back, I'll just keep changing them around. I've got all the time in the world, baby."

He smirks, a toothpick hanging loosely from his lips. I hate how much I love this fucking image, committing it to memory.

"Don't you dare," I whisper in mostly mock terror.

"Or what?"

I narrow my eyes, stand on my toes and grip him behind his elbows to steady myself. Putting my lips just above his, I whisper, "Or those lemon bars I made you Sunday?" His eyes get big. "I won't ever make those for you again."

"You love those too much to not make them for yourself."

I step back, crossing my arms. "Oh no, I'll still make them. For me."

"You are evil, woman."

Miles sets the generic tissues on the shelf, putting the Kleenex brand in his cart. He mutters something under his breath that sounds an awful lot like "best fucking lemon bars, devil woman, how dare she" and I laugh the rest of the way through the store.

seventeen

ASTER'S BEEN GONE A year next week. Five days, actually. It's Thursday and by Tuesday, it will have been a full three-hundred-and-sixty-five days since he left. Any way I spin it, say it, look at it, count it—I can't believe it.

"Briar?"

I look up from my quesadilla in front of me. *The Blue's* is hopping tonight. It feels crowded and loud. Though, that could be due to the extra person at the table with my family. It only took three weeks for everyone to harass me enough to bring Miles along tonight.

I look at Quinn, her eyes still on me after saying my name. I feel a finger twirl some of my hair behind my back and sigh into the presence of Miles at tonight's family dinner.

"What?" I finally reply.

"I asked how your quesadilla is. You usually get a burger. Is it good?"

I felt like switching it up tonight, which is, self-admittedly, odd.

"It's good. A little too cheesy for my liking but it's fine."

I push a piece around and then the plate is sliding away from me, and a plate of fries and a half-eaten hamburger are taking its place.

"You hate it, and that's fine, mo chroí. Have my burger, please. You said you missed lunch."

I smile at Miles and kiss his cheek, putting on far more PDA than I have ever been comfortable with.

But with him... With him it's *easy*.

I look up to find my parents and Quinn blinking at us before my dad chugs half his beer and my mom smiles like she just watched me get married. Quinn eyes me skeptically before eating more of her own chicken strips and fries. The rest of the meal goes on as it should. Small talk and light topics. Everyone takes their turn asking Miles about his life and I do my best to not buffer for him. He told me he'd love to answer anything they ask when I warned him about them and so I'm trying to respect that for him.

He's doing fucking incredible.

"Thank you for letting me crash your family dinner." Miles shakes my dad's hand as we stand by our respective vehicles. He picked me up from home and immediately my dad started asking about the specs of Miles's pickup, all of us arriving at the same time.

"Please, it was great meeting you!" My mom practically yells at him before shaking his hand.

I resist the urge to tell her to chill.

"I'm more of a hugger," Miles says, bringing her in for one and making her entire year.

"I love him, Briar! Keep him! Please!"

My cheeks redden and I duck my head down. Miles laughs and pulls me into his side, kissing the top of my head.

"Miles," Quinn says with narrowed eyes, holding her hand out. "Be nice to my sister. Or else."

I roll my eyes, but he shakes her hand and says, "As long as she lets me." Which immediately wins him a lot of points all around.

Once we're back at my house, settled on the couch together and watching *90 Day Fiancé*, I let my mind wander to Aster and the guilt I'm still holding on to. Not so much *let*, I suppose. More so... I don't put up a fight now that I'm in my own home.

The guilt I feel for feeling anything other than empty sorrow is overwhelming.

Miles and I have been seeing each other, frequently, for three weeks. It's been incredible. He comes here usually but sometimes I go to his apartment on the other side of town. Garrett and Catt are still seeing each other so we have all hung out a few times together. Usually, it's just the two of us though. We cook supper, watch shitty shows, cruise around town or through the hills. A couple weeks ago we went grocery shopping again.

Together. One cart. Parallel checkout lanes. It was great.

It was domestic as fuck.

And then tonight he met and had supper with my family. I ordered a new entree. And now I'm panicking.

Because what the fuck are we doing? What am *I* doing? I'm supposed to be alone forever. I'm destined to be sad and miserable, and this happy squishy feeling in my chest... I don't know what to do with it. It's out of place. It's foreign. It doesn't belong. I am not worthy.

And because I am an insecure shell of a human being, I sit up, pulling out of Miles's reach, and tell him abruptly and without context, "I think we should maybe call it."

He sits up, his smile kind. "A night? Sure, babe."

He gets off of my couch, his light-blue jeans hanging low on his hips until he pulls them up.

"No," I say, not moving. "Us."

Miles freezes and I avoid his eyes.

Better to do it now than later when we are in too deep, I guess.

"What?"

"I think we shouldn't-"

"Why?"

"It's not you-"

"Don't do that." His voice is calm but stern. "Don't do that. Not with me. Not after the last month. Don't fake it with me."

"I don't know what you're talking about. And it hasn't been a month."

He scoffs.

"Three weeks," I whisper weakly.

"Yeah, okay. Yes, you do know what I am talking about. And don't do it here, Briar. What's going on?"

"We're just moving too quickly, Miles." I get up and walk around him, putting space between us and making it so he isn't towering over me. "It's too fast."

He takes a deep breath and says, "I don't feel like we are. I feel like until a second ago it was a pace that we were both really liking." He pauses, weighing something out in his mind. "Listen, I very vaguely heard something about an ex of yours. Something bad must have happened and so I am completely fine taking things slow and going at whatever pace you need. But please don't think that means I will let you push me out completely. Not when I know you feel what I feel."

I freeze now, my eyes locking with his.

"Geez, Briar, babe. Don't look so scared. Garrett asked if I knew about how you had a hard time last year with someone important to you. How it seemed to have been pretty bad. I said no. We left it at that. But now I think I might be missing out on something vital. So, I'm asking about who he was and what he did."

I'm going to murder Catt.

"I'm not doing this. I don't need to defend myself."

I walk to the door and go to open it. A large, calloused hand stops me.

"Whoa, hold on. What happened between five minutes ago and now?"

"Nothing." I shake my head, looking at the floor between our sock clad feet.

"No, please don't lie to me. What happened?"

I shake my head again, feeling like a bobblehead at this point.

"I like you, Briar. A lot. And I think you like me too. A lot."

I say nothing and don't move to look at Miles. This isn't supposed to hurt this bad.

It's only hurting so much because he's fighting it. It's definitely not because I regret it already.

"Mo chroí, please." Miles puts both of his hands on either side of my face. "What's going on?"

My eyes connect with his. Mine are filled with anger and sorrow, his are worried and kind. We are not the same and that's the driving force here. But that name... He's called me it a few times over the last few weeks.

"What does that mean?"

"What?"

"Mu-" I try. "Mo chri-"

Miles laughs, not making fun of me but just amused by me.

He sounds it out slowly, "Muh khree," his tongue rolling the "r". "Mo chroí means my heart. It's Irish. My grandma speaks some Irish and-"

I pull out of his hands.

"My heart? *Your* heart? See?" I wave my hands around. "Too fast, Miles. It's better if we call it now."

Miles takes a deep breath. I would be annoyed at myself too.

"Am I supposed to be competing with a ghost here, Briar?"

My entire being freezes. The blood in my veins. The heart in my chest. The brain in my head.

"What? No, that's crazy."

Now we are gaslighting? Super job, Briar.

"Then tell me what the fuck happened with this guy that has him so far in your head right now. Because I am here, Briar. I'm right here and I'm damn near on my knees begging you to let us have a real shot. You ghosted me once and I let it go. But you gave us a chance again and you don't seem like the kind of girl to just change her mind like this. But how can we have that shot when you're looking over your shoulder waiting for some guy to come back? If that is even the case—I wouldn't know, you won't talk to me. Forget the fact that this isn't fair to me, mo chroí. What about *you?*"

"I'm not talking about-"

"I think I need to know what went down. If you're so against it that you can't tell me yet, fine. But I don't want to end this. Give us a shot. Give me a shot. Give me something. Please."

It's the please, combined with the pleading in his blue eyes, that shatters every lock and chain and wall I have built up inside of myself.

It's the fact that if I wanted to just keep going at this with him, this outburst be damned, he'd let it go tonight and just let me. No questions asked. For a while at least.

It's the fact that I so desperately want this man, this kind, good, gracious man... I want him to see me. To see what and who I am. To see that I am not okay and that I haven't been this entire time.

He'll leave then, anyways.

"He died!"

Miles blinks a few times, watching me for a moment. I sink down to the floor, crossing my legs under me and leaning back on the wall by the door.

"He died. He left me here, to mourn and grieve, and he *died,* Miles. He's gone. He's not a ghost. He's not alive to steal me back. He died in my fucking arms. And I loved him so desperately that now—now as I look at you and as I start to fucking enjoy you, like you beyond a flirting fun sort of feeling, I'm constantly choking on the fear that I'm not worthy of that. Of you. Of a second chance at something great."

I try to take a breath, to get myself under control. But I can't find the strength.

"Because he was my first, Miles. He was my soul mate, and my best friend, and the love of my life. And I was fucking lucky to have met him at fifteen-years-old. I was lucky to have loved him and to have been loved by him. And now here I am... Grieving his life, grieving the loss of his laugh and his smile and his heart. Day in and day out—*grief.* And up until I met you, I thought I was destined to feel that for the rest of my life. I didn't think I could feel *this*—feel *like* this again."

Miles hasn't moved. He's still standing by the door, his hands are slack at his sides and his eyes are wide. But then he moves, slowly and calmly, making his way over to me.

"Feel what?" It's barely above a whisper but he squats down next to me, keeping some distance between us.

"Fucking loved—in the loosest form of the word." I am freaking myself the fuck out, but he asked. "Or liked. I was sure that I had

had *it*. That *that* was it for me in my lifetime. The great love of my life—he loved me for a decade and then took his last breath while I held him."

I shake my head, scoffing at the thought now.

"I thought *"sure, that's fine, at least I got to feel that extraordinary love of a lifetime"*. I got to feel the love of the sun. And how many people can say that? And then I met you, Miles."

I look at him now, his eyes filled to the brim with concern.

"And suddenly my numb chest felt something again. It's like my heart had just been biding its time to feel. I thought I had lost all ability to *like* or love. But then you smiled at me. And you smelled like Old Spice. And your laugh made my knees weak, and you asked me out and that was it for me in a way."

He tries to push some hair off of my face but I shake him off, needing the space he's still offering.

"So, now I'm terrified. I am fucking scared to my core that you won't stay. That somehow, someway, I've cheated the system and whoever runs that system will find out and take you from me. No one gets two suns, Miles. Not here. You'll die, or you'll leave me, or you'll realize I'm fucking damaged goods. And then I'm shattered again and only this time, I had the fucking knowledge to prevent it."

"Oh, mo chroí."

"Don't *oh muh whatever that Irish word is* me. Don't pity me, Miles." I force myself to meet his gaze and see nothing but kindness directed at me. "I'm fucking fine."

"You're anything but fine right now, Briar."

"I am fine," I insist, the lie tasting like ash on my tongue.

"And it's okay not to be!" Miles says with passion.

"Nothing is okay!"

And at that, I break wide open. Completely and fully—a chasm of sorrow and anguish and darkness is exposed. One I have been hiding for a year.

eighteen

"Everybody moved on, I stayed there. Dust collected on my pinned up hair. They expected me to find somewhere, some perspective, but I sat and stared, right where you left me."
—Taylor Swift 'right where you left me'

My pulse is at a catastrophic level. I swear that if I got it looked at, it would be in a scary place. I could if I wanted to—get it looked at. I realize this as I rush through the halls of the hospital in Rapid City.

I've been here before. I visited Catt here when she had her gallbladder removed. I've tagged along with my mom visiting her friends throughout the years for various reasons—babies and broken hips or whatever ails the aging. But never have I ever ran through these halls, scowering each and every inch looking for Catt or Aster, or the crew of Punk'd, like I am right now.

I reach the elevator and punch, almost literally, the number for the floor Catt gave me. I tap my feet, my Birkenstock nearly falling off at how anxiously I'm doing so. Running my hands down my black leggings, I pull at the hem of my brown T-shirt, genuinely feeling like

I am about to crawl out of my skin. My fingers find the bun at the top of my head, pulling at the thick mass and making it even messier.

The bell dings, the silver doors open, and I rush to the white double doors that lead to where Catt said she and Aster are.

"Briar, thank God!"

I turn quickly and see her briskly walking towards me. Her hair is down and all sorts of tangled, messy and unkempt. Her face is bare and the bags under her eyes have me concerned. She's in brown sweats and a gray hoodie. It's all giving the impression that she's been here for a while.

I give her a hug and follow her to the desk by the doors.

"She's here to see Aster," Catt says from beside me to the lady behind the glass.

Her name tag says "Sammy" and her smile is soft but serious as she asks, "Relation?"

"Fiancé," I say quickly. Her eyes turn sad as she fills out a name tag for me and my body tenses even more.

I don't feel bad about the lie. It's what will get me in the door—to him. The romance movies have taught me that if you're not his sister or his wife, you won't be getting in to see whoever is beyond those doors if it's bad enough. And I have no idea what is going on. Best not to risk it.

No one can stop me from getting to Aster.

As Catt and I get buzzed through I grab her hand and pull her to a stop.

"What the hell is going on?"

She shakes her head, and her eyes fill with tears. "I can't... Just, go in and talk to him. Please."

I look around the area, searching for answers I won't find out here. The waiting room is empty. There's no one else here, it's about four in the morning. I don't see Fiona or Levi, no one but Catt.

"You call me, I rush up here from Omaha in the middle of the night, I don't ask questions. But now you won't talk to me?"

"I promised him, Briar. We all did. Please."

I say nothing else, feeling incredibly annoyed with my best friend, and also very confused. I walk down the hall, leaving Catt at the double doors and going to the number she told me. I stare at it for a minute—his door. It feels heavy, this moment.

Pushing the door to Aster's room open, I freeze as it closes softly behind me.

The smell, lemons and bleach, is the first thing I focus on. The sun is down still, the moon full and perched outside of Aster's window. I take in the bits I can see. The monitors must be silenced, making no sound. The light glow from the lamps on the walls and the moon outside illuminate the recliner in one corner, a computer in another, and then-

And then there he is. Aster. My-

Not mine, anymore I suppose.

Hasn't been mine for a couple of years now.

He's thin. Pale. Gaunt. Sick.

He's sick.

"What's going on?" They're the first words I have spoken to him in years.

I don't move from the door. His eyes locked onto mine the second I walked in and haven't strayed since. He says nothing, patting the bed beside him. I notice the tubes coming from his hand.

I say more firmly, "What is going on, Aster?"

"Come sit with me, sweet Briar."

"Listen," I say as I walk slowly to him. "The longer I stand here in the unknown, the worse the theories get. At first, I thought maybe you broke a bone. And then it became that you might need part of my liver somehow, though I don't know what our blood types are." Yes I do. "And now it's gotten so bad in here," I tap my skull, "That I'm thinking you're dying and have cancer or something. But that isn't possible. Because surely, you'd have called me here before now. Before it's too late."

"I do."

"Do what?"

I'm at his bedside now. He's not pale—he's fucking gray. And he's not thin—he's nothing but bones and skin and hospital tubing. I'm sick to my stomach at the sight, my brain running a million miles a minute.

"I do have cancer."

"No you don't."

He laughs, but it doesn't sound like his laugh. It sounds weak and sad. "Always stubborn."

"That simply can't be true, Aster. Because if you have cancer and you're this sick and just now calling me..." I shake my head, emotions clogging my throat and terror causing my hands to shake. "That's not possible because that would be cruel."

"I'm so sorry."

"No. Don't say that. Because that's not what's happening. Because there would have been time then. There could have been time."

I grab the railing near me on his bed to keep myself upright. "You could have called me at some point in the last two years. Because it was your choice to not speak, Aster. It was you that held that card—that ball. And so, it could have been you that reached out. We could have had time. There's no way you're just now speaking to me again. Just so I can, what, watch you die? No. Not possible."

I'm shaking my head like it's a pair of ruby red slippers and I'm Dorothy, and maybe if I do it hard enough things will go all black and white and I'll not be in South Dakota anymore.

I refuse to believe this.

"I'm so sorry."

"Stop saying that, Aster!"

I'm shaking. From my toes to the hair on the top of my head. My head is shaking. My hands are shaking. My heart is trying to keep itself held together. My knees threaten to take me out.

"Lay down with me, Briar."

My head doesn't stop its refusal. My heart breaks even as I fight it.

"Tell me the truth right now, Aster. This joke is sick. What's going on?"

"Please, love. Lay down with me. I even scooted over while I waited for you to get here."

His voice gets weaker the more he speaks, so I do as he requests and settle onto his bed with him. I'm careful to not catch any tubing and to not completely squish him.

"You couldn't squish me, Briar."

"Stop reading my mind." I sniffle. "What's going on?"

The anger has simmered, and the sorrow has taken over.

"It's like coming home," he says into my hair, avoiding my question. "I've missed you. I've missed running my fingers through your hair. I've missed rubbing your forehead right here and watching you relax."

He smooths the wrinkles in between my eyebrows, achieving the desired effect. But only for the briefest of a second.

"Just like that," he hums. "I miss how soft your lips are." His finger trails along my mouth, tracing the dip at the top. "I miss these." His hand cups a boob through my shirt and I can't help but to laugh, though it turns into a sob. "Apologies to your boyfriend. But I'm sure he'd understand the sentiment. First dibs and all that."

I don't correct him in the fact that I don't have one of those, it's only ever been Aster in the ways that count.

"I've missed the feeling of you next to me." His voice is quieter now, more serious. "I'm so sorry, my sweet Briar. I wish I had called sooner. I wish I had called every day for the last two years. I wish I had let us love each other—in whatever capacity we could have. I'm so sorry I took that away from us."

"I'm sorry you took it all away from us too." It's all I can think to say—to allow myself to say.

Because what I want to say is really mean. It's vicious and fueled by anger. So, I keep that anger inside. For now.

Aster sleeps soundly as I get up quietly and leave his room a little while later, needing to breathe air that isn't forced.

I don't see Catt as I walk the hall to the double doors. I don't see anyone, really. I find an open room with a couple of couches and close the door behind me. I fall to the floor, my face meeting the cold tile. I don't even have it in me to care that I'm lying on the floor of a hospital.

Aster is sick. He's dying. And he called me here to say goodbye.

I sob until my head hurts—until my tears and snot have created a puddle on the white tile beneath me. I gasp and hold in the screams I want to unleash until my throat is raw and sore.

I hold onto the anger, the fear, the resentment, the anguish. I carry it all back to Aster's room and keep it locked up tight for the next couple of days.

It's a Monday now, I think. Two days after I arrived back up here.

Aster's breathing is shallow and slow. Catt left an hour ago and the nurses have stopped coming in. His parents have been in and out, but I think Aster must have discussed something with them prior to me arriving because they've been giving us more space than I had anticipated. Everyone handles death differently and the Briggs family is no exception.

I'm sitting next to him, his body under several blankets and mine on top. He has one hand resting on my thigh and his head is on my chest by my shoulder as I hold him close. I'm reading a page from A Court of Thorns and Roses by Sarah J. Maas. When I told Aster it was about faeries and magic, he laughed until he coughed and asked me to read it out loud to him.

That's what I have been doing for two days. I don't remember anything by the end of the day, so I just start over from a random page and read.

When I asked his doctor on Saturday what the "timeline" looked like, his eyes filled with sympathy as he said a couple of days.

It's nearing the end of that "couple of days". I've kept the emotions at bay, the tears never flowing until I'm alone in a bathroom or somewhere by myself.

I haven't said so much as two words to Catt. I can hardly look at her. The only reason I'm saying the five I am to Fiona and Levi is because it's their son that's dying. But the anger towards everyone has taken root deep inside of me. It's sitting, settling for now. A dull throb when I think of how no one called me sooner. I'm sure that will all change after he's gone.

"Briar."

I look at Aster and hold in a sob.

I thought he looked sick two days ago, but nothing would have prepared me for today.

I think back on the fifteen-year-old boy that walked into my science class a decade ago. I see the boy I fell madly in love with. I remember his sandy blonde hair that is no longer on his head. His laugh and how full it was. How it had the power to wrap someone up like a warm embrace—like the sun. His hands... They were so strong once upon a time.

"I'm sorry."

"I know," I say. I run my fingers over his head, ignoring the cold feel of the smooth skin.

"I've loved you every day since I was sixteen," he rasps.

I swallow. "I've loved you every day since you were sixteen, too."

"Marry me."

I don't know how coherent he is anymore. He goes from lucid to not in a matter of what feels like minutes, all day, back and forth. But I don't question him. Instead, I lay us down a little bit, turning towards him and closing my eyes as I press my forehead to his.

"Marry me, my sweet Briar. Please."

And I would. I would run and grab anyone with the power vested in them. I would say those two words in front of whoever I could find, and I would marry this man in an instant. If I thought I had five minutes to track anyone down...

"Okay," I whisper onto his lips.

"I love you."

"I love you too."

I can't hold in the sobs any longer. My body continues to shake with them as his stops moving entirely.

I don't know how long I hold onto him. My tear-filled eyes don't leave his lifeless ones. Not while the nurse comes in to shut off any monitors that were left on. Not while his doctor comes in to do whatever it is he has to do. Not while Catt tries to comfort me, and I shrug her off, hating her. I don't move when his mom holds him from the other side and his dad rubs her back. I stay here, holding him to me and whispering how much I love him, hoping and praying that wherever he is he can hear it—that he can feel it.

"I wish you hadn't left me."

I whisper that into him over and over again, begging for a world where he's here and whole and I'm with him until the end of time.

I get up finally, my mom calling my name softly from the door, a group of nurses waiting behind her. Leaning down, one last time, I kiss Aster softly on his lips, my fallen tears pooling on the creases of his face. I try to ignore how cold and blue they are as I tell him I love him and that I will love him until the day I die.

And then I leave the room, and him, behind.

As if they were physically real, I feel the bars and chains and locks encase the cold empty chasm of my chest, sealing it off from ever feeling anything again.

<h1 style="text-align:center">nineteen</h1>

"The world just kept turning. I never forgave it for that." —Ben
Breadon

IMAGINE BEING THE KIND of man to spend a day with a girl,
that girl ghosts you, then practically booty-calls you for a wedding
with a lot of family drama attached, you're dating her for a month,
and she has a meltdown about a dead ex-boyfriend she still loves.

In what world would you ever stick around for that?

"He," I swallow, "Aster was gone a couple of days after I got
back up here. I had stayed with him, held him. He was gone and
then I left." I leave out our parting words, keeping those to myself.

"Oh, mo chroí," Miles says, rubbing my back with one hand
while he brushes hair out of my face with his other. "I'm so sorry."

I nod, not knowing what to say to that. What do you say to
that?

"Thank you." That feels weird.

"It's okay." It sure as fuck isn't.

"Yeah, me too." I am but what the fuck does sorry get me? Nothing.

So, I just nod and say nothing. Eventually, the crying slows and I go to stand up. Miles is far smoother and quicker than I, popping up effortlessly.

Then there's me where even on a good day my knees sound like there's gravel crunching away in there and my back pops like it's main mission in life to remind me that I'm aging.

Miles helps me up and pulls me into him, hugging me tightly. He's really threatening everything I've blocked and built a wall against over the last year. But when he asks if I want him to go, I start crying at just the thought.

"I'll stay, Briar. I want to. I'd love to."

I sniffle, wiping my snotty nose with a tissue he had grabbed at some point, and nod. I take his hand and lead him to my room.

"Make yourself at home," I whisper. This will be our first sleepover and how unsexy is this... "I'm going to use the restroom real quick."

I change swiftly into sweats before sitting on the closed toilet and taking a moment.

Alone behind a closed door, it all comes falling down on me again. Over and over I am bombarded with the smell of lemon and bleach. The way the moon shone on the white bedding. How gray his skin was and the feel of plastic tubing rubbing against my skin. I can hear him ask me to marry him, feel his last breath on my lips.

I'm sobbing and I don't even realize it until Miles is knocking on the locked door and asking to be let in. I open it and all but fall into his open and waiting arms. He leads me to my bed, setting me down and sitting behind me.

"My sister made me learn how to braid hair," he says softly as he starts to pull strands of mine together.

Once he's done, he lays down, pulling me with him, and covers us up.

"You're so brave, mo chroí. You're so strong. You're so good."

All night, he comforted me.

I fell asleep believing him.

I woke up feeling like a fool.

But that did not deter the man. Oh no, he has the patience of a fucking saint.

Miles made me breakfast and ate with me in much appreciated silence. He read the paper that I never even subscribed to, while I read some pages of *Second Chance* by Emily Keesee.

As if I didn't already have reasons to cry—whoever Emily is was out to get me with that story.

I don't usually work on Friday's, and Miles had the day off as well. I think he called in sick, but he shrugged his shoulders and winked at me when I asked.

I find his mother-henning to be incredibly adorable and quite welcome.

Which surprises me quite a bit.

The weekend was a bit foggy. Saturday, Miles and I went grocery shopping together for a few odds and ends. By Saturday night I was feeling incredibly exhausted and tapped out, bitter and angry, not ready at all for Tuesday to arrive. Having brought everything to the surface in discussing Aster with Miles, my feelings of resentment towards Catt were brought back to a bright and shiny light. So, like a mature adult, I avoided her Saturday and Sunday. Sunday was spent by myself, having told Miles that I'd love a day of just me to clean my house and mope solo. He didn't love it but he is nothing if not respectful.

By Monday I was ready to work. Ready to don the mask of "I'm fine and nothing to see here". And now, in Mark's office, I'm ready for it to be Wednesday and to just skip tomorrow entirely.

But time doesn't work around wishes and begging.

"Do you think you want to discuss with Catt the reason why you're feeling upset with her?"

I shrug my shoulders and warm my hands on my hot vanilla chai latte.

First a quesadilla and now a different coffee order? Who am I?

"Do you think she would try to argue with you? About why you're still feeling upset with her?"

I shake my head. "No, I think she'd understand. I just don't know if I understand. I hated her, Mark. Like truly and really hated her in that moment and for the days after. We didn't even sit together at his funeral."

"Briar please! I'm so sor-"

"No! You don't get to tell me you're sorry again, Catt. I don't want to hear it right now. Leave. I need to get ready for his visitation."

Tears continue to fall from my once-was best friends' eyes and I continue to watch them and feel nothing.

"Briar."

"Catt, I hate you."

She jerks her head back as though I had physically struck her. And I suppose that I may as well have by saying that.

Decades of friendship down the drain just like that. And I feel nothing about it.

Nothing but anger.

"Briar please..."

She showed up to my parents' house after four days of me ignoring her calls and texts. Tonight is Aster's viewing—his funeral is tomorrow. I have no patience for her tears. For her guilt. But I do have rage. And fuck, if she doesn't deserve to feel that from me right now.

I swing around, my wanting to storm off and leave her at the front door alone now changed to giving her all I've got by the door of my parents' home.

"You knew! You knew and you didn't tell me!"

"He asked me not to!"

"I don't give a fuck, Catt! How could you do that? You kept this whole thing from me! I could have had-"

"He didn't want you to uproot your life!"

"More time with him. I could have been there! Been here!"

"I didn't want to take that choice from him, Briar!"

I'm in her face now, anger radiating from my every pore. We are nose to nose and I am violently angry. She doesn't back down. She doesn't shy or cower away. I wish she would though. I want her to fear me right now, in this moment. I fear myself right now. I don't know who I hate more... Her. Me. Or him.

"No, you just took that choice from me."

"I didn't want to choose!"

"But you did choose! And you chose him!"

"What would you have had me do?!"

"I don't know! But I do know that he was my best fucking friend for years before he decided he couldn't be my friend anymore. And I know—I know that you two stayed friends. And I believe and trust that that was where that stayed with you two-"

"It is, Briar! I swear!"

"And I know you two were best friends too. I see that and I acknowledge it and I get it. But where the fuck did that leave me, Catt?! I know I was in Omaha, but I should have been told! I should have been given the choice and I should have been here!" The tears streaming down my face go unacknowledged by the both of us.

After this week I don't know that I will ever shed another tear again.

"Briar. He was losing weight by the day. His hair was falling out. His eyebrows were gone. He looked me in the eyes-"

"I'm done with this." I wave a hand between us.

I don't want to hear this. I wouldn't have wanted to see it, no. Obviously not. But I would have been here anyways had I had the choice. But no one wanted me here? No one thought I should be here? No one even gave me the option.

"No! Listen! He looked me in the eyes and he said I don't want to be the reason she comes back. I refuse to have had the last few years apart be a waste and her rush back to try and fix me or help me or whatever, and we all know that's what you would have done!"

"Of course, I would have come home, Catt! He is my best friend! He is the love of my life! He is everything to me and now he's gone! And I got two fucking days with him because you two decided for me that I was better off not knowing?! You were wrong. Both of you. And I'll never forgive you, Catt. Never. I would tell Aster the same thing but he fucking died."

I look her up and down, crossing my arms and forcing my tears to stop. I square my shoulders and step away from the platonic soulmate of my life.

"Briar." It's pleading that I hear in her voice now. Begging.

"He died," I say more to myself.

"I know."

I can't even hear her now. I don't see her. I just see him—sick and dying. I hear only him—his breathing slow and rattling.

"He-"

My breathing picks up.

"Briar..."

"He-"

My chest tightens and I'm back in that hospital room watching the sun fall out of my sky.

"Babe, come-"

And now I'm in the entryway of my parents' home, staring at Catt and wishing I wasn't.

"Don't fucking touch me. I want to never see you again. Grieve alone. Just like I have to."

"Briar," her voice catches on my name. "Please."

"I hate you both, Catt. And I will never forgive you for keeping this from me."

I sit down at the bar of *The Blue's* and wait for Catt. I practice my speech a couple times in my head, hoping that she forgives me for choosing anger over her the last few days. And hoping that I can allow myself to move past that anger.

"Hey, you."

Catt kisses me on the cheek and takes a seat.

"I'm sorry I've been weird since last week."

I blurt it out far less eloquently than I had anticipated. Catt stays quiet, giving me a minute to get it together.

"I was so mad at you, Catt. I was mad at Aster too but you aren't dead and so I took it out solely on you. I hate the things I said to you, but I don't think I regret them. I hope you can understand where I'm coming from when saying that. I love you. Deeply."

She nods at me and I go on. "And maybe that's part of why it all cut so deep. I felt like you chose Aster over me when he asked you to keep his diagnosis a secret. And then I was mad at him for even putting you in that position. But again, he was gone, and I couldn't scream at him. All I had was you. And then I didn't even have you anymore because I was so angry."

My voice breaks on the last word and Catt squeezes her eyes shut just for a second.

"The last year has been really hard for me, Catt. And I know that the last few days I haven't been doing my part of our friendship. I just... I told Miles all about Aster on Thursday and it brought up a lot of feelings from that time and then I got re-mad at you, and it isn't fair to you, but I needed time to sort through it."

"And did you? Sort through it?" Catt's green eyes are lined with tears, and I grab her hand, squeezing it.

"I don't hate you." She lets out a breath, her shoulders relaxing. "But I am still a little upset with how everything went down, and I don't know what to do with that. But I do know that I love you and that I will try to be better when my anger gets to me like it did the last few days. I'm sorry I blew you off. That wasn't right. You deserve better than that."

Catt wipes at her tears. "I'm so sorry, Briar. I hated doing it. I did. And I hate what it did to us. I don't blame you for being mad at me. And honestly, I'm pretty pissed at Aster still, for putting me in that position. For asking that of me. And I am mad at myself for going along with it."

She hangs her head. "I regret it. I do. And I know he did too by the end. But then it was too late to go back and we just, he—I don't know. We did the best we could, if that makes sense."

I let myself feel right now, refusing to be cold and numb to my best friend. And in doing so...

I gasp as a sob runs through my body. Catt wraps me in her arms and holds me tightly.

"I can't believe it's been a year," she whispers.

It all comes to the surface. The last year of feelings. The heartache and the sorrow and the grief that I never processed. The longing and the wishing and the anger. Every single thing I haven't allowed myself to acknowledge threatens to take me out in a very visceral way. It's all very dramatic but very real.

This impending breakdown that's bubbling right under the surface is getting louder and louder and before it claws itself free, I break away from Catt, telling her I love her and that I need to head home. I turn my phone off before I pull into my driveway.

And then I feel it.

I feel...

Everything.

twenty

"There are plenty of ways to die, but only love can kill and keep you alive to feel it." —Leo Christopher

MY FACE IS NUMB. My heart is broken. My lungs are raw. My skin is cold.

I open my eyes, but I don't see.

I open my mouth, but nothing comes out.

I try to think about what is happening, yet nothing makes sense.

I embrace that *nothing*.

I hold it close to me like I wish I could do with him still.

But I can't.

He's gone.

"Where is she?"

I come to slowly, not moving. My body feels like it's on fire while simultaneously being dipped in a bath of ice. I itch all over and the pain in my eyes and in my throat is almost breathtaking.

"She's in her room."

That's Quinn.

"Thanks for calling."

And that's Miles.

I look around, my brain still not working properly, and note that I'm in my room.

"How long has she been like this?"

At his question it all comes back.

Aster.

Dead.

A year.

A year without him. Without his laugh and his smile and his hugs and his warmth. A year that he hasn't taken a breath on this earth. A year where it's been past tense when speaking or thinking about him. A year of burying the anger and grief and sadness.

All of that came pouring out of me last night like the rain that fell from the sky.

I remember coming home after leaving Catt at *The Blue's*. I got here but didn't stay long—I paced my house and then got mad. I broke a vase. I'm sure it's still in pieces in my kitchen, dead flowers scattered along with broken glass.

I threw a chair.

Who did I think I was? Teresa Giudice?

I got in my car, not wanting to continue to rip my house apart. I drove for a while, aimlessly and almost a little blindly, and then I was staring at the dead end road by the airport.

Our spot.

I was there for three hours. I got out and walked the dirt road, cursing at Aster and God and anyone who would listen. I begged and pleaded for it to all be some horribly long nightmare. I sobbed on the side of the road, rocks digging into my knees. I welcomed the pain they caused.

For a year I had allowed myself, made myself, feel nothing.

Not anymore.

It started raining at some point. And I let it drown me. I felt every drop, heard every crack of thunder, and yearned for every strike of lightning to inch closer and closer to me. I didn't want to be struck, not like that—I don't think. I just wanted to feel it.

I screamed.

Oh man, did I scream.

No wonder my throat hurts so bad.

I remember staying there, as the dirt turned to mud, and my clothes became ice cold and soaked through. I recall the way my body eventually just stilled. My breathing slowed and my tears dried. I got up, walked back to my car, and came home.

It was one in the morning by the time I got back. My phone stayed off and is probably in whatever corner it landed in when I threw it after getting here the first time.

I try to think about how or when Quinn got here but I have zero recollection of that. When I got home, I came straight to my room and crawled onto my bed. I sobbed myself to sleep.

I can feel my pulse in the front of my skull. But I welcome this pain too. Because at least now I'm feeling something. Pain is taken for granted, I think. But perhaps I only feel that way right now because I haven't allowed myself to feel it about Aster's death.

I'm sure they'll leave soon.

"Mo chroí."

I don't notice I'm crying until he whispers his nickname for me, causing a sob to escape my throat.

"Fuck," he swears quietly. I feel his hands on my thighs. "Baby, you're soaking wet and freezing."

"It was raining," I whisper, my voice raspy from the raging.

"I know. Let's get you changed and get new sheets on your bed, okay?"

He eases me up and holds me close to him. I don't have the energy to mention that now he'll be wet too. I don't know that he'll even care.

"He died," I cry.

"I know, mo chroí. I know." He eases my shirt off of me, taking his time, not being too quick with his movements. "I'm taking your bra off okay, sweetheart? No funny business. It's just too wet to sleep in."

I say nothing as he takes it off, sliding one of his own T-shirts on, one that he left here over the weekend, over my head and arms. I'd smile at the memory of that incredibly respectful sleepover—if I could smile. This is the first time Miles is seeing me completely naked and it's in the least sexy setting.

I should feel embarrassed, I think. Perhaps I will come morning.

He then stands me up and moves me to the chair in the corner of the room, sliding my leggings and underwear off before sitting me down. He inhales at the cold, red skin under my pants, but doesn't say anything. As he dries me off, slipping on a pair of underwear and sweatpants, he remains quiet.

"I'll be right back to change your bedding, okay?"

I say nothing, staring out the rain-soaked window. I listen as he makes his way to the living room. His footsteps are quiet but steady.

Like him.

I hear him as he asks my sister, "What the fuck happened? Is she okay? Did someone hurt her? Is this about Aster?

"Today just isn't a good day for her. I didn't know what else to do or who to call. She would have killed me if I had called our parents. I don't know that she won't still after calling you but she really cares about you and I think you really care about her-"

"Of course, I do."

"And she just needed someone to care today. Someone that she'll *let* care... Aster died a year ago tomorrow. Or I guess, a year ago today."

I shiver at the fact. Or the cold. I'm not sure.

Miles is quiet as he brings in a new sheet and a blanket from the couch with a glass of water.

"Drink this please, mo chroí. While I make your bed, okay?"

I don't answer him or move to take the glass. It's as though I'm here but I'm not. I can see him. I can hear him. I can feel him. I can logically understand that I need to move. To speak. To do *something*.

But I can't.

I'm frozen in this space where it's just me and this cloak of grief that's covering me up, swallowing me whole. And it's as if I want to move my arms, try to find the space for them to fit through, to get them out from under here and grasp onto something—the water or Miles or *anything*. But the weight is too much and the cloak is almost suffocating. So, I stay there. Unmoving and stuck.

Miles squats down and sets the water beside me onto the dresser. He puts his hands on the sides of my face, the warmth seeping into my tear-soaked cheeks. I close my eyes, soaking it in.

"I know what today is. I know you're feeling it all right now like it's a rock crushing you flat. But you need to drink this or you'll get dehydrated. Especially after all of the rain and..."

Tears...

"You just need to drink some water. For me, Briar. Please?"

I blink at Miles, his eyes bright even in the dark. His hands being on my face have lifted the cloak of grief ever so slightly, taking some of its weight from my shoulders, making my arms free to move again. I take the water and start sipping slowly, having the wherewithal to know that if I chug it, I *will* throw up. He sighs, content, and gets up to make the bed. When he's done, the glass is empty and I'm no longer actively crying.

"Let's get you back in bed, okay?"

Miles helps me to my bed, covering me up and brushing my hair away from my face before leaning down to kiss the bridge of my nose.

"I don't want to overwhelm you, mo chroí. So, I'm going to the living room, okay?"

I grab his hand as he moves to walk away. I don't often ask people to stay.

When you feel like you're an easy person to leave, why bother stalling what feels inevitable?

But right now, the thought of him walking away from me leaves me despondent—more so than I already am.

"No. Stay. Please."

My eyes fill with new tears, and he says nothing, sliding off his sweats and getting into bed. He pulls me close, my back to his front, and presses a kiss to the back of my head. A few minutes of silence go by before my body starts shaking with quiet sobs. He says nothing. Just holds me tighter.

"I'm sorry I'm so messed up," I say, now beyond tired from it all.

"You stop being sorry, baby, and you just keep being strong. You're the bravest person I know, mo chroí. But you don't need to carry the weight of your world by yourself. Let me help you. We'll talk more in the morning. I'll still be here. For now, sleep."

I listen, falling asleep at some point to the feeling of Miles pressing soft kisses to the back of my head, while quietly telling me how strong he knows I am.

twenty-one

"Like rain, I fall. But like water, I flow. Like the sun, I'll shine. Everything takes time and I'll be fine (again)" —Dika Agustin

QUINN DIDN'T SAY ANYTHING other than "Okay, I love you" when I texted her asking her to tell mom and dad that I would be skipping family dinner tonight.

I worked like normal this week after Tuesday's... *spell.* I turned Catt down on her taco date night Wednesday. Miles has been over, bringing me food and making sure I actually eat it. He also fills my "giant-ass" Trek cup with fresh ice and water before he leaves, commenting on the size and heftiness of it every time.

I haven't asked him to stay the night since Monday, or I guess Tuesday, not wanting to become a burden or an obligation to him.

I'm sitting with Mark again now, our Thursday session feeling incredibly somber. His salt-and-pepper hair looks to be freshly cleaned up—the sides shorter than they were on Monday. His dark blue sweater and khaki slacks make him look extra professional.

"Why do you wear such business-y clothing?" I ask, my random thought tumbling from my mouth. "Like, you listen to sad people whining to you all day. Don't you want to at least be in something comfy while you do it?"

Mark laughs and picks up his tea to take a drink. "I like to feel like I look professional," he says. "And the slacks aren't uncomfortable."

I shrug my shoulders and turn my attention to my ring.

"Aster gave me this ring when I was seventeen," I begin. "We had been doing this thing where we watched planes take off at the airport. And the night he asked me to be his girlfriend we had made up a story about a couple of best friends going to Ireland. He gave me this and told me that it seemed special because of that. I'm Irish, like fifty-ish percent of my muddled genes, so I didn't feel weird wearing it. I thought it was sweet. We Googled the rules of them, and I wore it the right way—on my right hand, the point of the heart facing towards my arm. That's what Google said is the correct way when you're in a relationship. When we broke up, I remember wanting to take it off but also not ever wanting it to leave my hand. So, I had to Google it again. Turned her around and she's been like that ever since."

My gaze meets Mark's.

"Would you like to talk about yours and Aster's break up today, Briar?"

"Well, 'like' is a pretty strong word. But..." I take a deep breath. "Yeah, I guess maybe I do."

I cross my legs underneath me, sitting down on the new-to-me couch. It was the longest day in the history of days today at school and as I look at the carton of Chunky Monkey ice cream in my hand, I sigh at the relaxation I am about to enjoy. The first bite is only halfway into my mouth when a knock sounds at the door of my apartment.

She's tiny—my apartment. And perfect. I'm a few months into my second year of college in Omaha and decided I wanted my own place after a long year with roommates. Was my decision based almost solely on the ease it would create in having Aster come visit?

Absolutely.

Privacy is priceless.

It's cheap and cute though, so I'm happy with my decision. The walls are all a really bright white, older appliances sit in the very dated kitchen. It's got one room that barely fits my queen size bed and dresser. But what else do you need a bedroom for? I'm on the second floor so it's not a huge journey up and down.

I forget to check the peephole like my dad always lectures me about doing and almost pass out when I see Aster on the other side of my door after opening it.

I jump into his arms, my own instantly going around his neck, and his going around my back. We stand there for a moment, breathing each other in.

"What are you doing here?" He sets me on the ground and that's when I see the worry etched into his face. "What's wrong? Is everyone okay?"

He sees my panic and says, "Everyone is fine. It's me. Or us, I guess."

I step back into my place, letting Aster in. I try to rein in my concern, the panic. My chest feels heavy though, and my breathing is picking up. I swallow hard, trying to calm myself.

"I'm not any less confused here, honey."

Aster slowly enters my apartment, hands in the pockets of his black sweatpants. His blonde hair is longer than he usually keeps it, falling in thick waves over his forehead and ears. It's messy, like he's had his hands in it a million times.

It's as I turn to face him that my brain acknowledges that he doesn't have a bag of clothes with him. My eyes meet his and I see the bags underneath, the frown marring his perfect mouth, the sadness in his gaze.

"Aster, you're freaking me out. What is going on?"

"I think we should break up."

Stunned. That's what I feel. Just... stunned.

I stare at him for a moment, eyes wide and blinking slowly. He says nothing. Does nothing. I move then, pacing my small living room.

"Briar." My name on his lips, usually like a breath of fresh air, is a storm moving in.

I hold up my hand to silence him, needing the quiet to try to calm myself. I am known to be a bit overreactive at times of stress. And I am most definitely stressed. After a minute or two, what felt like hours really, I stop and look at him.

"Why?" It's the calmness in my own tone that should alarm the both of us.

He starts to speak, and I cut him off, not caring at all right now about giving him grace. It doesn't matter to me that I was the one that just asked him a question.

"Is it because of the distance? Because that can be solved. Is it because of someone else?" My throat feels like it's going to cave in, the calm tone from moments ago now gone. "Because I gained a few pounds? I'm not small to begin with but that college whatever really took hold and I know that, but I can work on that and-"

"Absolutely nothing you're saying is anything that should even be thought of, Briar."

He walks to me, his long legs getting him here quickly. His large hands, soft and kind, grasp my cheeks and hold firmly.

He is the sun. Yet I have never felt colder.

"Then why?" If it were anyone else, I would feel embarrassed by the crack in my voice. But this is Aster.

My Aster.

"Briar..." His thumbs swipe at the tears that I didn't know had started to fall. "Please understand this. You are incredible. You are beautiful—every ounce and centimeter and rogue strand of hair that I can't stop finding in every space I occupy. You are everything to me and I love you."

Aster takes a deep breath, putting his forehead to mine. "But this fucking sucks. This space between us. The time difference, just the single hour is awful. And the state line that separates us might as well be an ocean some days. And the fact that neither of us are visiting like we had originally planned to. And I know you love it here-"

"I love you-"

"And I know when you're done next year you won't want to leave and I love that for you, Briar. Fuck."

He pulls his head back, his gray eyes hold that storm I mentioned a minute ago.

"I love that you found somewhere you enjoy being. That you found friends and people that are good to you. That you've found a place to just exist in peacefully. Being yourself and loving it."

"But you-"

"I can't be the reason you leave all of this. That will kill me, and eventually you will resent me for it and do the 'what ifs'. And I refuse to be that for you. I refuse to be chosen just to be regretted in a couple decades. This isn't it for us though, Briar. Not by a long shot. We aren't over for forever. Believe me when I tell you that I will ask you to marry me someday. But you deserve to live before that. I'm not even talking romantically. Just in general..."

"I don't want to be without you in my life." My voice is quiet, the tears falling faster now. My heart is erratic as it breaks, like she's her own being entirely, fighting for her life right now.

"I know, love. I know. And I don't want to be without you."

"Then why are you doing this?" I step out of his arms, the sadness turning to anger.

"Because I love you. And I want to love you until my dying breath, Briar."

"You're not making any sense, Aster. You love me but you want to dump me?"

"I love you and I want you to have the space and life you might need now before we're sixty and you hate me for never having had any of that."

"You're basing your decision on what ifs, Aster. How is that fair?"

"It's not."

He says it so simply, like he hasn't just broken every promise we have ever made to each other in the four years we've been together.

"And I'm just supposed to be fine with this?"

"I don't expect you to be fine with it, no. Not right now at least."

"Well, that's good, because I'm not."

"I know." He puts his hands into the pockets of his sweatpants, his shoulders slumping as his eyes well up with his own tears.

"So, what now?"

I'm pissed. I have never been so mad at this boy standing before me. I have never wanted to grip him by his stupid broad shoulders and shake him. My head is telling me to do that. To tell him that he's making a huge mistake. That we aren't going to be anything to regret when we are sixty. My brain is telling me to be mad and scream at him that he will never have someone love him the way that I can. But my heart...

That sad bitch is telling me to hug him. To lean on him as he breaks us. She's whispering to me that it's okay and that he hasn't ever led us astray and that we need to trust this beautiful man that we love.

"I'm going to go home."

His voice breaks me out of my inner thoughts. I go for a happy medium—or a sad medium, I suppose.

"I won't pretend to understand why you are doing this. I also won't pretend that I don't think this is a major mistake on your part. But..."

I loose a breath and step into him, putting my arms around his waist and looking into his eyes. I lean up, kissing a tear on his cheek away.

"But I love you. And I trust you. And I will respect this terrible decision if it's what you think is best. For now. But Aster, I won't wait around for you to realize this is a mistake. I'll be your friend and I'll be yours when you decide this is stupid. But I won't allow myself to wallow for long. I can't even fathom ever looking at someone the way I look at you. But I never imagined you driving eight hours to break up with me—anything is possible. Keep that in mind as we try this out. I love you with everything I have. I won't live my life waiting for you to amend your mistakes, though."

Aster's breath is shaky as he cries into my hair, his cheek resting on the top of my head. I join him, my own tears soaking into his shirt. We stay like that, holding each other.

"I love you, Briar. So much. And this isn't for forever. I just can't risk you hating me someday for making you come home when you didn't want to..."

But he will risk me hating him now. Always the one to think long term.

I don't say that though. Not aloud.

"I love you."

I watch him walk down the hall and go down the stairs. When I can't see him any longer, I close my door and lock it.

I hold out hope that he'll turn around. That he'll get to his car, and he'll realize how stupid this whole thing is and he'll run up the stairs like he's Mr. Coulson in "Never Been Kissed" and bang on my door. Or maybe he'll let himself get on the interstate and that's when it will hit him.

But it doesn't happen. Because this isn't a romantic comedy. I'm not Drew Barrymore.

No, I'm Briar Davies. Twenty. Newly single. Sad. And suddenly bitter.

"Do you think he regretted it?"

Mark's question surprises me. Usually, he doesn't ask questions about how someone else might have felt.

"I know he did."

I twirl my Claddagh ring some more, hating myself for still being mad at Aster.

Mark sighs, resigned to the fact that my share-O-meter is maxed out for the day.

"Alright, kiddo. We'll pick up here next time, yeah?"

I sigh at his nickname that he knows I secretly love. Daddy issues and all that.

"Okay, next time."

I open my phone when I get into my car, a text from Miles waiting.

McMan

Dinner tonight?

I've been so reclusive lately and he's been so patient about it. I look at the time, noting that it's barely after five. I don't feel the pressure to get all dressed up for Miles. He's seen me naked and it wasn't even for anything hot.

I'm in. Pick me up at six?

See you then, mo chroí.

twenty-two

MILES LETS HIMSELF INTO my house, knocking softly twice before opening the door and walking in. He looks good tonight. I mean, he always looks good. But I'm in the headspace to notice it appropriately this evening.

His dark brown shirt has the long sleeves pulled up a little bit, showing off some of his perfectly sculpted forearms. Light blue jeans over brown boots round out his very signature look.

"Hey, sweetheart," he says as he toes off his boots and makes his way to where I'm standing in the kitchen, filling my water cup.

"Hi," I say back softly. "You look handsome."

He presses a kiss to the side of my head before leaning back on the counter next to me. "You're beautiful."

"How was your day?" I ask, mirroring his position next to him.

"It was good, productive. Nice day to work outside. How was yours? Work? Mark?"

I love the ease in which he asks me about therapy. Taking care of your mental health is so important and being supported by those around you is incredibly under appreciated by some. Knowing that Miles both supports and cares about me taking care of myself is huge.

"It was good," I slide closer to him, leaning my head on his arm. He takes that arm though and tosses it around my shoulders, pulling me into him. "We talked about when Aster and I broke up, we were twenty. I was living in Omaha at the time, in college."

"Can I ask what brought that up?"

He asks it carefully but not in a scared kind of way. His fingers twirl the loose pieces of hair that are fanned out over my arm. I hold up my hand, showing him my ring and spinning it around.

"He gave me this when we were seventeen."

Miles holds my hand up, looking at the ring. His question next isn't one born of anything remotely malicious, but more just curious. "Are you Irish?" He sounds excited.

I chuckle softly. "Yeah, like half or something. All a part of the mixed, mutty blend. My mom's mom was some percentage of Irish, and Jack is about half Irish."

He mutters something under his breath that sounds like "of course she's Irish, blessed fates" and I laugh.

"Let's talk more as we go, yeah? Where should we eat?"

He laces his fingers through mine. "I was thinking we could get some sushi at the small place on the west side? Shouldn't be too busy but not quite empty."

I nod, that sounding actually perfect. Gets me out of the house but not in a room that's completely overwhelming.

"So, what about you?" I ask after we get in his pickup. "Any tragically sad or remotely bumming break ups for you?"

He laughs as we leave my neighborhood, his hand grasping mine in between us. "Nothing terrible. I dated a chick in high school for a year or so. Thought we were great together but then I found her making out with one of our friends. That was a bummer, but it wasn't too bad."

He shrugs before going on. "I hung out with some people after, stayed fairly single for the next few years. I dated one pretty seriously for almost a year again but by the end of that we just felt like we weren't in the right places for each other long term. That was, oh, six or so months ago. I hadn't really hung out with anyone else."

He looks over at me, pulling my hand to his mouth and pressing a kiss to my knuckles. "But then I saw you that night at *Phresh*. Now, here we are."

I smile softly at him, squeezing his hand. "Here we are."

I go quiet. I haven't had feelings like this for anyone other than Aster. And I don't really know what to do with that. I wasn't even allowing myself to feel *anything* prior to like, this week. And even now, I'm not really acknowledging all that I probably should be. So, tack on the fact that I actually *like* someone new...

"I haven't dated anyone other than Aster," I say as we pull into the parking lot of the restaurant.

I don't wait for Miles to get out, letting go of his hand and rushing out of his pickup. That admission felt like a lot for some reason. I find myself hoping he'll let it go and almost forget about the whole thing. But of course, he doesn't.

Had to go and find yourself a good one, eh?

We finished ordering our rolls and drinks and immediately Miles jumps back into our conversation.

"You didn't date anyone after you two broke up?"

His questions are never rude. He's never condescending or judgmental. He shows genuine curiosity in everything he asks. Which I think is a big part of why I *want* to answer him.

"No. We broke up when we were twenty. I spent that next school year super focused. Busted my ass, really. I even spent that summer doing schoolwork and finished a whole year early. We had been broken up for six years before we stopped being friends and in those years I only came home twice. Both times were awful—being around him but not being with him."

I shove away the emotions that come along with thinking of those years. "I think that's what kind of broke him, seeing me that last time. The driving force to ghosting me, I suppose. So then in the two years we didn't speak, I don't know, I just didn't come home. I hung out with some guys in those years after we stopped speaking. Nothing ever beyond a night kind of thing..."

"You didn't date while you were friends? Why?"

"It was a lot. Emotionally. Aster and I had a decent friendship over those six years. A good friendship, really. He didn't date either. That I know of, and I think I would know. I don't know if his was intentional, unlike me where I was just too busy. But neither of us ever brought up other people. We would text at least once daily. It was probably unhealthy, really. But he was my best friend."

I don't look Miles in the eyes as I recount all of this. It feels so strange to talk about Aster in such an open way with anyone, let alone the man I'm dating. But I push on.

"When I came home those two times, we had made plans to hang out. Neither of us ever broached the subject of getting back together. The first time when we saw each other it was this big emotional thing. We met at the park on the west side of town and immediately were in each other's arms. We cried and held each other like that was the end of the time apart."

I pick at my lip while I talk. "But he didn't ask and neither did I. Eventually we went and walked around. Then the second time I came back, it was nearly the same. Less tears but no talks of getting back together. I wasn't in school anymore, it had been towards the end, before he disappeared. But both times I would go back to Nebraska feeling less whole, more empty. I felt like we were re-breaking up both times. So, we decided we wouldn't see each other in person again."

Miles never once looks down on anything I say. I find anywhere else to look but his face, but he stays in my peripheral. His hand takes mine, putting them in the middle of the table. His thumb moves over my ring—gently and lovingly.

"Is this weird? Me telling you all of this?" My nerves are taking over as I finally meet his gaze.

"Not for me, at all." His voice is so sure. "I want to know every-thing there is to know about you, Briar. I want the good and the bad. The sad and the happy."

"Why?" I ask it so quietly, so meekly, that I don't know if he heard me.

But of course he did. His hand stills, tightening slightly around mine. He leans forward on the table and smiles softly.

"I like you, Briar."

I don't even wait for more before I dive in.

"But I'm a mess, Miles. I'm sad, and honestly... pretty angry. I'm grieving, and that whole *thing* just fucking started, really. I'm almost thirty and every relationship I have in my life, aside from my therapist, is strained in one way or another. I'm not the kind of girl, even when I'm not this messy, that laughs easily and smiles at everything. I don't enjoy being around a million people all of the time, going out a lot, or doing really much of anything. I almost never get dressed up to impress anyone and I definitely swear too fucking much for what society might deem appropriate. My waist is bigger than yours and I've got stretch marks nearly everywhere. I'm not even that nice most of the time. I'm crabby and sulky and hostile..."

I sigh. "Even at my best I am all of those things. Like, sure, you've caught me at an extra not-great time in my life. But even before Aster died, before we broke up... Do you know what he called me before we had even started dating?"

Miles shakes his head, his face one of kindness and curiosity. *This fucking man.*

"Sweet Briar. Like the bush with thorns. Prickly. He called me a prickly shrub. And he wasn't wrong, Miles. I'm not happy-go-lucky. Not even remotely."

I finish my rant, my hand still in his, taking a deep breath and looking into his eyes hoping for two things at the same time.

One, that he understands me and sees how genuinely crazy and not worth it I am.

Two, that I didn't just scare him away from me and my insanity.

I am beyond a mess.

Just when I'm about to tell him I should leave and call a cab or something, he laughs.

Miles fucking *laughs.* Fully and loudly, covering his mouth with his other hand and causing himself to cough slightly from laughing so hard.

My jaw drops and my eyes go wide. I fight the urge to get up and shove him because I feel like he's laughing *at* me, but can I even blame him? I'm certifiable.

"Are you done?" I take my hand back and cross my arms over my chest, sitting back in my chair.

He leans forward, prying my hand away from my body and back towards him.

"I'm sorry, mo chroí," he says after getting himself under control. "That prickly bush thing got me."

"What?" I am shocked.

He laughs again, this time more softly and gently. "What six-teen-year-old knows what a sweetbriar is and why am I so impressed with him for thinking up that whole comparison?"

"You... You're *impressed*? With my ex-boyfriend for comparing me to a prickly shrub when we were teenagers?"

"That and for the fact that he had the balls to say that to six-teen-year-old Briar." He smiles. "Absolutely. He sounds like he was great."

I don't know what to say to that. He says it so honestly. And he isn't wrong.

Our sushi arrives a second later, breaking up the weirdness. Momentarily.

"Before we dig in, let me just say," Miles begins, sliding the extra side of eel sauce that I ordered towards me. "Everyone is messy. Your mess doesn't scare me. I can understand your hesitation to let someone new in. I can see why that would make you nervous. But *you don't scare me*. So, let me be happy-go-lucky for the both of us. Let me show you that you are worthy, that you're incredible. Let me help you find that part of yourself—*for yourself.*"

He flashes me a dazzling smile. "It shouldn't matter what I think, what Jack thinks, what anyone thinks. The only one that needs to find you worthy is you. I already think you're enough and I hardly know you. I don't need forced laughter or done-up hair. I don't want fake smiles and perfection. I like *you*. I like that I have to work for a smile, because then when I get one... *fuck.* It means even more. I like that you swear like you're some backwoods trucker with no filter. And..."

He leans close, making me follow suit, dropping his voice. "I fucking *love* the curve of your waist. The way your ass looks in leggings and jeans. I can't wait to see every single part of you, every mark and freckle, up close and personal someday. Don't think for a single second that I base my feelings for you on anything other than who you are. And I hope to God you believe all of that. I pride myself on honesty, Briar. I don't say things I don't mean."

I stare at Miles, my mouth slightly open and my heart beating fast. My stomach is swirling as my brain processes his words. I believe him. And that freaks me out entirely.

"Okay," I choke out.

I feel my cheeks blush and his smirk tells me he sees it—sees what he does to me. He squeezes my hand before releasing it and picking up his chopsticks.

"Let's eat so we can go back to your place and watch some more of that Real Housewives shit you had on all week. I need to know why we're mad at Vicki."

I shake my head in disbelief and allow myself to laugh like I want to at him. His smile widens, his perfectly straight, bright teeth giving me butterflies.

"I love earning that laugh."

twenty-three

MILES STAYED OVER FRIDAY night, showing me exactly how much he enjoys the entirety of my curves. It was such a spontaneous decision, to not just sleep together but to *sleep* together. I thought that I would wake up Saturday morning feeling unsure and guilty, not about taking that step with Miles but about the fact that I hadn't thought of Aster for nearly an entire evening. I didn't though.

I did go through the majority of Saturday thinking of him, then. Apparently when you process grief, actively thinking of who you're grieving is a crucial part. Or so Mark tells me twice a week when I complain about it.

The light feeling from Friday is still floating throughout my body now on Sunday. I've got Noah Kahan on shuffle over my Bluetooth speaker from my kitchen as I clean my house. I'm singing along to *"Stick Season"* as I put clothes from the washer into the dryer when the song suddenly pauses. I make my way to the kitchen and scream when I round the corner.

"Quinn!" My hand is on my chest, my heart nearly stopping. "What the hell? You scared me. Did I know you were coming over?"

Quinn runs her fingers over the small braid that's resting over her shoulder. She looks odd today.

"Are you okay?" I ask as I step into the kitchen and stand opposite her.

"I'm fine."

"Okay..."

"Listen, Briar," she begins. "I want to talk to you, and I know you're going through a lot, but I've waited a super long time to do this and now I don't want to wait anymore so if we could just sit down for a minute and talk I would appreciate it."

I nod and walk to the table. Both of us sit down but before she says anything more, she gets back up and begins pacing.

"Quinn, are you alright? Is something wrong?"

She stops her pacing and puts her hands on her small hips. "I have a girlfriend."

Oh.

Oh.

Neither of us say anything. I don't want to overwhelm her, our relationship being weird as it is. But also like, does she want me to react *largely*?

"Well! Say something!"

I jump at her demand and stand up. "Is she nice?"

Quinn's hands drop from her waist and her mouth opens. I hold back a laugh at the fish-like gaping she's got going on.

"What?"

I smile. "Is she nice? To you."

"Uh," she fidgets around. "Yes. She's really nice. But that's it?"

"What do you mean?" I hate that she thinks I would react poorly to this. "I couldn't care less who you're with as long as they aren't mean to you, Quinn."

Her head bobs up and down as she watches me.

"What do you need from me here, Quinn? Excited support? Calm support? Silent support?"

She makes her way back to my table and takes a seat. I follow her, doing the same.

"I didn't think you'd be weird about it," she says. "I guess I just thought... you wouldn't, maybe, be, like, happy for me?"

My chest threatens to cave in on itself. I take both of her hands in mine.

"Why?"

"You're so sad, Briar. You're distant and sad and mad and now here I am, dropping this new... life on you, I guess. And I'm happy and she's great and you're just..."

"Not?" I offer gently.

She nods.

"Oh Quinn. I hate that you were nervous to be happy in front of me. I hope you know that we all support you though. Mom and dad, do they know?"

"Mom laughed when I told her and dad said 'okay, and?' like I had told them I got a cat." Quinn looks at me with a straight face before we both burst out laughing.

"A cat would surprise me more than a girlfriend." We get serious. "I love you. I'm sorry I made you think I would be anything other than happy for you. I am working on it—on me. I'm trying at least."

Quinn goes on to tell me all about Adelaide and how they met at a teaching convention in Pierre. She sounds very nice and nerdy, which made me giggle because Quinn has never played a video game in her life. But the entire time, talking about Adelaide and then Miles, we laughed and smiled and just... hung out together. She stayed for lunch, and we ended up sitting on the couch together to watch "50 First Dates".

"I want to be a better sister."

Quinn leans her head on my shoulder. "I think you're a good sister."

I laugh slightly. "I want to be better. I want to be involved and included. And I want to involve and include you. But not just you..."

The topic of Jack's kids, my siblings from him, has always been odd for me to just openly talk about. Not because I don't love them, but we did grow up apart. My relationship, having grown up with Quinn, is way different with them, and it always feels a bit awkward.

"I'm missing out on so much with Kyle, Christine, and Madeline. They're getting married and having babies and I don't even know them. It makes me sad to think about all of the things I've missed out on with them because of my feelings towards Jack. And then it makes me sad to think about what I have missed out on with you because of how closed off I let myself become."

I try to keep my voice level while I finish saying, "And I think I'm finally starting to acknowledge the fact that I started shutting down before Aster even got sick. After I moved to Omaha. And I hate that for us. For me. I hate myself for it. I want to do better—be better."

"I love you, Briar. And I don't want to hurt you but since we are being honest…"

"Please," I encourage her.

"I miss you."

I fucking hate myself.

"I hated when you left because it wasn't just distance between us then. You left the state but then you also left me too, I think. And never fully came back. But I don't hate you. I'm not mad at you. Not anymore. I want to have a better relationship too. We just have to try."

I hug my sister. Feelings of inadequacy and anger with myself threaten to take over but I don't let them. I allow myself to feel them but not be driven by them in this moment. And I make a promise to myself and to Quinn to do better. Not just for her or my other siblings. But for me.

Later that night I find myself thinking about the last time I visited Rapid City when I still lived in Omaha.

"Do you think you'll see Aster again before you leave?"

I sit up on my elbows, laying down on Catt's bed. I've been in town for three days and I haven't seen him yet. We've talked and made plans to get breakfast tomorrow morning before I leave to go back to Omaha. I tell Catt that and she gives me a sad smile. I wave her off.

"Nope, we aren't letting this make us sad today. I'm fine. He's fine. We are still friends. It's okay."

Catt shakes off the sad-eyes and smiles brightly. "Let's go out tonight!"

I laugh. "I'm game but not like, to a bar-bar. So, where?"

"There's that pool hall! We could go there. Just hang out, listen to music and play some games."

I lay back down and sigh. "Okay fine, but we're getting tacos first."

"Deal!" she yells as she jumps on top of me and smothers me with her love. "I miss you when you're gone."

"I miss you too." I allow her to cling to me, knowing I need it too. The affection. The love.

Later that night we are taco-ed and happily singing along to the jukebox.

"I don't know who keeps playing Taylor Swift," an all too familiar voice from behind me sounds. "But I think I want to be her friend."

Catt can't help but smile over my shoulder, Aster's her best friend too.

"Can I join you lovely ladies?"

I roll my eyes playfully and scooch in a seat giving mine to him.

"Hey, Catt."

"Hey, buddy."

He then looks to me, his smile not meeting his eyes.

"Hey, you."

My initial instinct still, after two years, is to lean into him. To hug him. To kiss him. To love him. To be loved by him.

"I need some air. I'll be back."

I get up, grabbing my small bag and going outside. Running, really.

"Hey," I hear Aster call after me as I walk around the corner of the building.

It's June. So, it's hot and a bit muggy and the bugs are heavy—like my fucking heart.

"Briar, hey, hang on a second." Aster catches up to me and I sigh.

"Why are you here?" I can't help the snap in my voice.

"I saw Catt's Snapchat and wanted to see you. I should have asked. I just didn't think about anything other than seeing you. I'm sorry."

Looking at him in the eyes finally, his gray hue making me feel like I'm home for the first time since I pulled into town, I relax slightly.

"It's fine. I'm sorry. I just didn't expect to see you. I'm sorry."

"Don't be. I should have asked. I wasn't thinking."

"It's okay." I smile sadly, feeling the unwanted sting behind my eyes. "It's okay," I repeat quietly.

"We don't have to have breakfast tomorrow..." He offers.

I jolt upright, leaning away from him. "You don't want to?"

"No, no. That is not it at all. I promise."

I sigh.

"I just hate this. I hate seeing you sad. I hate knowing I'm the reason for it."

Then don't be—that's what I want to say.

"Catt's waiting," is all that escapes my lips though.

We don't touch each other the rest of the night. We laugh and joke and talk as a trio. But that's it. And the next morning, I "forget" to set an alarm and wake up too late to make it to our plans. I leave Rapid City more sad than I was when I arrived.

We make it three more months before Aster and I speak for the last time.

I let a tear fall as I finish recalling the last trip I made up here before Catt called telling me to hurry and get back home quickly.

The last time I saw Aster before he died.

twenty-four

"No matter how many times she was told she was loved, there was no recognition that the proof was in the abandonment."
—Markus Zusak

I SETTLE INTO MY spot in Mark's office. It feels unreal that it's only been a week since my breakdown. Since Aster's one-year... it feels odd to call it an anniversary but I suppose that is what it is, no? My head is a jumbled mess. My heart is sad and heavy. My soul is tired. But I'm here. And that's what matters.

"How are you, Briar?"

I sigh. "Honestly?"

"Please."

"I'm fucking tired, Mark. Last week was a lot. This weekend was fine. I had a really great day with Quinn, I feel like we had a good breakthrough. But then last night, when I was alone and with my thoughts... I started thinking about the time after I quit coming home. About why I did that and when Aster quit talking to me. I started thinking about how I felt and how fucking mad I am at him."

I look at Mark, taking my attention away from my ring that feels heavier and heavier every day.

"What kind of person stays mad at someone who died? What does that say about me?"

"That you're human, Briar."

"I'm so angry at him."

It's as though the tears I didn't let myself shed are now trying to make up for lost time as they fall down my cheeks. Mark stands softly and hands me a small box of tissues. I mumble a thank you.

"I wanted him to ask me why I stopped coming home. I would daydream about it," I laugh at myself, the sound feeling a bit sad though. "I would imagine coming home. I would run into him at *Fresh Family* or something and I would be sad because I loved him and wanted to be with him and missed him. But we wouldn't be speaking then. Our carts would hit, and we would look up, ready to apologize to the stranger across from us. But then he'd see me, and I'd see him and the store would go quiet and our eyes would be the telling sign of heartache. And he would ask me why I'm so sad. And I would tell him."

I swallow down the emotions, forcing the tears to stay put for a while longer. "I would say... 'It's you. It's always you. Every time I come home—I search for you. I look for you in every Jeep that looks like yours did in high school, or every stupid souped up little car like the one I've been told you have now. I watch for you around every corner of the grocery store, or in every restaurant and bar. *I wish* to find you. The whole time I'm here, I just hope that this is the time I accidentally run my cart into yours in the store. Or it's the trip where I meet your eyes from across the dimly lit Chili's and we raise our drinks to each other and smile."

I take a breath, closing my eyes tightly and letting myself picture his warm smile and what this all might have looked like had anything been different.

"But every time I come back... I leave, and you're gone still. I don't see you. I don't hear your laugh or feel your gaze on me. It's like you were never even here. You disappeared all those years ago, leaving with not even so much as a goodbye, and you're just... gone.'" I finish my monologue and take a grounding breath.

I say to Mark now, no longer speaking to the hypothetical, "Sometimes it feels like I imagined the whole thing—us. Like we never happened. He was my boyfriend and the love of my life. And then he was my friend, but we still had plans for forever. And then he was gone. Poof. How ironic that he once ghosted me and now he's the ghost that haunts my every moment—awake and asleep. He was the sun and I craved his warmth, and now I'm blinded by memories of him. It's exhausting, Mark. I am living in a constant state of then and now. I'm fucking tired."

I let myself cry. I don't have much of a choice at this point, really.

"If Aster were still here, what would you want to say to him? To ask him?"

I don't hesitate. This thought has gone through my mind for years.

"Why did you disappear like that? You just quit talking to me. I've got this vision in my probably-narcissistic brain that it was because you still loved me. That you wanted to be together, but you felt the timing was still wrong or something. That you were doing what you thought was best—which would be bull shit because we were what was best. But that can't be the case. Because you would have told me then. You would have been honest, and you would have come and got me. You would have waltzed into my apartment, declared your love for me, packed my shit, and taken me home. You would have let us build a life together. You would have chosen your truth. You would have chosen me. Chosen us."

I take my first real breath. Saying that aloud was cathartic. My heart rate settles back to a normal level, and I look at Mark to find a soft smile gracing his kind face.

"What?"

"I'm proud of you, is all. Voicing all of that. You should feel proud of yourself."

I look away, needing reprieve from his knowing gaze.

"Switch gears?"

I nod, "Please." I cross my legs under me.

"I want to discuss your family, maybe."

I nod. "Sure. What about them?"

"You're doing all of this healing with Aster. I wonder if perhaps we should start to work on some healing with Jack and your siblings."

I sit with his statement, his idea. "I don't know what I can do with Jack but I have been in small contact with my sisters and brother."

"That's incredible, Briar. Have you thought about that letter I mentioned previously?"

My eyes go wide and my pulse goes high.

He raises a hand at my clear sign of anxiety. "You wouldn't have to send it if you chose not to. But writing your feelings down might be beneficial to you. Just like voicing what you just did was beneficial."

I sigh. "Okay..."

"Give it a try. Bring it in or don't. It's all up to you, Briar."

I leave feeling unsure. But once I arrive home that evening, I find myself setting up my laptop at my dining table.

Jack,

My counselor gave me some homework. That homework is this letter. I had mentioned to him the letter I wrote you when I was fourteen years old and the fact that when I asked you about it at a later date, you had said that you received it but just "didn't know what to say". I don't know if you know or knew then, or honestly if you cared or care, but that cut me deep. Then and now. So, even though you will more than likely never see this and even if you did, I would bet nothing would come of it, here it is. My letter to you, 14 years after the first one.

I sit here and I look around at my life. I look at my good job and the degree I got for it. I look at the house I live in, the people in my circle—as small as it may be. And even against my wishes, my desire, I see your absence in it all. While I understand that you did not ask for me to be conceived and born, I still was. And had you purely just been one hundred percent absent from my life, I think that would have been better. I don't wish to not have your side of our family in my life. But I wonder what it would look like for me had you been gone completely. But instead, you made as little effort as possible around family and friends of family, always putting on a show. Father-daughter dances at weddings, introducing me as your daughter and just blowing past the shocked look on your friends' faces as they find out about me for the first time, making conversation like you cared at all about what I was doing with life. All of those things, all of my life, were any of them sincere? I ask that because how could they be when it is evident that the loss of any form of relationship with me has no effect on you.

It honestly makes me mad—at you and me. I'm an adult now. I have always had an incredible mother who never shut the door on you. I have the best dad that loves me like I am biologically his, even though he doesn't have to. Then why do I care so much about the fact that you just... don't?

Do you know that you, not Marnie, you have never wished me a happy birthday?

I recall in my first letter I asked you why I wasn't good enough for you to love. Had I played a sport well like your other kids, would you have made more of an effort? Had I gotten better grades, would you have visited? I wasted years of my young adult life yearning for a better relationship with you and in turn, almost ruining the one I have with the man that raised me because of my own bull shit.

Do you wish it were different? Do you wish that my love of music was cultivated from your teachings instead of Brian's? Or that when someone says I have your eyebrows or chin that I felt like that was more of a compliment instead of an annoyance? Does it bug you that when someone calls you my dad, I correct them that you are not my dad, and that Brian is?

Did you ever want a relationship with me? Does the fact that half of who I am biologically is YOU matter at all to you?

You missed out. On prom and Aster. On college and my first house. You'll miss out on my wedding and children someday, if I am BLESSED to have them.

My aunts and uncles, my cousins, grandparents. I believe they all think I'm the drama queen. Like it somehow is annoying that my heart gets so heavy over the lack of relationship between you and I and your other children. Maybe it is annoying but honestly, it should be talked about or at the very least acknowledged—the fact that you just really failed me.

Your lack of parental effort has never just affected you and me. You may not be the sole reason your other children and I have no relationship, but you are a major contributing factor. Does that bother you? It makes me sad for them, for me. You can only miss so much of someone's life before you've missed too much. I wonder sometimes what it will be like to explain who you are to a new partner or to my future children. But realistically, I know you and everyone else will just go on ignoring the weirdness and the disappointment I always feel having you as my father, making the explanations pointless.

I wish you weren't that... my father. I love my grandparents and all that you being my father has given me in that aspect. But my whole life I have felt out of place, unloved, and unwanted because of you and your lack of acknowledgement. Am I easy to leave?

I don't hate you. I don't love you. I nothing you.

But perhaps that is untrue. How can you be so angry with someone you feel nothing for?

I wish you were different. Hell, maybe you wish you were different. It is so sad to me though, that you clearly don't want to be different enough to make a change for me. Someday when you are old, maybe even ill though I would not wish that upon you even now, and you're reflecting on your life and the things that have transpired in it... will you think of me? Your first born. The daughter with your chin and none of your affection. Will you think of me and wish things were different?

I won't. Because I did my best and I tried—even though I am the kid, and you are the adult. I tried when I had it in me to do so.

Can you say the same?

The "other" daughter,

Briar Davies

I save the word document as *"A Letter to My Father"* and send it to Mark, leaning back in my dining room chair and swiping a tear from my cheek.

<h1 style="text-align:center;font-style:italic">twenty-five</h1>

"All she wanted was the effort that she gave." —R.H. Sin

THURSDAY CAME UP QUICKLY this week, auto-pilot getting me by. My mood hasn't been great. Thoughts of Aster have become best friends with thoughts of Jack and the repercussions of his inaction. I've set up a lunch date for Saturday with my brother and all three of my sisters. Quinn was the one that talked me into that—having all four of them together. She said something about "cultivating a relationship where we all coexist with each other."

Now, as I walk up to *The Blue's* with Miles' hand in mine, I feel myself get nervous because the train of thought from Aster to Jack has led to thoughts about how my parents, mainly my mom... How she has been fairly blind to how I've been struggling.

I'm not so crazy that I would blame them for not noticing. I am at fault for not being honest and open with them. It's nothing against them that I haven't been. It was my decision to hide my feelings—*myself* from them. And it isn't even just everything that has to do with Aster.

The feelings of anger and sadness towards my father are not new. But growing up we all just kind of swept them under the rug, not appropriately dealing with them. While I'm in therapy *now*—I should have been far sooner. I know my mom did her best, dealing with all of that the best she knew how.

But I can't help but feel a little bitter about her not seeing *me.* Under the façade of being alright... I wish she would have seen the hurt I was dealing with. I don't blame her, necessarily. But something *has* to change and give. And I have to start that process.

"You ready, mo chroí?"

Miles came over after work so we could ride together to supper. I told him about the letter to Jack and how it kick started all of these feelings that I feel like I need to express to my mom. He sat and listened, offering small smiles and reassuring nods.

It's not so much that he made me feel like I *could* talk to my mom about all of this tonight, but rather he made me see that he believes in me that I can *handle* doing this. It's not a false sense of security that I'm feeling with him around. It's just the security he's offering by being around that's helping strengthen me.

I nod and squeeze his hand as we enter the bar, immediately feeling an excited sort of nervousness to finally be open with my mom about how I've been struggling.

Everyone needs people in their corner. I just struggle with keeping that corner open sometimes.

"Hey, sweet pea," my mom says from her chair. "Oh, and hi, Briar." Her joke makes everyone laugh.

They love Miles which makes my heart swell with a feeling I haven't felt in a long time. But that's not very true, is it? Considering I haven't ever stopped loving Aster. That's all something to dig through another time, though.

"Hi, everyone," I say as I sit next to Quinn, putting Miles between me and my mom.

We all exchange the standard Midwest "How's it going?" "Good, you?" greetings. I mix it up again this week, ordering a club wrap with a salad. Quinn smiles at me after she orders her chicken strips. It's the little things, for me, that are making a big difference in feeling better about anything lately. Like switching up my typical food order. Taking back control over something so minor to me, in this case good food that I enjoy, is under appreciated.

Supper goes fine. Conversation flows and laughs are had. It's when we all get up to leave that I start to get nervous again. I wanted to do this here, outside where after it's all said and done, I can get in Miles's pickup and go home.

"Hey, mom, listen." I pause at the curb by our vehicles. Somehow, we all parked next to one another. "Can I say something quick?"

"Of course, honey. What's up?"

She's fiddling with her keys, not looking at me.

"Um," Miles rubs his hand across my shoulders, putting his around me. "Can you look at me please?" I feel so small, like a child, requesting something stupid.

"Oh, sure. What's going on?"

Quinn and dad are standing next to us, some sort of malfunctioning circle forming. My mom's eyebrows push together in concern and confusion.

"I'm having a hard time."

Get it together.

"What do you mean?"

I look to Miles and then to Quinn, both of them smiling at me in encouragement. My dad tilts his head and asks, "You okay, Briar, honey?"

"Um, well, not really, I guess. I'm not having a good time with things. Like, Aster. I'm having a hard time dealing with his death and also some feelings about Jack have resurfaced recently and I'm having a hard time with that now."

My mom huffs, not in annoyance but also not-not in annoyance. She hates when I bring Jack up. She gets defensive for me immediately, like overly on my team, which is nice in theory but also a little overwhelming in reality.

"Oh honey, I didn't know that you were still having such a hard time with the whole Aster *thing*."

My guard goes up more than it was already, and I'm instantly irritated.

"Well mom, that's because you're emotionally unavailable ninety-nine percent of the time. And what do you mean the Aster *thing*? It's not a *thing*—he died." With every word my breathing quickens, and my voice rises in volume.

"Honey, take a breath and relax." My dad tries to soothe me from the side, always the peacekeeper.

"Dad, tell me I'm wrong, then. Tell me she's not emotionally unavailable and that since he died no one has hardly even noticed that I was drowning in my own grief, damn near numb and unable to move on from anything-"

My mom interrupts my spewing. "I'm sorry we didn't notice sweetheart, but you don't need to be so mean."

"But this is where I'm at mom. It's not about you right now. It's not about being mean. It's about me telling you that I needed help and that I still need help. I'm not doing it very well, but I don't feel like I know how to do it the right way. And it's hard to tell you that I want to talk about it, and I want to visit his grave, but I don't want to ask to do it all alone, but I don't feel like I can lean on you guys because you hardly notice that I'm a walking ghost." The majority of that came out in one breath, anger and sorrow mixing for a heavy dose of what my reality has been.

I look around then, the silence overwhelming. Quinn has her arms wrapped around her. My dad looks shocked and concerned and sad. My mom has tears running down her cheeks. I take a deep breath and rein in my emotions. Or try to. Miles is running his thumb over the spot where it rests on my shoulder.

"I am sad. Therapy is helping but only recently since I started talking about Aster, a name I have only started saying again recently by the way. I haven't been doing well. I wasn't doing well for the last year. Quinn and Miles found me damn near catatonic last week."

At that my parents both gasp and take small steps towards me.

"And I've cried at least once every day since. Which is completely new because up until last week, I hadn't cried in almost a year. And

Mark asked me to write a letter to Jack and I did, and it made me sad about all of that so now I'm navigating both of those things and they're both weighing me down heavily and I just don't want to do this all alone anymore."

Tears are falling down my own face now. And it's as if that was the proof my parents needed, the girl who doesn't usually cry—crying. That's what causes them to snap into action.

"What do you need?"

"What can we do?"

"I can't kill Jack, but I would if you asked."

At my dad's offer I laugh.

"I just don't want to do this alone anymore," I say again.

I'm suddenly engulfed by three warm bodies. Arms and faces press in on me. Miles steps back to give us a moment. Until my dad yanks him back towards us.

"You helped my girls. You're in this now, son."

Miles laughs and hugs us all back, his massive arms squeezing tightly.

"You tell us what you need, give us a direction to go in, and we'll do anything for you. Okay, honey?"

"I just want you guys to know, I guess. To be aware. I don't think I want hovering or anything like that. Just like, know that I am trying to figure it all out."

"And what about Jack?" my mom asks as we separate.

I swallow, looking at my dad and then my mom. "I'm meeting him on Sunday. I called him earlier and asked if he had plans and if he could make time to sit down with me. He said he's got friends coming over Saturday but Sunday he had time."

Quinn rolls her eyes and my mom scoffs while my dad says, "Glad he could fit you in to his fucking schedule."

We all leave it at that, saying goodbye and our 'I love you's.

"I'm proud of you," Miles says a little while later as we sit on my couch together.

I don't respond beyond a kiss on his cheek.

My mind continues to over think what Sunday might look like.

What after Sunday might look like.

Tomorrow is my meeting with Jack. But today... Today is my lunch with my siblings. All four of them. To say that I am excited would be an understatement.

To say that I am kind of freaking out... Would also be an understatement.

"Ready?" Quinn says from my passenger seat.

She's all cute in her baggy, ripped jeans and ACDC T-shirt. Her hair is in a clip and her face is makeup free. She's never needed it.

"I think you're beautiful. Have I ever told you that?"

She gives me a disgusted look like I just told her she resembles the bottom slice of summer sausage.

"Ew, too soft, Bri. Like, you're pretty too but we're not really those kinds of sisters, yeah?"

I roll my eyes. "The kind that compliment each other?"

"Exactly." And with that she exits my car and waltzes her smart ass into Panera.

Without me.

I follow in after her, making sure my own ripped jeans are sitting where they should and that my *"Fireheart"* T-shirt is straightened and not tucked into a roll it doesn't belong in. I resituate my hair clip, leaving half of the thick mass down. I also kept my face bare, not wanting to feel like I'm trying too hard.

Even though I really want to try hard with these guys.

Quinn is sitting with my three Nebraska siblings and I have to pause in awe for a minute and rein in the small amount of jealousy I feel towards the ease she always carries with her. I can't hardly say hello without stuttering through my nerves but she's over there laughing with Christine like they're best friends.

"Hey, Briar." Kyle gets up and hugs me, the twins follow after him. "Nicole sends her love. Can't wait for you to visit after the baby comes."

I smile and hug him tightly. "I can't wait to meet her."

"We're going to be aunties!" Madeline says excitedly, hugging me before Christine does.

I sit on the end, not between anyone and feeling better because of the small amount of space.

"It's so exciting!" Christine says.

I nod my head, smiling.

We all go order our food, having wanted to get a table first.

Things are going well. We all chat about the basics—life and jobs and catch up on the day to day. Quinn kicks me not-so-gently in the shin after a while. I look at her in alarm and annoyance and she just raises her brows at me and nods her head at the Warrens. I nod, taking a deep breath.

"Um, so," I clear my throat and they turn their attention to me. "I was wondering if I could just say something quick?"

The girls look at me like they don't know what I could possibly be needing to say and Kyle looks at me like he can see right through me. Which is alarming and also very cool.

"Of course, Briar. What's up?"

"So, it's no secret that shit is weird. With us. Like, the four of us, I mean. And I don't really know that there is an exact reason. Like, I don't know if I did something and my brain has blocked it out, or if there's just this weird wall up that we can't get down. But I would like to start trying. To get it down, I mean. The wall. I would like to have a relationship with you guys." I look around and they all just watch me.

"You just never seemed like you liked to be around us."

Have I mentioned how much I hate myself?

"I'm so sorry, Madeline. And Christine and Kyle. It was never you that I don't enjoy being around. It's your dad. And I'm sure that's so weird for you-"

"He's your dad too," Madeline says softly.

"He's not," Quinn says quietly but firmly.

I smile softly at my bold little sister.

"He's not though. He doesn't do what a dad should for me like he does for you. And I love that he does what he does for you. Please know that. That he's provided for you guys and that he was there for proms and birthdays and first dates and he'll be at weddings and there for your kids and everything he should be there for..."

I fold my hands in my lip, twisting my ring around my finger. "But he's missed the first half of that for me. Willingly. And I don't foresee that changing. I've sort of accepted it—as much as I can, anyways. But I don't want my lack of relationship with him to affect my relationship with you guys anymore. I want to visit. I want you to visit. I want to get lunch and call you and meet your boyfriends or girlfriends. I want to be there to meet my nieces and nephews and come to birthday parties."

"But he'll be there for all of that," Christine says.

I nod my head. "Right. And he should be. I'd hate him even more if he didn't show up for you guys. But what he is to you isn't my business anymore as long as he's something and it's enough for you. I'll be chill. I probably won't do much differently than I do now, honestly."

"So ignore him?"

We all laugh even though it's really not that funny. "Yeah, basically." I shrug. "I just want to be your sister. To support you and love you. If you'll let me. If you want me."

"I want you to be." I smile at Kyle and he takes my hand in his. Christine puts hers on top, then Madeline.

Finally Quinn, sighing like the drama queen I love, says, "I'm in this too, in case anyone was curious. Auntie Quinn and all that."

We all laugh and hug when we leave. The girls and I make plans to get lunch in a couple weeks in Chadron with Nicole. A little pre-baby girls day.

My heart feels the fullest it's ever felt, I think.

twenty-six

"If she could put the hollow ache that haunts her into words, she would tell him 'I miss the father you never were.'" —John Mark Green

THE DRIVE TO WHERE Jack lives isn't long. About two and a half hours—if I went the speed limit. I arrive in Chadron anxious and wishing I had taken Miles up on his offer to come with me. The SiriusXM station I haven't paid attention to is at a low level as I pull into the parking lot of the *Runza* here.

At least I'll be able to eat my weight in onion rings and Runza ranch dressing on the way home after this.

He's here when I arrive, waiting at a booth in the back corner. It surprises me, seeing him here before me. I sit down, quietly saying hello. I set down the printed sheet I brought with.

"Thanks for making time," I say, not looking him in his eyes.

"Of course," he says back. His voice isn't cold or warm. It's somewhere in the middle.

Isn't that almost worse? The middle? A parent shouldn't be in the middle of love or hate with their child. Of like or dislike. Pro or con.

I look at him then. I see the gray blending in with his already light hair, take in what my eyebrows would look like if I hadn't started waxing them when I was fourteen, notice the way his eyes have more wrinkles on the outer corners going downwards rather than upwards—As if he frowns more than he smiles.

"Is everything okay?" His question is cautious.

Which is fair because I bet I give off "Don't fuck with me, I'm crazy vibes."

"I wrote you a letter. You can either read it yourself or I can read it to you. I don't mind either way. It's up to you."

His face shows a small amount of surprise. He holds out his hand, wanting the paper. I hand it over, folding my hands in front of me and focusing on a chipped spot on my dark red nails.

I give him time to read, trying to not look as if I might burst into flames from the energy coursing through my body. Every now and then I hear him sigh deeply or take a harsh breath in. I avoid looking up, not wanting to get mad before necessary.

Eventually I see the paper get set back down in my line of sight. Not in front of me—he keeps it in front of himself. He folds his hands in front of himself, waiting for me to look at him. I take a deep breath and meet his gaze.

"Well, you're quite the writer."

"Thanks. Think I should write a book someday?"

My joke misses its mark.

Disappointing.

We sit in silence for a minute before I ask, "Do you have anything you want to say?"

Jack sighs. "I'm not sure I know what to say."

I roll my eyes and under my breath say, "Go figure."

"That's not fair, Briar."

"No, what isn't fair is you abandoning me but loving your other kids like they deserve. That isn't fair."

"Briar."

"Don't 'Briar' me, Jack. Be honest. For once in *my* life, be honest and own your shit. Is it me? Was it me? I guess now, at this point, I can see why I would be part of the reason we don't have a relationship. I don't like you so I'm sure you don't like me. I'm not very nice to you but with good reason, in my opinion. But before that? Before I started not accepting the placating bull shit and the fake niceties? I was a child, and you didn't want me. Why? What did I do that was so unlovable? What made me so easy to leave?"

I feel my eyes water, but I don't care at this point. Let him see the pain. Let him maybe remember the tear stains on the letter from fifteen years ago.

"Briar, that isn't the case. I don't know what to tell you. Nothing is going to help. I wish I could say that I will do more. Be more. But I honestly think we both know that it would be a lie. I wish I could give you a tangible reason as to why things are way the way they are."

I rein in the urge to roll my eyes at him.

"But I've got nothing other than that I *am* sorry I have caused you so much pain. I don't know what else to tell you or do for you. I want to have a relationship with you, but I have very little I can offer you in terms of emotions and support and anything that you are wanting. It isn't just you, either. Please don't think this is isolated to just you. Ask your siblings. I am not a good parent to any of you. I provide for them. That's almost it."

I try to remember that overreacting would do me no good, trying to stay calm and collected.

"We talk sometimes when it comes time for things we enjoy like camping and hunting but otherwise, Briar, I am absent in their lives. I invite you to things. I pass on invites from others in the family like I do for the kids. I don't know why that can't be enough."

That's all slightly bull shit—he's far more involved than he's portraying. He helps with household projects if Kyle asks and he works on the girls' cars and he does *some* things for and with them. But I won't mention any of that.

I can't believe what I am hearing, though. Poor Marnie—having chosen a man like this to marry and procreate with. Suddenly I look at Jack and I don't feel anger. I feel pity. What a pathetic excuse for a "father".

"I don't know why that can't be enough."

"Because I deserve better. I get it—you think a last-minute invite to Christmas is okay. But I disagree. I don't deserve to be an afterthought or a late-thought. I deserve..." I take a moment. "I deserve a first-minute invite. I deserve to be thought of initially and remembered right away. I want nothing from you. I will be trying to get closer to my siblings. But from you, I want nothing."

Jack sighs like I am putting him out.

"I feel sad for you. Your brain must be such a dark place to live in. I pity you for not being able to feel love and give it like you should. Please stop sending me Christmas cards. I will get them from my sisters and brother themselves. Don't pass on invites to me anymore, I always know about the events prior to you mentioning them anyways."

I blink away the single tear that is trying to escape.

"I don't want to be the 'other daughter' anymore, Jack. So, I am asking you to consider me as nothing from here on out. I will do the same. I will make an effort to no longer scowl at you and make backhanded comments in your direction. I can't promise immediate results. I am only human, and I'm still pretty pissed about the whole being abandoned thing."

Taking a deep breath, I finish my speech. "But I'm going to do my best to heal for myself. When anyone asks, I would hope you have the balls to not lie to them about why we don't speak. And in the same breath I would hope that you see the truth for what it is. *I gave you chances, you told me to fuck off.*"

With that, I leave the letter where it lies in front of him and get up. I don't say anything else to him and I don't give him a chance to respond. Not that he would. I get in my car, take my first full breath since I pulled into Chadron and then I allow myself to cry. I sit in the feelings of disappointment and anger. I ruminate in the sadness and pain. And then I drive my car through the drive-thru for some onion rings.

On the way home I talk to Quinn, Catt, and then Kyle. I give them the rundown. Quinn expresses her anger for me. Catt expresses her pride. Kyle also gets very mad at Jack and lets me know that he wasn't lying when he said their relationship is of the lowest standards.

"I get it. I understand that he doesn't hardly talk to any of us. But I'm not okay with it. If you are, that's fine. I won't judge you for that—*ever*. It's just not enough for me. I deserve a father that wants to tell me happy birthday. I deserve a dad that loves me even quietly. One that wants to see me and mine. He doesn't, and that's his choice."

I inhale deeply. "But just like that—it's my choice to want better and hold my standards higher. I won't fault you, ever, for having him in your life. He's your dad and he is more active as yours than mine. Just please do the same and don't fault me for choosing the opposite."

"Absolutely, Briar. I understand. I hate that it is this way, but I don't fault you for any of it. I want us to be good. That's my priority where we're concerned."

My heart swells at my brother choosing to love me despite our father.

"I love you, Kyle. Thanks."

"Love you too, Briar. Drive safe, okay?"

We say goodbye and hang up. I call Miles and give him the details last, wanting to just talk to him now. I get all warm and fuzzy while he lets his anger at Jack out on the phone.

"I'll meet you at your house, if that's okay? I don't have to stay. I just want to hold you for a minute."

"I'd love that. Bring work clothes if you want to stay the night." The last part comes out more quietly, the nerves taking over as if he hasn't spent many a nights at my house by now.

I hear his smile over the phone though as he says, "I'll see you at home, mo chroí."

twenty-seven

"HOW ARE YOU FEELING?"

I look at Miles in the mirror and smile. Last night he held me and reassured me that I am not a drama queen. At least not for the decisions I made where Jack is concerned. He thinks that my decisions were thought through and fair. He then reminded me, in great detail and efficiency, just how much he enjoys me—how wonderful he thinks I am, and vice versa.

This morning as he stands behind me, leaning his large frame on the doorway, he smiles broadly. His arms are crossed over his chest and his gray T-shirt hugs every inch of his tanned muscles perfectly. He has yet to buckle his belt over his jeans and the sight makes me almost dizzy. I force myself to not look down at myself, wearing one of his T-shirts that I slept in. In the romance books and movies when the girl wears her guy's shirt, it's all cute and big and swallows her up, right? It's huge because she's small and he's large and that's the norm.

I'm not the norm. And it's very apparent in the snug fit of his black band tee that he says he loves to see me wear. I scoff when he says it, not believing him. But then... he does what he did last night and reminds me just how much he loves every inch and ounce and curve of my body.

So, I swallow down my insecurities now as I eye my incredibly hot, um, *Miles*... Haven't quite worked my way up to the "B" word. But in my defense it's been almost a decade since I have had one of those and the last one I did have... Well, anyway.

I finish brushing my teeth before answering him. "I'm feeling alright. My heart feels heavy, but my head feels clear. I found myself thinking of Aster while I made our coffee."

I smile softly and turn to face him, leaning on the bathroom counter.

"I think he would be proud of me for how I handled everything with Jack yesterday. I wish I could tell him about it. And after talking to Catt last night and hearing how proud she is of me for all of it, I feel even better about the whole thing."

Miles smiles his knee weakening smile and holds one hand out. I take it in mine and he pulls me to him, making me laugh and smile in a way I haven't in so long.

"I didn't know him," he says a little sadly. "But I would bet he's incredibly proud of you, mo chroí." He kisses the tip of my nose. "Mark will be proud tonight too when you talk to him."

I smile at that too. "He's going to be stoked."

"Hey, so listen." I look up at Miles, his tone carrying some nerves. "My family is doing a thing this weekend for my uncle. It's his birthday next week. My mom mentioned wanting to meet you and I floated the idea by her of inviting you."

My body tenses and my eyes go wide and I hate it. I hate the nerves I get from hearing about maybe meeting Miles's family. It's like my heart isn't ready to open us up to that kind of life, that kind of potential for love, again. Not even with just Miles—his whole family.

I had that once... The boy with the incredible parents. He senses it—my apprehension.

Kissing my forehead he says, "It's okay. You don't have to come. It was just a thought."

This sweet, patient man.

"I want to." My voice wavers slightly.

He leans back, gazing down at me. "You don't have to, sweetheart."

"I know I don't have to. I want to. I do. I promise. It's just..."

Miles gives me the space he knows I need to work through it in my head.

"I haven't dated after Aster, right? So, I've never met anyone else's family. And his mom and dad loved me, like immediately. But that was easy because I was barely fifteen meeting them. Even after we broke up, they stayed fans. I haven't spoken to them since his fune-" I cut myself off. "I'm not fifteen anymore... And I'm all sad and messy and I don't want your parents to hate me."

"You won't believe it until you feel it, but I'm telling you right now—my family will love you."

"I'll go. I want to. Please."

"It's Saturday afternoon." His smile lights me up inside.

We both leave the house at the same time, kissing each other goodbye from the driveway.

I go to lunch finding a text from Mark that he has some sort of flu, and we have to cancel our session today. I briefly text him about Jack, after wishing him to get better soon, and he radiates pride in his texts back.

Miles and I decide that we'll have supper tonight, I'll cook since I'll be home earlier than normal now. This Monday is looking up and I can't help but find myself feeling better than I have in weeks.

I run to the store after work for some groceries, deciding I want to be ambitious and make a lasagna for us.

I don't know if perhaps God has a weird sort of sense of humor. Maybe he thinks I am far stronger than I am. Or perhaps he isn't even really real and it's just a fucked up sort of fate that as I round a corner inside of *Fresh Family* I run, and I mean that in the most literal of sense, right into Fiona Briggs.

My basket tips into her cart, our groceries mixing together like a weird ode to how our lives used to be mixed together, but I don't think either of us notice.

I almost admitted out loud this morning to Miles that I haven't seen or spoken to Fiona or Levi since Aster's funeral. And how shitty of me for that, really? They lost their only child to a terrible death, and I just ditched them?

But do you know how hard it is to even *think* about stepping foot in that home? Or to hear her sweet voice? Look into these eyes of hers that are almost exact replicas of Aster's? And his dad—by the time Aster's voice had dropped fully, they sounded identical. It's torture just thinking about it.

So, I'm selfish. I've been selfish. And now I'm face to face with a woman that shares in some sort of grief that is adjacent to mine, and I silently beg whoever is laughing at my pain to open up the floor I'm standing on and swallow me whole so that I don't have be here in front of someone I love so much but can't stand to be near.

"Briar." My name is barely a whisper on Fiona's voice. I see the tears in her eyes. "Sweet-"

I say nothing. I need to say something. But what can I say?

"I'm sorry your son, the love of my life, died?"

"I'm sorry he and I weren't speaking, and I wasn't there until the very end?"

"I'm sorry I haven't called since we left the cemetery?"

"I'm sorry that I am so incredibly angry with your dead son for leaving me like he did?"

"I'm sorry there will never be a "we" again?"

"Oh, and also, while I'm being honest, I'm pretty pissed at you too?"

None of that seems like a good start to any sort of productive conversation in the middle of a grocery store on a Monday night. So, I stand here—frozen and silent.

"You look wonderful, honey." I track a tear as it falls down her flawless cheek.

Here's the thing about Aster's family—they are *perfection*.

Think Princess Diana—looks and heart. That's Fiona. Married to a man like Hugh Jackman—kind of rough but good and kind, right? That's Levi. And then they produced this perfect Josh Hutcherson-esque boy that stole my heart a decade and some odd years ago and then he died with it still in his grasp, and now I can't hardly look at this incredible woman in front of me without wanting to rip myself in half for her because she's obviously and rightfully devastated and I'm a selfish twat that doesn't deserve her kindness.

"We miss you."

"I have to go."

We say those two very different sentences at the same time, and I think I would much prefer a semi-truck to literally run me over than to have this interaction with Fiona.

She smiles at me. And it's a true, honest to goodness, genuine and kind smile.

Princess Di, remember?

"You just come home when you're ready, Briar. We love you."

And then this wonderful, resilient, beautiful woman walks around her cart, picks my few things out and sets them gently into my basket. She slowly and gently, like I'm a fragile and feral stray cat on the street, sets my basket in my hand, squeezing tenderly around my fingers. She presses her perfectly pink lips to my cheek in the softest, most nostalgic kiss. And then she walks away. Chin up, shoulders back, pace even.

I internally curse Mark for bailing on our session tonight because now I need Thursday to be here quicker than I did five minutes ago.

Fuck.

"Mo chroí," Miles calls from the front door. "It smells amazing."

I came straight home from store, focused on making the best fucking lasagna ever, and tried my hardest to not spiral about Fiona and Levi.

Only the first bit of that worked.

"Did you make this?"

I fane offense at his question, placing a hand on my chest. "From scratch. Ish. I definitely didn't make the noodles."

"It looks incredible. What can I do to help?"

"Grab plates?"

We set up the table, get food dished up and dig in.

"Holy shit," Miles says around a full mouth. "Baby. Don't ever tell my mother this." I've never seen him so serious. "But this is the best lasagna I've ever had."

I burst out laughing, he does not. His seriousness makes me laugh even harder, tears forming in my eyes.

And I don't know if it's the release of oxytocin that kind of kicks shit into overdrive, Fiona at the grocery store and everything that comes along with that, Jack and his bull shit from yesterday... I don't know exactly how I get from point A to point B, but one second I'm laughing at Miles and his tone and the next I'm gasping for breath and sobbing uncontrollably.

Both, the laughing hysterically and then the actually being hysterical, are incredibly unlike me on a normal day, freaking myself and Miles out.

Wide, bright blue eyes are level with mine suddenly, searching for answers that I don't even know the questions to.

"Baby. Briar. What's wrong? What happened? What do you need?"

I can't answer him. Even if I wanted to, which I think I do, I can't. I can't breathe. I can't get anything in, let alone anything out. Everything is choppy and my lips are starting to tingle, and my vision is going a little weird at the edges and I want to laugh at the fact that literally not sixty seconds ago I *was* laughing.

"Okay, up we go."

Miles lifts me off the chair, his hands under my arms. He picks me up like you would pick up a baby and if I weren't in the middle of a panic attack, I would protest that I am far too large to be carried like this. But he does it, and he does it well. He hauls me off to the bathroom, not setting me down until he's turned the shower on.

"I'm so sorry about this, Briar."

His words mean nothing to me right now. I'm still breathing like a dying fish. I can't feel my face now, my fingers feel like what the tip of a sparkler probably feels like during the Fourth of July. I'm not able to pay attention to anyth-

"Holy fuck!"

Cold. So cold. Very cold.

"I know, baby. I'm sorry."

I didn't know I said that out loud.

Time is weird when you feel like your chest cavity is literally imploding in on itself while simultaneously exploding out of itself. I don't know how long we sit here, Miles holding me to him, my back to his front. His back is against the shower wall and we're both under the frigid spray of water. Fully clothed, mind you.

Eventually my breathing slows, my gasping sobs turning to soft cries. He continues to hold me, reaching up and turning the dial to make the water warm. We stay there like that for a while. Every now and then, his chin will move away from where it's taken up residence, perched on my shoulder, and he'll kiss the back of my head. Some sort of silent reminder that he's choosing to be there or something. That's what it feels like, at least.

"Do you know I have cried in front of you more than I have cried in front of almost anyone?"

I feel him silently chuckle. "Quinn?"

"Oh, absolutely."

"Catt?"

"Yeah, actually. She's seen me cry more than Quinn has but still not by much. I always just cried alone if I needed to cry."

There's a long pause from Miles. "Aster?"

"No," I say quietly. "He saw me cry the most."

twenty-eight

"Now I have to remember you for longer than I have known you."
—C.C. Aurel

"Do you think you and Aster would still be friends if you hadn't been together and things had... gone differently for him?"

Miles almost chokes on his question, but I don't. I love that he asks me about Aster. He's the only one, Mark aside, that has ever just brought him up and made him feel real.

That's something I've struggled with immensely since he died—the realness of it all. Aster was very much a living, breathing, loving person. And then he was gone. And for me it was all pretty quick, losing him. But I pull myself back to Miles's question.

"Yes, definitely. I don't think, though." I give Miles a shy sort of look. "I don't *think*... I *know* we were going to be together. We would have been again. I don't say that to make you uncomfortable-"

"No, no, I know. It doesn't." I give him a look. "Maybe it does a little bit. But only because you're my girl-" he cuts himself off.

I perk up from where I'm sitting on the couch with him, my feet curled up under me. He's a cushion over, his feet propped up on my coffee table. We've been watching The Discovery Channel since my meltdown, which I haven't told Miles the reason for yet, and sort of just mindlessly coexisting. He's given me some space which I've appreciated. Every now and then he'll look over at me, lean his entire body across the couch and kiss whichever part he can reach. It's very sweet.

"Well, do go on," I say, amused.

I'm far more excited for this label's conversation than I had anticipated I would be. Distraction aside, I thought I would be terrified of labels.

Turns out I think I want them...

His smile is crooked, and his eyes are all bright as he puts his feet down and gets on the floor, crawling over to me on his knees. That does something to me, most definitely.

"Mo chroí," he whispers.

I rein in my shiver, setting my feet on the floor and giving him the space to settle between my legs. He takes it, resting his hands into the crooks of my knees.

"Hmm?" I'm not trying to be a pain—I simply can't speak now with his big body so close to mine, on his knees, all smiley and broad and cute and about to tell me we're like, official and shit.

He laughs at me, knowing how much he undoes me.

"I guess I hadn't really thought about asking, which is a damn shame now that I see how pink your cheeks are."

I press my fingers to my face, knowing he's not wrong.

"So, I guess now I'll ask. Briar, my heart, mo chroí," he smiles and winks and I roll my eyes because I'm prickly like that. "Will you let me call you my girlfriend? Let me be your boyfriend? All *out loud and shit?*"

"Will *you* let *me* be your girlfriend?" I say, putting my hands on either side of his stubbly face. "Miles, I hate to tell you this, but I think you've grossly miscalculated the one who might come out on top here."

He winks at me, the flirty bastard. I shake my head.

"That's the plan here, baby."

I roll my eyes. "You're far too good for me," I whisper, serious now.

His face goes soft. "Oh, Briar." He turns and kisses one of my palms before doing the same to the other. "Lovely Briar." Never *sweet*, not yet. "I think *you* have miscalculated just how good you are, my love. But that's okay—for now. I can show you as we go."

I melt. Right there, into my couch, into him.

"I guess when you introduce me to your family this weekend, this makes the whole 'this is Briar my...' less difficult," I joke.

He laughs and lays his head in my lap. "Yes, definitely makes things much clearer."

I run my fingers through his dark hair, twisting a few strands every now and then.

"Hey," he says quietly. "Can we talk about what happened during supper?"

I take a deep breath. I want to be open and honest with him, I do. And I am. I will be. But it's new for me—talking about everything. So, it takes me a minute to gather my thoughts.

"I ran into Aster's mom at the store today."

He doesn't move. Doesn't make it a thing. Doesn't react in a way that shuts me down or shuts me up. He stays still and calm, keeping me still and calm.

"I haven't seen Fiona, that's her name—Fiona and Levi. I haven't seen them since Aster's funeral. We were close. Really close. They only had Aster and so then when he brought me home and Fiona was all *'oh look a daughter I get to love now'*, she was stoked. And it never stopped. Not even when we were broken up."

I look from my new tattoo to Aster's new tattoo and smile big and wide.

"I love them!" I say, jumping up and down and clapping.

We did it on a whim. We're both eighteen now, adults and all that. So, we didn't need our parents to come with us and sign off on these. We just decided this morning while lying in bed together that we should get them done.

"An aster flower for you," he said, pointing to the aster on my arm. "And a flower from a sweetbriar for me." He points to "me" on his wrist.

So, that's what we did—two little black outlines of flowers that match our names. Aster put his on the inside of his wrist and I put mine above the inner crease of my elbow.

"I love them," I say again, quieter this time.

How special—having this with him, for him.

A little while later, after getting lunch and going back to Aster's house, his mom walks in and we hug. She pulls back, her hands on my shoulders like she does, looking me in my eyes and smiling.

"Honey, how are you?"

I smile and hold her arms with my hands. She spots the little plastic on my arm and guffaws.

"What's that?"

"Oh!"

"Mom!" Aster says from the couch because he doesn't get up to hug his mom and she doesn't make him, just me and I like that fact. "We got tattoos today!"

I see her try not to freak out and I laugh inside. She's so funny.

"Oh, kiddos..." Her voice is all high pitched and fake-excited. "What did you get?"

We laugh and tell her to relax, nothing big and major. We both show her and tell her what they mean.

She loves them immediately.

Her face goes a little serious though and she says, "What about, and don't hate me for this, kids, I love you both and can't wait for the day you get married in like, ten years, okay? But... what if, God forbid, something happens and you don't, I don't know, end up together?"

We both look at her and then each other before we burst out laughing.

"Good joke, mom. We're forever, me and her." He puts his arm around my neck and gives me a big, loud kiss on the side of my head.

I smile and my heart about bursts. And then I look at Fiona, who truly wants us to be end game, so I know she's just being pragmatic, and I don't fault her for it at all!

I smile at her and say, "Sure, we got these because we are in love. But it isn't just because of that—it's more than that. It's because we are best friends. And honestly, even that term doesn't fully encompass what he is to me, or me to him. He's it for me in every facet. Long term, short term. I love him... more." I shrug like it's a no-brainer, common knowledge.

She smiles at me and kisses my forehead before doing the same to Aster. "I love you both very much."

"So, I saw her today for the first time in over a year after leaving her high and dry after her son died and I didn't say anything to her, Miles. I blacked out. I think all I said was 'I have to go' as she told me she misses me. It was awful."

His head is still in my lap, his hair in my hands. His fingers are pulling at my leggings, rubbing up and down my legs. "Do you want to see them?"

"Yes."

It's such an easy answer. I've missed them every day. Even since before Aster died, I missed them. I still spoke to Fiona often, even when Aster and I weren't speaking. She would text or call and we talked at least once a month. Not even about Aster, no. About life. Us. She was mom-adjacent.

"I didn't just lose him when he died. I lost them too."

"They aren't lost though, baby. Not to you. Maybe start with a text, go from there. I can tell you miss them. It hurts you to hurt them and I would bet they don't blame you for it. But you said you want to start moving forward. This might be a good place to start."

He's not wrong. I reach for my phone and it's like it's still in my muscle memory to find her name in my favorites list that hasn't changed since I was sixteen.

> I'm sorry. I miss you too.

I didn't expect an answer until tomorrow at least, it being well past ten. But before I even get my phone set down, it vibrates.

Mama Fi<3

> Lunch Sunday? Xoxo

> Yes, please.

We don't need to narrow down a time and place because it's been the same for a decade, before I stopped coming home. My heart feels like it might burst out of my chest and my stomach does this weird swirling feeling but it's all sort of this excited kind of nervousness.

"I'm proud of you, mo chroí." Miles kisses my knee before getting up. He holds his hand out, pulling me up and leading me to my room.

I'm kind of proud of myself too.

twenty-nine

NOT HAVING SEEN MARK since last Thursday is very strange. It's been months of twice a week. So, it kind of threw me for a loop, if I'm being honest. Thankfully, we're back on track. I'm in my spot on Mark's couch in his office watching the same white car I've been watching for months now just sit there in the same spot it seems to park in every time I'm here.

"How's your week? You had a big weekend—Your parents and Jack. Big conversations."

I nod. "Yeah, yes. That went well. Fine. I was nervous but Miles came with to talk to my mom and dad, and kind of like, stabilized me? Does that sound healthy? Like, I don't feel like I'm depending on him in a big way but he's definitely taking up a role in some fashion in my emotional welfare and I don't want to mess that up and so I'm kind of panicking but that's new and just started and oh my gosh-"

"Kiddo," Mark interrupts my spiral. "Breathe."

I do.

"It sounds like it's perfectly healthy, him being there for you. It doesn't seem like you're letting him lead you on any of this, more like he's just there for you to hold your hand when you need it. Which is great."

I nod my head a few times. "Great. Okay. Cool. Didn't realize I needed to hear that so badly until just now. Sorry."

"All good. Good question to have, good thing to be aware of."

"He talks about Aster."

Mark raises his brows. His glasses are black today, going nicely with his polished, office vibe. A bright blue V-neck sweater over a white shirt, black slacks, black shoes.

"Like, randomly he'll ask a question. Monday morning he told me he thought Aster would be proud of me for that whole meeting with Jack thing."

Mark smiles and I smile. "That's very cool of him, to be so comfortable talking about Aster with you."

I nod. "Miles is really great. I'm meeting his family this weekend."

"And how do you feel about that?"

"Well, I was nervous to begin with. But then I ran into Aster's mom, Fiona. And I hadn't seen her since his funeral because I'm horrible-"

"Not horrible."

"And so that got in my head and I had a pretty bad panic attack..."

"Did you? What happened? Can you explain it?"

I take a second, breathing deep. "Yeah, I think so. I talked about it after with Miles and didn't fall apart. It all just kind of like, hit me I guess? Miles brought up meeting his family and then that night I saw Aster's mom for the first time since his funeral. It felt like a weird sort of sign. A sign for which direction, I'm not sure." I shrug. "But she was so kind, like always, loving me still. And then there I was, a total spazz. So, I got home and focused on a lasagna and then Miles got home and he made me laugh. And you know, I Googled it that night, what could lead to sobbing from laughing."

Mark's eyebrows inch up.

"Came up short, if I'm being honest on that one. But one second I was laughing at Miles and then I couldn't breathe because I was panicking and sobbing. He put us in the water, in the shower, and got me to calm down. I told him about it after and he mentioned texting her. So, I did. And now we're seeing each other on Sunday. The whole *trying* thing you both keep bringing up."

"How are you feeling about seeing her Sunday?"

"Fucking terrified. She's like another mom to me. Or was, maybe, I guess? And now... I don't know what we are. I was going to be her daughter one day and now I'm just her dead son's ex-girlfriend. We weren't even together when he died." That last statement doesn't sit right in my mouth. "Did I ever tell you his last words to me?"

My voice is quiet, and Mark shakes his head. I swallow deep, spin my ring around and smile sadly to myself.

"Marry me, my sweet Briar. Please."

I look up and watch Mark watching me. I hold it together quite well, if I do say so myself. Though, I don't think that's the goal these days.

"I said yes. I said yes and he said he loved me, and I said I loved him and then he stopped breathing while I held him. So, I guess I say we weren't together when he died but like, also, that feels like a lie because maybe we were? In that moment? Had he had two more hours or even twenty minutes... We would have found someone to do it, you know? We would-" My breathing gets choppy. "We-"

"Briar." Mark gets up and walks over to me, pulling my feet down so they are flat on the floor, and he squats in front of me. "Watch me breathe and try to copy me."

I watch and try, and I wasn't far enough into my own thoughts, so I come out of this one rather quickly.

"Great job, kiddo. You're alright. It's alright."

I nod my head and feel my eyes burn.

"I would have married him," I whisper, tears sliding down my face. "I would have."

I show up to family supper a few minutes late, needing to pull my shit together in my car. I was super bummed this morning when Miles told me he couldn't make it tonight, and now I'm extra sad because I could really use his strength. But, alas, I'm solo on this one.

I walk in, makeup free because I had to wash it all off after crying in my car. Quinn notices immediately but waits for me to sit down.

"Hey, honey."

"Hi, Bri."

"Why have you been crying?"

Ever the one to ease into shit, my sister.

I sigh and look at her next to me. "Can I order a drink first?"

"You wanted us to pay more attention."

She's not wrong.

"Have you been crying?"

"What happened?"

My parents can never *not* talk over one another so like, that's always the most fun.

I thank God as the waiter comes up and asks if we're ready to order. We all are, me being the only one to mix it up today by getting a hamburger for the first time in weeks.

Quinn gives me a questioning look when I order it and I tell her, "I need easy right now and that's easy."

She nods and says nothing else about it. The very second my beer is placed in front of me though, the three of them are on me like it's their job, and I'm both bothered and thankful.

It's all new, I'm learning.

"Okay, settle down. I had a weird week. I will tell you all about it. But you will sit here quietly and reserve your questions for when I am done."

They all nod like little prairie dogs, and I bite back a smile before telling the story, for what feels like the eight hundredth time now, about running into Fiona.

"And that's it. I'm having lunch with her Sunday."

Everyone is silent and the food arrives a minute later.

No one but me moves and finally I look at them and say, "You may speak now," in my most sarcastic voice. Quickly I add, "One at a time!"

They all had their mouths open, gaping and ready to go. Just like that, they all slam shut. Looking at each other, determining who goes first, Quinn clears her throat.

"Ah, the chosen one."

She rolls her eyes, and we all start eating. "Are you okay?"

I look at her, really look at her. I see the sadness for me there. I debate telling them about Aster's final moments, but I don't. It doesn't feel like the time or place. I don't know. And I kind of want Miles to know about that first for some reason? Not ready to acknowledge why that is right now.

"I'm not *not* okay. I'm nervous to see her. To sit down with her. She's going to ask why I haven't been to his grave and I'm not going to have an-"

My dad nearly chokes on his fry. "You haven't visited him?!"

Not since the day after we "buried" him, but we don't think about that day.

I frown at him. "Well, no. I haven't hardly begun saying his name and discussing it all, let alone going... *there*." I say it like it's a bad word.

"Briar..." He looks so sad now. Sadder, I think, than he did at the actual service. Which, by the way, was very sad. Not a single person at this table wasn't in love with Aster in some way.

"I just don't want to go there. He's not there, not really."

I shrug and try to brush it off like it's nothing even though I know it's something. I'm very much someone who loves the thought of leaving flowers at someone's grave. Of speaking to someone like they are sitting next to you—remembering them out loud. Setting up decorations for the holidays to make it more... more. But not his, not him. Not yet.

We all let it drop. For now.

"What can we do for you, honey?"

My mom's question catches me off guard. I look at her and smile, genuinely and truly.

"I think just... be here. For me. That's it for now, mom."

"Always, Briar."

thirty

"He was Christmas morning, crimson fireworks and birthday wishes." —Raquel Franco

LOOKING BACK NOW, I should have perhaps asked Miles about what kind of party his family was having. Because this was not what I was expecting.

He picked me up this afternoon, a beautiful late April day, and drove us out into the Hills. His aunt and uncle have a good chunk of land out here and it's all open and spacious and perfect for hosting parties. I'm talking wedding reception level perfection.

Like, I almost would have felt out of place in my cropped mom-fit jeans that are fitted on me because your girl has some thighs and calves on her, along with my black V-Neck and Birks. Almost—But I didn't because everyone else dressed almost exactly the same at Miles's uncle's birthday party.

It's all green, spring having sprung, and flat here. Old buildings that are charming, string lights and tables, chairs and benches, baskets of thin blankets for when it gets darker and cooler, fire pits scattered all about. There's a freaking dance floor, okay?

And boy, oh boy, do they use that dance floor.

I watch Miles twirl his mom, Freya, around the wood plank floor. They are both all smiles and rhythm and I'm most certainly not falling in love in this very moment.

"They sure are good at swinging each other around, aren't they?"

I look over at his dad who snuck up on me and rein in my yelp at the last minute.

I laugh. "They look like they're having so much fun."

He eyes me, looking down with a smirk so much like his son's.

Miles has his mom's eyes, bright blue, and icy but warm. But literally everything else is all Declan O'Brien. Freya isn't even five and a half feet tall. She's got the Irish red hair, freckled pale skin, a fuller figure. Her accent is very faint, her parents being from Ireland. Declan is an inch under Miles, six-foot-two-inches. He wears his dark hair a few inches longer than Miles wears his, and his beard hangs a couple inches long. His skin is tan, and his voice is smooth and honestly, so is he. Besides the eyes, the major difference between Declan and Miles are their noses.

"Did Miles break his nose?"

My question surprises Declan slightly. He looks to his son and wife who are still spinning and two-stepping all about, laughing loudly and having a good time.

Declan nods before saying, "When he was sixteen. He got into it during hockey practice. His cousin," Declan points to a fit, gorgeous red head across the yard. "Someone on his team had said something really unkind about her. Miles wasn't having any of that. Jumped on the guy the second he refused to take it back."

My eyes are wide. "The guy broke his nose?"

Declan laughs. "Nah. Miles got yanked off the guy after hitting him a few times. Whoever pulled him off didn't have the best grip and so Miles threw himself out of his hands and into the plexiglass. Broke his own damn nose."

I stare at Declan as he stares back at me before I break out in a full-on cackle. He joins me shortly after, both of us just howling away. I'm bent over, trying to catch my breath. Declan's wiping at his eyes, laughing still, one hand on my shoulder. I stand up straight, pulling myself together, and look around for Miles. My eyes catch his and he's got this sort of awed look about him. I tuck some hair behind my ear and smile shyly, looking back to Declan.

"Come on, kid. Let's show my son that his old man can still two-step better than him."

I shake my head. "Oh, no. I don't know how-"

He grabs my hand that I was holding out in protest. "I'll teach ya, honey!"

We get to the dance floor far too quickly for my liking and I don't have to look to know Miles is watching. I can feel it—his eyes on me.

After a very brief, and quite unhelpful, set of verbal instructions, Declan grips my hand in his, placing my other on his shoulder and his other in the middle of my back. He nods, smiles, and just literally starts dancing. And I don't know how I do it—it definitely wasn't hardly me doing anything... But the next thing I know, I'm two stepping with my boyfriend's dad. All around the dancefloor like a couple of jigging fools.

"That's it, honey! You've got it!"

I laugh and it's not forced or uncomfortable. I truly laugh as I tip my chin up to the sky while Declan spins us around and around to a song I don't know. I laugh and then I'm not in his arms anymore—I'm in *his*.

"Mo chroí."

I straighten a bit, opening my eyes and finding Miles'. I smile widely before saying, "Mo mhuirnín."

When I tell you that the weeks of practicing that one single phrase paid off the instant his eyes went big and then soft within the same second...

He leans in close, slowing us down far too much for the song playing. "Say it again." His voice is all rough and deep and *holy shit...*

All the YouTube videos and literal hours making sure I could pronounce "my dear" in Irish correctly—muh voor-neen, just so you're aware... All worth it for this singular moment in time.

"Mo mhuirnín."

His smile grows and if I ever reflect back on us—Miles and I... If I ever look back and wonder "When did I fall in love with him?" it will be this moment that I see. This lighting, the sun nearly beneath the horizon and the string lights creating this halo effect behind his messy head of hair. His fitted white quarter-zip pull-over and his dark blue jeans with his dirty boots. This smile, these eyes, that crook in his nose from the plexiglass of an ice hockey arena.

Miles kisses me then. Hard and with probably too much tongue for his mothers liking. But then again, I think it is Freya that I hear say "whoop whoop" with her faint Irish accent from a few yards away.

I laugh into his laugh, smiling into his smile.

And then we're spinning and two-stepping again, together. His eyes are locked on mine, and we're both smiling and laughing. Eventually I tilt my head up again, Miles puts both hands on my waist, I hold my arms out to my sides. He spins us in circles. I feel like we should feel sick, like we should slow down or something. But we don't. He just pulls me closer, and I keep my eyes closed while we just laugh together as we go on.

Eventually, because time isn't endless, we come to a slowing stop. I rest my forehead on his chest, both of us a bit sweaty and sticky now from the dancing. Though, I'm not sure I would really call it that.

"Let's take a breather, sit down for a bit."

I nod my head against him, and he leads us to a table with some benches, throwing a leg over either side of one and pulling me to sit in between them. We sit like that for a few minutes before his mom and dad make their way to us.

"Sweethearts," Freya croons as she sits across from us. "Having fun?"

We both nod, a little sleepily but enthusiastically.

"Thank you for letting me crash the party. It was very cool to be here."

They laugh and Miles leans in and kisses the back of my head.

"You're welcome here anytime, sweet Briar."

You know in a movie or show where things are going so well? And then the music changes just ever so slightly? The screen maybe dims a little bit and the vibe just kind of... *shifts*. Just the slightest, smallest, tiniest bit. The actors get a little tetchy and even you, the viewer, you get a little... AHHH?

That's this moment. And it shouldn't be. It's just a name. It's not even *a* name. It's *my* name. But yet, here I am. Frozen in Miles' arms. His parents are looking at both of us in an odd sort of way, confused by what just changed.

"Um-"

"Hey, ma. Can you not call her that, yeah? The sweet part?" He says it so sweetly, so respectfully, but also firmly. "She had a really good friend call her that and he passed away. It's just something that makes her feel a bit sad is all."

I think Briar pre-one-year-anniversary-breakdown would hate that Miles is sitting here saying this. But Briar today... Briar, the girlfriend of this kind man behind her...

I smile softly at Freya and Declan. "His name was Aster and I met him when I was a sophomore in high school. He was my first boyfriend, actually. But really, my best friend. He died last year. He used to call me that—sweet Briar. I just haven't really had anyone else call me that and-"

Freya gets up and walks to me quite briskly, sitting in front of me on the bench. I sit up straight, but Miles doesn't take his hands off of my hips.

She grabs my face. Her hands are rougher than I would have imagined, had I ever had the chance or need to imagine the feel of them.

Her eyes, the same as her sons, bore into mine as she says to me in the softest, sweetest, almost fairytale-like voice, "You will be okay. I see you, Briar. I see your pain. Your sadness and anger. I see *you*. You must allow yourself to be those things. They will take over, mo chailín. You must let yourself be sad, be mad. You will be okay. I see that in you too." Freya leans in and kisses my forehead. "Take her home, Miles mo mhac."

We get up, no one saying anything else. Literally—nothing. It would all feel odd, perhaps it should feel odd, but it doesn't. It's rather comforting, being seen like that after living the last year as a ghost. Declan smiles softly at Miles and I, pecking us both on a cheek. His mom hugs us each and kisses her son on the cheek before letting us go.

"You alright, Briar?"

I look over at Miles as we walk hand in hand to his pickup. It's well past ten now, a full moon though, so it's bright enough to see with the help of the string lights' glow and the lamp posts spread throughout the lot. He's so handsome—Miles. His dark brows, thick and a little crazy but in an attractive way, they're pushed nearly together in the middle. I bring my index finger up, smoothing them apart.

"I'm okay, Miles."

And I am. I'm actually alright. Was it a bit weird to just kind of like, casually discuss Aster like that with near but not strangers? Yes.

But only for a second. The way Freya saw me... Like, genuinely saw me... It was unlike anything I had ever experienced. It's not like she saw through me, but she *saw me*.

"Hey," I say, looking over at him as we make our way back to his pickup still. "What was it that your mom called me? And then you? When she was saying goodbye."

He smiles softly, wistfully almost. "Mo chailín means my girl. And mo mhac means my son." He raises our hands to his lips, pressing a kiss to my knuckles.

He relaxes more as we reach his pickup, opening my door for me. Before closing it, he stops and pauses, looking at me from outside.

"Thank you for coming with me to this. They loved you. Like I knew they would." His smile is soft. "I hope you had a nice time."

I lean out a little, grabbing his face and pulling him close to me. "I had a very good time. Please do not think anything otherwise. I love your family. They're great and I very much am glad I came with you." I kiss him in between his brow, on the tip of his crooked nose, sniffing a laugh.

"What?"

"Your dad told me about your incident..."

He rolls his eyes, pulling away.

"Lose a fight with a window, did ya?"

I break out in laughter as he shuts my door and huffs his way to his own side. And then I keep laughing the whole way home with him.

thirty-one

"And sometimes it's loss that truly makes us understand how much we loved." —Dane Thomas

"Briar, babe. She loves you, you'll be fine."

"Catt, I almost ran away from her at the store. How am I going to sit in front of her for brunch?"

I fidget with my ring, spinning it around my finger.

"Well, how did you sit with me at the bar that first time again?"

I take a deep breath then. "I missed you."

"Right. And you miss Fi. She misses you too. You'll be fine. Just... Be honest with her. She can handle it. She loves you."

I nod my head, picking my phone up off of my kitchen counter and checking the time. "Alright, I've got to go or I'm going to be late. Love you."

"Call me after. Love you!"

I wipe my hands down the front of my leggings. Wearing jeans for an entire evening last night was plenty good enough for me. Met my quota for, oh, the year. And Fiona has seen me in much worse than black leggings and an oversized graphic tee. Though, now that I just realized this is one of Miles's shirts...

Oh gosh, I'm going to be sick.

I wipe the tears, taking a deep breath before getting out of my car. I try to not notice how terrible I look. Fiona won't care. She never has. She's been asking to see me for months. I'm back now and I won't be back for a while again if I can help it—seeing Aster without being with him makes me want to actually die.

I get out and make my way to the front door of the Briggs's home. Fiona opens the door before I'm even halfway up, bounding out and down to hug me. Her hug feels like a semblance of home. I take comfort and also feel pain in that thought.

"Sweet Briar, my girl!"

"Hi, Fi." I try to hide the anguish inside of me, but I simply can't. I almost take us both down to our knees on the sidewalk as my legs buckle and my chest caves in.

"Let's get you inside, honey."

We make it in, on to the couch, and I crumble. I didn't even cry like this to my mom when Aster and I broke up. Not to Quinn or Catt even. Not in the time since either. But Fiona... Fuck. She's seen it all. Literally watched us fall in love in a way a mother does.

And then she's watched us try to navigate loving each other as friends now. Not sure how much longer that's going to last if I'm being honest. But I'm not ready for that whole thought process.

"What do I do? Tell me what to do? Should I move back? Beg him to move to Omaha? I don't know what to do Fiona." I sob into her chest, her hand runs down the back of my head.

"Oh, my girl. Shh, shh. You're alright. Take some breaths, my girl. Please."

I do as she says, settling down and sitting up. We both scooch away, slightly turning to face each other on the couch.

"You just keep doing what you're doing, Briar. I know it's hard. I'm so sorry for it. But you're doing such a great job. And so is Aster. And soon enough you'll find your way back to each other."

"What if we don't? What if he finds someone else while I'm gone? And she's here and not prickly or difficult or sad sometimes? She'll keep her chapstick in the same spot of his center console that I did. She'll have her side of the bed that was once mine. She'll know what shirts make his eyes look brighter or lighter, or how different his laughter can be based on who he's with or what he's doing. I miss him every single day. And what if he stops missing me?"

I start sobbing into my hands, big gasping, choking sobs. Fiona wraps me in her arms and stays quiet.

Eventually she tells me, "Briar, honey. Look at me." I do. "I love you. Please understand that when I say this—I love you. No matter what, you will be okay. Whether you two figure it out or not, you will be okay. Whether you fall in love with someone else,"

I pull back in shock and she gives me a very much settle-down look.

"You will be okay. Whether he does the same, you will be okay. You are strong and beautiful and smart and brave, and don't you ever doubt yourself for more than a single second at a time because you are worth more than that, Briar."

I don't know how long I cry on Fiona for. Aster doesn't come home until after I leave, I know that. And I know it was on purpose to give me space.

But it's space I never asked for.

I remember that being the moment my anger towards Aster began. Anger for putting space I never wanted between us. He could have moved to Nebraska, or I could have moved home. He made a choice that sucked.

And as that anger starts to bubble up now, Fiona steps into view. It's eleven in the morning at *The Ham & Eggs*. Our time, our place. We started coming here when I turned seventeen. We would plan it monthly and after the third one, just stopped choosing the time and place because it had been the same. Just her and I, a monthly brunch. I didn't realize how much I had missed it over the years.

She looks the same but different today. Her hair used to be a cute little bob. Now it's longer, to her shoulders. A natural, bright blonde. Her blue eyes always pop against her tan skin, high cheekbones on a heart shaped face. My height, five-nine. Thin and fit, gorgeous. She walks with an elegant, kind air about her. Her warmth is infectious—you can catch a smile from her after a second of being in her atmosphere.

Aster was the same way.

"My girl," she says against my hair as she hugs me tightly. "I have missed you so much, sweet Briar."

I start crying.

Just like that and I am a puddle. I am a mess. I am distraught and breaking in the middle of a restaurant at eleven in the morning hugging my dead ex-boyfriend's mom.

What a picture to paint.

She says nothing about it either, the saint. But then I hear her sniffle and I jerk my head back in shock.

"Fiona?"

"I've missed you so much." She says it on a gasping breath.

I look at her in surprise for a second longer before I pull her to me, holding her head to my chest now. She keeps saying it.

I've seen her cry. Her cries are the sounds in my nightmares, along with the last breath Aster took. The sound she made as Levi carried her from the cemetery was the most heartbreaking sob I never want to hear again. But outside of that, before he died and then even after he died but before his funeral... She was a quiet griever.

"I've missed you. I've missed you. I've missed you."

And then, I don't know when, it turns into, "I miss him."

"I miss him. I miss him. I miss him."

And if that doesn't just fucking wreck me.

I wait. I don't know if that's the right call. I don't know if I should try to comfort her immediately, or how I would even begin to do that with her.

I lost the love of my life.

She lost her son.

Adjacent—not the same.

Eventually, her crying slows and mine is down to a trickle, I say, "I miss him too. And you."

She backs up, holding my shoulders like she always has, and nodding. "Let's sit."

We wipe our faces, and the waiter finally makes his way over, looking beyond nervous and terrified. And honestly—fair.

We sit there, quiet and a bit nervous I think, after we order our meals.

"You're seeing someone." It's not a question.

And she isn't being mean, I know that. She would never. Not even when Aster was alive would she have faulted me for dating. But regardless... I freeze. We've never discussed another boy aside from her son.

I nod, smiling softly. "I am. Miles."

She smiles back. "Your mother says he seems very nice."

I nod again, unsure of how to navigate any of this.

"Fiona, I am really sorry I haven't been around."

"Why haven't you? I mean, I guess I know the why... but also, I don't. We love you, Briar. And you love us. And I know you're furious with Aster for waiting to tell you, probably mad at us too for going along with it-"

"I am."

She blinks at me.

Here goes.

"I am. I am," I swallow, bracing myself and wishing I could brace her a bit. "Fiona, I love you. I love you almost neck and neck with how I love my own mother. And nothing will ever change that, ever. But Fi... I am furious with you. With Levi. With Catt still. With Aster. I'm mad at all of you for keeping that from me. I don't understand it." I pick up and put down the rolled of silverware in front of me before I go on. "I don't understand any of it. I don't know why any of you thought it was a good idea to keep me out of the loop. I don't know why anyone thought it was best for me to not be here immediately. Had I done something wrong? Did I seem like someone that would not have been helpful through all of that? Did I do *something*?" I'm getting choked up again, so I take a breath, reining it in.

"Oh, Briar. No..."

"Then why? Because I've been drowning in this for a year. I've been sinking in a ship by myself with no one and nothing, not even a life raft. And no one noticed and I didn't call for help because no one called me for help. And I don't know why."

"I have something for you. It's from Aster. And I want you to open it soon but in your own time. I know you haven't been by to see him... I think maybe that would be a good place for you to open it. It's a letter. Open it wherever, whenever—but maybe with him. It's in my car. But I think with him... It might be a good spot to read it."

That doesn't answer my question now, but it sounds like the letter will answer my question then.

"I don't want to not discuss things that you want to discuss. I don't want to avoid things. But... Briar, I also don't want to live in grief with you. I want to just live in life with you, honey. If you aren't ready for that, then when you are, I'll be here for you."

I think that over. I don't want to live in grief, but I haven't let myself grieve yet...

"I haven't grieved him yet," I say it barely above a whisper.

"I know, honey. I know."

And I'm sure she does even on her own. Without talking to anyone. Just looking at me, she can see it.

"I miss him, and I hate him, Fiona."

She sucks in a breath, and I feel bad for a second but then she says, "He knew you would, Briar. We all did."

thirty-two

"Do you think you want to visit his grave soon, Briar?"

That stupid white car that is usually parked in the same spot every time I'm on this dumb couch in this overly clean office is gone today. And I'm mad about it.

Not even just mad—*irate*.

"Where are they?"

"What was that?"

I look at Mark. His insufferable black glasses and his stupid brown sweater and awful khaki pants, annoying brown loafers. How can loafers be annoying? I don't know. But today... his are.

"What?" I shake my head, glaring at Mark.

He doesn't even flinch—this guy. "You asked where they are. Who?"

I shrug. And then get mad. "That white car! That stupid white car that parks in that stupid spot on that stupid parking garage every time I'm here! And today! Today?! It's not here! Why? Where is it?"

Mark stares at me for a second and I can tell he's trying to not laugh. I can tell only because who the fuck wouldn't be holding back laughter at my absolute insanity.

"That was my car, Briar. I uh, upgraded over the weekend. The gray one next to the spot I used to park in, that's my new car." He smiles softly at me, and I stand up. "New car, new spot, I suppose."

"Well." I settle my hands on my hips. "Did I tell you Aster wrote me a letter? He did. He wrote me a letter, and no one gave it to me until yesterday when I had lunch with Fiona. And! She said I can't read it until I'm ready to and then said she can tell I'm not. Like! How dare she? How does she even know? Maybe I am ready, and she just doesn't even know me anymore! How would she know! I don't even know me anymore!"

I'm breathing shallowly and pacing the room now.

"And how dare he! How dare he write me a letter before he dies when he *chose* to keep me out of the loop on that? How dare he get sick and die on me like that? How dare he ask me to marry him and then take his last breath against my fucking chest the next fucking minute?"

Now I'm sobbing—heavily.

"I loved him. Fuck, I *love* him. I love him so much I wish I was the one that had died instead of him. He left me and he didn't even give me time with him first. I love him with everything I have and now he's gone, and I don't get to ever tell him how much loving him has made me fucking hate him."

I fall to my knees, holding my face in my hands.

For a year I have wanted to say that out loud. That I hate him. I don't, obviously. Not in the whole never-speak-to-or-about-him-loathe-him-can't-fathom-anything-nice-about-him kind of hate.

More like a...

I miss him in everything I do and am. I miss him in the way the sun sets and rises, because he won't ever see those again. I think of him in every breath I take and every exhale I give. I love him in the way you love the moon, in any phase on any day.

And I hate him for it all because he died and didn't give me time to love him like he deserved before then.

Once I've settled down, taken some breaths and asked Mark about his new car to get my mind off of the reeling, I relax back into the couch.

"Can I ask again about whether you think you're up for visiting Aster's grave yet?"

I sigh and mutter, "You can ask..."

I sense an internal eye roll from Mark before I go on.

"I don't know if I can do it. I want to. I think. Alone. But also, I don't want to do it at all. Ever. Because seeing his headstone there... He's not there. Not spiritually or physically. He's in an urn in his parents' home. But still... His name on that stone... I don't know Mark. It's kind of a lot."

"It absolutely is a lot, Briar."

"I'll do it. Eventually."

I drop my keys on the table by the door, sighing at the smell of whatever Miles made for supper.

Have we moved a skosh quickly? Yes, maybe. We see each other almost daily. It's weird if we go a day without seeing each other for at least a thirty-minute meal. He also spends like, five out of seven nights a week at my house. Which I actually love. We talk all day, little texts and calls throughout. So, again, have we moved a skosh quickly? Actually, I don't think so.

"Mo mhuirnín," I say, wrapping my arms around his waist from behind and leaning my head on his back.

I love his back.

His grabs my hands with one of his, squeezing them once. His black long sleeve shirt smells like dirt and I know that's a weird compliment, but it is that—a compliment.

"Mo chroí, how was Mark?"

"He was good." It's an automatic response that I catch. "Actually, I kind of freaked out."

He turns slowly after turning the stove top off. "I made spaghetti, it's ready whenever." I move to pull away, but he stops me. "What happened?"

I smooth the crease in his brow away like I've started doing, feeling good about doing something small for him like that. Even though I'm the one that puts it there... but that's beside the point. I tell him about my meltdown at Mark's office and he stands with me in his arms, rubbing his thumbs in small circles on my back and looking at me like he might love me.

And then because I have the biggest fucking mouth in the world and zero filter when I need one, I ask Miles, to his face, "Do you love me?"

My eyes go wide immediately, my hands go to my gaping mouth, and I try to get out of his hold. He doesn't let go though. Oh no, this man holds tight.

He smiles at me, wide and full and unashamedly. "Is my honest answer going to freak you out more than you just freaked yourself out?"

"Probably yeah, but like, honesty is the best policy, or whatever the fifth graders are saying these days," I whisper.

He laughs my favorite laugh, and my heart nearly stops and starts at every octave change.

"I love you, mo chroí. Very much. And you don't have-"

"Shh!" I put a finger on his still smiling lips. "I hate that part of books and movies. Just... Hang on."

I take a deep breath. Close my eyes. Brace myself to say something that I have only said and felt for one other person in my entire life. It's something I never thought I would get to feel or say again. It's something that terrifies me every day.

I wake up in the morning next to this man and I think these three words and I panic because the last boy I loved, *love*, died. I go through the day talking to him and at the end of every phone call I fight the urge to say this one phrase because the last man I used to end phone calls saying it to... he's not here anymore. I go to bed every night telling this man in front of me that I love him in my head... because the guy I used to tell that to at the end of every day, the one I still might say it to before I go to sleep in my prayers, if you can call them that, left me fucking shattered and alone.

But what is living if you don't do it honestly?

"I love you too."

No taking it back now. It's out there. It's said. It's done.

I loose a breath.

Miles picks me up, his hands sliding under my butt to grip me. "I don't really feel like spaghetti right now, yeah?"

He's kissing down my neck, up my neck, anywhere near and far from my neck as he walks us to my bedroom.

"Yeah, no, totally. I'm good," I breathe out.

"You most definitely are, baby."

thirty-three

IT'S JUNE NOW. JUNE in South Dakota is gross. It's fine, but it's hot and there's a lot of bugs and it's just not my favorite. My favorite is November. Mostly because my birthday is in November but that's still very far away. So, anyways, it's June.

May was busy. There was a lot of "why does Jack not love me like a father should" and "did Aster think I couldn't handle watching him be sick" moments in therapy. A few "am I easy to leave" moments snuck in there.

I had my monthly brunch with Fiona, we both cried again. I told her I'm not ready to come by the house or to see Levi... To hear his voice. That made her sad. It makes me sad too. But she understood. I wish I did.

Miles has all but moved in with me, which I love.

We are disgustingly in love, or so Quinn says.

But she's one to talk, having sat next to her own freaking *girl-friend* at family supper earlier!

I tried to be chill. I did. But like, I just got so dang excited to finally meet Adelaide. And the girl did not disappoint. At one point I literally whispered, or as Quinn then yelled at me, screamed that Adelaide is the most beautiful person I have ever met.

And she is.

You know those Native American women you see in the movies? With the smooth, perfect, dark tan skin? The dark, silky hair, and the deep eyes, and the incredible noses with the long bridges that you just can't help but be in awe of? Adelaide is that and more. Petite and short, five-three. Hilarious—and I mean it. The funniest person in our group now. Which would probably be a real bummer for Quinn herself if she didn't like her so much. Adelaide says it's her "rez humor" that makes her so funny.

Our parents are enamored with Adelaide. Miles might have some competition if things keep going like they are for both Quinn and me in the in-law department.

He made that joke himself, just so we are all on the same page.
In front of everyone.

I almost passed out from the nerves and excitement of it all.

Miles is twirling a piece of my hair around his finger while scrolling through TikTok, my head on his chest. We're lying in bed and I'm reading a book on my Kindle—*Of Night and Blood* by Brea Lamb. I'm in the middle of really, quite an emotional part between Asher and Bellamy-

Okay, a smutty part.

Miles sets his phone down and asks me, "I know I've asked... And I don't know why I am again. But it just keeps coming up in my head."

I sit up and turn around, setting my Kindle down and facing him.

"Putting me aside, which I am sure is tough," he smiles a slightly sad smile, and it makes my heart hurt for him. "What would life look like right now if Aster hadn't gotten sick?"

I take a deep breath and settle into the spot I'm in on my bed. I've got no pants on, so no rogue strings to play with. Just my bare legs that now that I'm looking this closely really need shaved and that's not the point of this.

"Well, we would be together. At some point, we would have gotten back together. We got together when we were sixteen, fell in love at the same age. Stayed together until we were twenty. Stayed close friends, as close as we could be for the next few years. And then..."

I pull at a loose string on my pillow. "He just kind of dropped off the face of the Earth. It had been two years by the time Catt called me to come home before I saw him again. So, together for four, friends for six, didn't speak for two. I like to think that had he not gotten sick, that I would have come home shortly after that timeframe."

Swallowing, I say, "I would have come home, and he would have known. We would have reunited and that would have been that. We would have gotten married a year later and had babies and all of the things from there."

I never looked away from Miles as I said all of that and he never looked away from me. And maybe I should feel stupid, putting so much blind faith into that "could have been". But that's the truth of it. That's what would have happened.

"You really believe that?" He's not asking it to be doubtful or rude. It's a genuine, and honestly fair, question. "Why? How?"

"At fifteen I had found the person I was going to spend the rest of my life with, you know? I can't explain how I knew, how *we* knew, but we did. We would have done it all. We would have found our way back to each other and done it all like we had planned—like we were supposed to." I smile sadly. "Neither of us doubted that. Not even after the break up. We always joked to Catt, never to each other, that we would just call them "The Absent Years". He was absent from me, me from him. But they weren't lost or anything. We just weren't present. But we would have been."

I swallow and look away, feeling sad. For me. For Aster. And for Miles who has a girlfriend that loves him and also her dead ex-boyfriend.

Look at me getting so good at calling him that though...

"He asked me to marry him." I say it so quietly.

I don't think that Miles even heard me until I feel his fingers grip my chin lightly and tilt my gaze to his.

"Don't stop."

"This can't be fun for you..."

"I admit it's not my favorite thing to do in bed with you," he winks, albeit weakly, at me. "But I asked, and I care, and I want to know these pieces of you."

I nod and bring his hand from my chin to my lips, kissing his palm, before placing it on my cheek.

"Aster—the day he died... He asked me to marry him. Right before, actually. Before he, um, passed away."

Miles doesn't flinch or look away. His thumb brushes a tear I didn't even know was there off of my cheek.

"I said yes."

He wipes away a few more now.

"And then we said we loved each other."

And some more.

"And then he-"

And now there's too many tears for even the most productive of thumbs to take care of.

"And I would have, Miles. I need you to know that. I don't know why but I do. I need you to understand that I would have married him had we had even a fraction of enough time to make it happen. Because I love him. Present tense. I love him today. In a very real way. And I hate myself for it. I hate him too for all of it."

My breathing is coming faster now. "But I hate me because I love him, and I love you, and I feel like that's horrible of me. I didn't want this—you and me. And not because of you. You're wonderful. That's just it... I didn't want to fall in love with another incredible man that loved me back. Because nothing lasts forever. And then when, or if, this doesn't... I'm going to be really honest, this one might just fucking do me in for real, Miles."

I put my hand over my heart, feeling the fast paced beat through my shirt. "And I don't quite know what to do with that. I don't know what to do with the love I feel for you, and the love I have for him because it's there, both of those things. I went from not feeling a fucking thing to feeling everything and it's all because you fucking smiled at me like you liked me in that bar, and then you smiled at me like you loved me in my kitchen and now... I'm in this so fucking deep and-"

His lips are on mine and he's breathing back the breath I was losing. He's giving me back the life I hadn't been living.

His hands have my heart, and mine his. And it doesn't matter that there's a fully formed shadow of the hands that have held my heart since I was fifteen resting next to Miles's very real, living ones—caging them in, encasing his hands and my heart. It doesn't affect either of us as we lay the other down in one way or the other, exposing ourselves in more ways than just our skin.

"I love you," I give him.

"My love," he takes, "I love you so much."

"How do you do it?" I ask Miles as I snuggle into him.

"Do what?" His voice is that calm, sleepy, rasp now.

I don't sit up to look at him, not really wanting to if I'm being honest. There's something odd about being on the other side of this—being the one to ask the questions.

"How are you so okay with Aster and me?"

Because there is an Aster and me.

"With the way I am-"

"The way you are?"

I sit up now, turning myself to face him as he sits up and leans back on my headboard.

Gosh, he's handsome. All disheveled, his hair a mess from my hands running through it. His scruff is a little longer than normal tonight and I debate on asking him to just grow it out for a few days. His eyes are bright, even in my dimly lit room.

"You know..." I shrug. "I'm like, therapy-girl."

He smothers a smile and runs his hand over his jaw. "Therapy Girl? Like a superhero? Seems fitting, actually."

I roll my eyes. "Therapy-girl, like the girl who's dependent on her therapist and going twice a week because I can't manage shit on my own."

"Whoa, first, Mark sounds like he's the kind of guy who wouldn't love hearing you say you think you're dependent on counseling. Maybe mention that and see what he thinks."

Not the point.

"Second, you are not unable to manage shit on your own, Briar. Are you asking why it doesn't bother me to ask about Aster or listen to you talk about him?"

I nod, chewing on my thumb.

"Alright well, it's easy. He's a part of you."

And then he shrugs. He just *shrugs* like he told me it's sunny outside. And I don't know if he knows that actually what he said to me is essentially the equivalence to decoding the Voynich Manuscript.

"What?"

Miles reaches out, taking both of my hands in both of his. How there's room there next to where he's holding my heart... I'm not sure.

"Briar, I know what he is to you. What he was and will always be. You have loved him for half of your life. I didn't have to be there to know that. I saw it in the way you hated the idea of letting me in when we first met. I didn't question it when you peaced-out—it makes more sense now."

I wince an apology.

"Fuck, seeing you on the anniversary of his death... Baby, you might as well have ripped my heart clean out of my chest—it would have hurt less. No one is devastated the way you were because of someone who isn't everything to them. And I can't fault you for that. He didn't leave you in a way that can make a man in my position hate him. I don't hate him. I'm sad for him and I'm sad for you. And maybe I ask about him like I do because I feel a little guilty..."

Miles shrugs, grabbing the back of his neck and looking away for a moment. "Like, I get to be here—with you, right? I get to hold your hand, and I get to see how you are after you get out of the shower, and when you just wake up, and how fast you can eat a fucking burrito. He'll never do those things with you again and honestly, that makes me so fucking sad for him."

And it does, I can see it in his eyes as he looks into mine. I squeeze his hand.

"But then... I feel like an ass hole because it makes me so happy for me. And how can I be so selfish like that? So, I guess maybe I ask about him to keep him here. To let him have a piece of you still and to hope that will maybe absolve me of some guilt or something. I don't really know. I just know that because he *is* important to you, he's important to me."

His eyes bore into mine. "Aster's dying isn't anything that is ever going to be something that I can remedy or resolve or fix or replace for you, Briar. And I know that. But I also know that I can be your best friend and partner that's *here*. I choose to be that. To be the one that asks about the first one—the one before me. I want to know how you loved him—how he loved you."

Miles pauses and smiles at me. It's a mix of sad and happy, this smile. But isn't that just kind of the definition of life at this point?

"I want your joy and sorrow, your therapy-girl and Sunday-drives, to be the one that helps you through the bad and gets to be there for the good. I didn't say I love you in the terms of short, Briar. I love you in the way of forever. I see it all with you."

I get up onto my knees and straddle his lap, putting my hands on his scruffy cheeks.

"You see it all?" I ask quietly.

I saw it all once with Aster. The marriage and the house and the kids and the jobs and the vacations and the Christmases. The life. We all see how that went, though...

Miles nods, his hands resting firmly on my hips. He's in just a pair of boxers and I've got on one of his shirts and a pair of, and don't judge me here, incredibly comfortable granny-panties. His thumb plays with the hem by the crease of my thigh, and he hums in answer.

"I do see it all with you, mo chroí. Long haul, end game, life. I can see it all. In time of course, zero rush. I love you."

I nod empathetically, "Zero rush, for sure. I'm a wreck. And I love you too, mo mhuirnín."

"Not because you're a wreck," he laughs. "Okay, well kind of because you're a wreck and I don't need to scare you off."

I rub my nose on his slowly before kissing him softly.

"Do you think we will ever lay in bed together and I won't bring up my deceased ex and cry to you?"

He laughs into my neck. "Honestly, I don't know that I mind either way, my love."

thirty-four

"And I don't know what can be done. Catching up with you is like trying to touch the sun." —Charles Wesley Godwin 'West of Lonesome'

I HAVEN'T BEEN THIS nervous to step foot into the Briggs' home since I lost my virginity and thought for sure that Fiona and Levi would be able to just like, *know.*

They didn't. They had no clue. But I was a wreck. I was all sweaty and had a fast pulse and nervous babbling. Aster eventually just hauled me over his shoulder, carrying me inside.

I was mortified.

"You ready, mo chroí? Or we can stay out here a bit longer? Whatever you need, Briar." Miles brings my hand up to his lips.

I smile softly at him, thankful for him extra today.

Fiona asked us to come over for lunch. Levi wanted to grill for us. I wanted to say no because stepping foot in this house, seeing Aster's dad, hearing the voice they essentially shared...

271

I genuinely might be sick.

"His voice is the same."

"What was that, Bri?"

I turn to look at Miles, trying to not look like I might vomit before we even step foot off of the curb in front of this house.

"Levi, Aster's dad... He sounds just like Aster did. Like, in a super kind of weird way actually. It was wild when it happened, the voice changing thing. Aster's voice was already like, post-puberty or whatever when they moved here. But then like, six months into our sophomore year, he woke up and just sounded like his dad. Exactly like his dad. I called their house one morning before school and Aster answered and I was all 'hey, Levi. Can I talk to your son?' and he was all 'haha very funny, babe' and I was like 'ew, levi, gross' and then when we got to school, and I saw Aster and he said 'hey' I about had a stroke right there in the hallway because he sounded just like his dad. It was wild. And I haven't heard that voice in over a year now. Longer, really. Aster didn't sound like Aster that last day..."

See, nervous babbling.

Miles is holding back a smile at my rambling and probably the story too, which—fair. I look from him to the front door and feel my eyes burn as I spot Levi and Fiona standing in the doorway waiting for us, hand in hand.

They're all blue jeans, crisp T-shirts, shiny hair, bright eyes, sad smiles.

Miles squeezes my hand and I take a deep breath.

"I cry too much these days," I say more to myself.

"It sounds like you're catching up on crying, actually," Miles says as we take a step forward.

We make our way up the sidewalk, and I can tell that Fiona is having to keep Levi from swooping down to meet us. It hurts my heart that we are where we are but I'm grateful for the effort to ease me back in.

"Briar, honey," Fiona says as we get to the door. "And you must be Miles."

I am going to lose it. The way she looks from my eyes to his eyes, to our joined hands, back to his eyes and then smiles...

"Yes, ma'am. It's nice to meet you." He lets go of my hand to shake hers, and I instantly want his back. He turns his attention to Levi. "Mr. Briggs, sir." Miles extends the same hand to him, and I swear... Levi looks like he might be sick too.

Aster took after Fiona in the looks department. Levi has short brown hair and brown eyes. I've never seen a single strand of facial hair on the man in the almost fifteen years I've known them. He's six-foot and has broad shoulders and is muscly but like, not muscly-muscly. Very quarterback-esque? Handsome. And kind.

Usually...

Miles leaves his hand extended, and I feel offended for him. So much so that I open my mouth to say something but then Levi is grabbing Miles by the hand and pulling him to him, hugging him. Everyone is quiet, unmoving.

Miles has a pan of brownies I made this morning in the crook of his other arm and the hug lasts long enough that eventually Fiona quietly takes the pan from him, smiling softly at me and nodding her head towards the living room, leading me inside.

I look back at Levi and Miles as we walk towards the back of the house, headed to the backyard. Levi is still hugging him... tightly. Miles has both arms around him now, holding him back. I think I see Levi's shoulders shaking a bit and it's then that I stop and realize where exactly I am.

I'm in *his* home. I'm in his living room. I'm by the couch that we used to lay on together.

I'm standing literally in a spot where he hugged me on several occasions.

Over there, by the stairs, that's a spot that I used to love to stand and be kissed on, made me feel very Cinderella-y.

There, on the wall, is a picture of us at our high school graduation.

By the door I just walked through for the first time in well over a year, on the same rug they've had since I was sixteen, is a pair of brown Vans. Size elevens. Ten years old.

I know because I bought them for Aster for Christmas one year and they've been there, in that same spot, since we broke up.

I look to the stairs, taking a breath, and walk over to them. I look back once more. Levi has Miles by the shoulders now and he's saying something to him, and Miles is just watching and listening, and I love him so much in this moment. Fiona went to the kitchen after walking in here.

I slowly walk up the stairs, running my fingers along the wooden banister as I go.

You know how wood is absorbent? Water and smells—it can soak them in. I wonder what the wood of this house has absorbed over the years that the Briggs have been here.

Does this banister hold the smell of Aster's hands after a day of holding mine?

Do these walls house the scent of us holding each other, nothing between us but love?

Do these floors still know the sound of his steps as he would walk me in the dark to my car well after midnight?

I push the door to his bedroom open slowly, closing my eyes. They could have made it into a crafting room—sewing or beer? Maybe it's all dust and cobwebs from months of neglect and anguish. Perhaps when I open my eyes, the ghost of Aster will be staring back at me, room empty, wide hollow eyes.

I take a deep breath, leaving the door open and stepping inside. It feels warm, this room. It has always felt warm but that was always just Aster.

He was the sun—bright and good and always whole.

I was the moon—ever changing and a bit dark, always missing him.

My eyes are still closed, my hands resting on my chest.

"I miss you," I whisper.

I open my eyes on the count of three, trying to be brave like I know he would want me to be.

It's him—this room. His room... It's still his. His bed is the same. The same dresser and photos and random trinkets. I haven't stepped further than one foot in and I'm shaking, tears falling from my eyes. I move to his dresser, picking up a pack of gum. His favorite—Trident peppermint. I put it back exactly where it was. Fiona must come in here to dust, not a speck to be seen. I run my finger over a photo of Aster and I from right before we broke up, pressing my other hand to my lips to silence my crying.

"I miss you," I whisper again, this time coming out a little choppier.

I move to his bed. I loved this bed. We spent so much time in this bed. For various reasons. The majority, truly, was spent fully clothed and just together.

We would turn on the radio he had on the floor at the end of his bed, open the curtains to the massive window that his bed sits against, and then we would just curl up together and exist. He would run his fingers through my hair, and I would draw different shapes with mine on his stomach, watching his muscles flex every so often.

I can see us here now—seventeen-year-old-us. Young and in love and dreaming of the forever they would never see.

I give myself a few minutes here, with him in his room. I pick up his pillow and I hold it up to my face, smelling it and not feeling like the weirdo I thought I would.

I don't hold it for long, not wanting to take away from the smell of him. It's already so faded, I can tell. And that realization crushes me. It's faded so much in a year? What will it smell like in another year? Or a decade? Will anything be reminiscent of Aster by then?

Once I've stopped sobbing, having skipped makeup altogether today for this reason, I make my way back to his open door and pause, looking back at the picture of us. I don't have anything at my house of us. I kept it all in boxes in my parents' basement when I moved back, and I haven't touched it since.

I walk back over, picking the frame up and touching his young face, smiling softly at the boy I fell in love with.

"Can I take this home with me?" I ask gently from behind Fiona in the kitchen.

She turns around, looking at the picture. Her smile is soft and sad, her eyes meeting mine.

"I wish you would, sweet Briar."

I nod, setting it on the counter for now. I look around. "Where did Levi and Miles go?"

"They're out back. I was waiting in here for you. You alright?"

I nod, holding back tears as my chin wobbles. Having been given away though, I opt for honesty and shake my head. She opens her arms and I walk right into them. We hold each other, grieving.

Grieving, I think to myself. *I'm grieving.*

It dawns on me then that I am. That I am finally in Aster's home, speaking to his parents again, speaking to *him* again, letting myself miss him and love him and hate him out loud.

Took me long enough...

But there isn't a timeline on grief. There isn't a playbook or an instruction manual. There aren't rules and regulations. There isn't someone telling you what to do next and how to do it. Sure, there are books that might help, guides and things that give generalized directions on what route to maybe take.

But there is no one set way to deal with loss.

And so what, it's taken me over a year to deal with the loss of Aster?

It took me longer than that to love him how I do. A second to fall in love, yes. Years to love him so irrevocably, though.

I don't think he would want me to be focusing on the has been.

Just everything that comes next...

Fiona and I make our way to the back porch. It's well past when we had decided to eat, an hour at least. What with me stalling at the curb, Miles and Levi having their moment, me and Aster having ours... I still haven't even spoken to Levi yet and the thought makes my stomach sink.

"Is he angry with me?" I whisper to Fiona as we step outside.

She looks at me confused. "Levi?" I nod. "Honey, no! Never. No." She squeezes my hand before walking ahead of me to the table of food.

Miles spots me from where he's standing by Levi at the grill. He smiles at me and winks, asking me without asking me if I'm alright. I smile back and nod my head once. His shoulders relax ever so slightly with relief, and I love him for it.

Levi notices where his attention went and looks to me, his eyes lighting up a bit. I wave like a dork, like I haven't known this man for fifteen years, like he hasn't seen me grow up practically. Best and worst days, he was there.

He motions to Miles to watch the grill before making his way over to me.

"Briar, my Briar. Hi."

He stops a few feet away, hands in his pants pockets.

"Hi," I say, trying to keep it together for longer than thirty seconds.

"Can we take a walk, you and me?"

He nods his chin to the gate that leads to the front of the house, the sidewalk. I nod and we mosey on out.

"Miles seems great."

"I'm sorry I wasn't here."

We laugh after we both talk at the same time, some of the awkwardness leaving. Levi bends his elbow, giving me his arm. He knows this is one of my favorite ways to walk with someone, and my heart melts.

"You sound like him," I say after looping my arm with his.

"Yes, I do. I'm sure that's very hard."

I shake my head, tears lining my eyes. "It's not. Not as much as I thought it was going to be."

And it isn't. It is—but it isn't. I can't explain it very well, I don't think—this part of missing him.

Hearing Aster in Levi is like... It's like your favorite blanket that you hardly ever wash which is probably kind of gross, but that's beside the point. It's soft in the right spots, smells just so, feels familiar in a way that nothing else does. But then your mom washes it because you had the flu and obviously—germs. And like, that's fine, it needed it. So, it's okay that it's clean now. It's still your favorite blanket. It still smells good, and it still feels soft, and it's still familiar. But it's not the same. It won't be the same. There isn't anything that can or needs to be done about it.

It is what it is.

"We miss you. I miss you, kiddo."

"I miss you too. I'm sorry. I hate myself for being so absent. I can't imagine how angry Aster would be at me for leaving you and Fiona alone like that. But I just..."

"He would understand. Just like we do." He squeezes my arm with his. "You'll come around now, though? Yeah?"

His voice cracks slightly and with it so does my heart.

"You'll never get rid of me. Told you that when I was a teenager. Meant it then, mean it now." My chin quivers as I say it.

We pause as we make it back to the gate of their fence. Levi grabs my face in his hands, holding me and looking into my eyes.

"Whatever you need, Briar. We're here for you. Okay?" I nod. "I love you, kid."

"I love you too."

We laugh as tears escape our eyes and hug tightly before making our way to Miles and Fiona. I sit next to Miles, turning so my knee is leaning into his leg, needing to feel him without being all over him. He puts his hand on my knee, smiling at me.

"Alright, mo chroí?" he whispers softly.

I nod, leaning in to kiss his cheek.

"Alright, mo mhuirnín."

thirty-five

"I miss the memories we'll never have." —Ranata Suzuki

MARK AND I DECIDED on Monday that it would be kind of cool to have Miles come with me on Thursday to my therapy session.

So, on Thursday, Mark and Miles then convinced me, without much argument, that a lunch with both my family, Catt, and Aster's family would be a nice idea. A good place to tell them about those final moments with Aster.

They both, and admittedly I, think that those last few moments, those last words and choices we made, are quite important. To me, they are important. And apparently that's all that matters.

They weigh on me. Heavily, if I'm being honest.

I always imagined Aster proposing to me. It would be when we were around twenty-five. We would be on a date, just like any other. It would be fall or spring because those are my favorite times of the year. The two of us would walk hand in hand to the little gazebo that needs a paint job in the middle of this park on the west side of town. He would start saying something sweet, which he did often, and I would smile at him and then watch the geese flit around the lake. He would go quiet, and it would take a minute or two to notice because I would be in my own little world. But then I would. And I would turn my head and he wouldn't be there anymore—not at my eye line anyway. He would chuckle and I would look down, see him on one knee holding a little box with a ring he picked out just for me. One that's perfect, that I hadn't had a single hand in, that he knew I would love endlessly because it's from him, and also because he knew me better than anyone ever had or would. I would start crying even though I wasn't a crier. And he would cry because he kind of was. And he would tell me how incredible I was, even though it was him that's incredible. And how much he loved me, but I loved him more than anyone has ever loved another person. And how wonderful our life would be, no argument on that one. He'd laugh at my gaping silence and then I'd notice the aforementioned gaping silence and rush out eighty-six thousand 'yes, oh my gosh, yes's'. He'd stand up and slide a bright, beautiful ring on my finger and then grab my face with both hands and kiss me like it's just the two of us in the entire universe. Because for us, it was. And then I'd hear his mom sobbing and my mom crying and my sister cheering. Our dads would be clapping, and Catt would be all snotty and excited.

But that's not how it happened. That isn't how Aster asked me to marry him. So, for the third or fourth time, after never even thinking I'd tell anyone this story, I prepare to tell our families.

We decided to have a Sunday supper at my house. I'm comfortable here. If I need to freak out or sob or break something, I can do so in and to my own shit.

Miles is grilling—summertime in the Midwest demands it. Everyone brought a side and a dessert, and it's all too much but it's also just enough. I hated asking Quinn not to, but she was really chill when I asked her to not bring Adelaide. So, it's just Levi, Fiona, my parents, Quinn, Catt, Miles, and me. I thought about having my Nebraska Siblings come over as well... But they didn't know Aster and I think I want them to hear it from me in our own time.

We're all sitting around a large folding table that my dad brought from their house. Everyone is eating, chatting, laughing. The sun is starting to set, turning the sky a million different kinds of reds, oranges, yellows.

Miles puts his hand on my knee as I tilt my head to the sky, taking a deep breath and clearing my throat.

"Can I talk to you all about something?"

Everyone quiets down. I feel it then—this calming breeze. And call it bull shit or fate or God or whatever you want... But I know it's *him*. It's Aster.

I square my shoulders—my nerves having been settled by the hand on my knee and the breeze on my neck.

"Mark, my therapist," like they all don't know who he is by now. "Thought that it would be a good idea if I shared something that happened between Aster and I with all of you." I swallow. "It's not anything like, super crazy. Nothing major-"

"Mo chroí," Miles whispers into my ear. "Don't take away from it."

I nod and smile softly at him. "Right. It is kind of big but not like, whatever. Okay. Um. So, Aster, on his last day..." I look to Levi and Fiona, wincing slightly and saying sorry. They hardly flinch, happy to be here with me—for me. "I was with him when he um, when he..." I shut my eyes tightly, unable to go on. "Oh fuck. Hang on."

I get up to take a minute. I walk inside of my house, going to my kitchen first and washing my hands, running cold water over my wrists.

Like, yes. What we said to each other was big. And I know that. But is it big enough for a formal conversation with our families? Are they going to care about it like I care about it? What if they think it's nothing, when to me... To me it was, and kind of is, fucking everything?

I walk to my room, pacing. I walk to my bathroom, telling myself to pull it together. I go to the living room and my eyes snag on the picture I took from his room a couple weeks ago. I don't go to it, though.

We have a standoff, twenty-year-old-us and I, a yard or so between us. I chew on my lip, tapping my foot on the floor. Taking a deep breath, I nod my head once and spin on my heel and head back outside.

"Aster asked me to marry him, and I said yes, and then he died."

Well, sure. That's one way to do it.

Both of our mom's gasp, their hands going to their mouths. My dad gets really sad, Levi doesn't look surprised at all. Catt starts crying and shaking her head. Quinn looks at Miles and he just nods.

I sit back down, feeling calmer now that I've said it out loud to them all.

"Okay, that was a bit aggressive. Sorry. Um, so. Questions?" I look around and everyone is all wide, teary eyes and sad, sorrowful faces.

Everyone except Miles. And Levi.

"You knew."

He nods. "He told me he was going to ask."

My dad kind of yells, okay totally yells, at Levi, "You didn't think to tell him that maybe that might end up hurting my kid in the end?"

Levi shakes his head at me when I open my mouth to defend him.

"Brian, my kid was dying," Levi says on a sigh. My dad looks regretful but still perturbed. "What did you want me to do? Tell him to not ask the girl he'd loved for a decade to marry him like he wanted to on the day he was dying?"

Everyone looks around a bit uncomfortably. I don't. I just watch Levi watch me.

"He loved you, Briar. More than anyone probably really understood or knew. And when he asked me for my opinion, I wasn't going to be the one to stand in his way. Cancer was doing that enough. I couldn't tell him that it would probably hurt you in the long run. I'm sorry, Briar. I am. I am so sorry."

I get up and walk to Levi, throwing my arms around his shoulders from behind him.

After a moment, Quinn asks, "So, what all happened?"

I move back around, sitting back down. Miles catches my hand as I go, though, and pulls me onto his lap.

"I'm too big for this, bud."

He rolls his eyes. "Tell your tale, my love."

I take a deep breath, holding on to Miles while he holds on to me. And then I tell our families about his final moments. From the second I walked into his hospital room to the moment I kissed him that final time.

Everyone is crying. Literally everyone. Miles is running the tip of his nose across my back lightly, sniffling every now and then, pressing soft kisses to my spine through my entire retelling. My mom is holding Fiona, and they are full on sobbing into one another. My dad is holding Quinn and Catt, one arm around each woman, all three of them crying in some varying degree. And Levi has his hand on his wife's back as he wipes tears from his face, his eyes never leaving mine.

It's an odd feeling, now knowing that I didn't walk this plane of existence being the only person to know what Aster and I had talked about in those final moments.

I've never been alone, it turns out. I had Levi in my corner this whole time, knowing and sad for me, probably a little upset for me at Aster. But I had no idea because I had closed myself off from so much.

Not anymore. I will no longer allow myself to walk through this alone. I won't suffer solo. And I won't make other's watch me do so. I won't force anyone else to have to grieve Aster without me and vice versa.

thirty-six

*"How lucky am I to have something that makes saying goodbye
so hard." —Winnie the Pooh*

THE SUMMER FLEW BY in a blink. Fall is here now and this weather is some of my favorite kind. It's all cloudy and dark, cool and a bit gray. Moody.

"You like moody-fall because you're moody-Briar,"

"That's what you told me once," I say to him.

Well, to his headstone.

ASTER LEVI BRIGGS

1994 – 2023

THE BEST SON

THE BEST FRIEND

I've been discussing coming here for months now with Mark. Ultimately, I decided I would come alone, after much debate. Miles was supportive and is waiting at home, a phone call away. I gave Fiona and Levi a heads up that I would be here today, and they said they would give me space. Otherwise, I think I would be looking over my shoulder the entire time I'm here, waiting to see if anyone else were to show up.

I trace the engraved bouquet of flowers on the cement stone.

Asters and sweetbriars.

Fiona told me yesterday that she had them put those on here. I smile at the ode to *us*.

I take a deep breath, pulling out the sealed envelope from my sweater pocket.

"Apparently you wrote this. Which I believe. You're quite dramatic like that." I sigh. "And your mom gave it to me earlier this year. Said to wait until I was ready to open it. That you knew I would be upset with you. She said I wasn't ready then. I told her yesterday that I'm ready now. But honestly... I don't know that I'll ever be ready, Aster."

My eyes burn and I look to the sky. It's quiet here. No traffic nearby, no one else is visiting any loved ones around Aster's grave. His little plot is nice. His stone is beautiful, the flowers his mom planted this spring and spruced up over the summer are perfect. Bright poppies.

"They make me smile," she said.

"I'm so fucking mad at you, Aster. I have noticed your absence every single day since the moment you left. It's in every breath I take. It's in every thought I have. It's in every song I can't listen to still. Every restaurant I can't go to because it was ours once upon a time. I can't eat Skittles anymore, did you know that? Because they were your favorite and if you can't enjoy them, how can I? And Adam Sandler movies?! Fucking forget about it. Can't hear his laugh without hearing you trying to mimic it horribly."

I choke out a laugh at that.

It was really bad.

"I miss you every second of every day. Someday I will have missed you for as long as I got to be loved by you... Do you know how unfair that is? And do you know how selfish I feel for finding that unfair? Because how lucky am I at all to have ever been loved by someone so wonderfully beautiful like you, Aster..."

I wipe the snot from my nose with the sleeve of my sweater, forgoing breaking the moment with a pack of tissues. I sit in silence for a few minutes, soaking it in—the moments before. Before I read his parting words.

Before I have this last piece of him that he's giving to me.

"We chose each other when it mattered most though, didn't we?"

That's what gets me the hardest sometimes. The Absent Years. The years we didn't have because I wasn't here, and he wasn't there.

"Gun to our heads, we chose each other. Cancer in your body, death knocking at the door, we chose each other in those last minutes. In the moment it mattered the most, I think."

I slide my finger through the tiny hole in the envelope, opening it. It's notebook paper. Like proper, eight by ten, college ruled, lined notebook paper. Front and back.

His handwriting. Handwriting that I have seen hundreds of times in my life. Handwriting that I never thought would mean so much to me to see again for the first time. I take a deep breath and I read through the tears.

My dearest, sweetest Briar,

Fifteen-year-old me would've been pretty annoyed at the amount of people that call you that by now, but cancer-ridden me is pretty happy with it. I love that the name I called you might be something that someone you love calls you for the rest of your life. Even if I won't be the one to do it.

I'd like to start this by telling you that you might need a Kleenex or two for this letter. I hate making you cry. It's one of my least favorite things to do, but I think this one might be inevitable, love.

I know that my dying—it's going to reshape you. Not to toot my own horn or anything, but I think that it will move the pieces of you around a bit, losing me. You'll still be you, of that I am certain. But you won't be the you that you were before my death. And I want you to know, if no one has told you yet, I love both versions.

If I could go back in time, keys to the DeLorean in hand, I wouldn't go back to the moment in your apartment where we ended things. And don't scoff like that, **we** did end things. I would go back to that following year.

I would have given you that year. I would have been the better man for that amount of time and then I would have gone back in time, said fuck it, and made you come home or let me make home wherever you wanted it to be.

You were my home, Briar.

I need you to know that. And believe it. I know you're going to be mad. I understand why. You're going to hate me for all of this. And it was selfish of me. It had nothing to do with you—not having you here sooner. It was me. I couldn't watch you see me like this. Not long term. I wanted to leave remembering the way you used to look at me. The way you looked up at me. With nothing but love and fire. I didn't want to see the sorrow and disease reflecting in your eyes that I know will be there the second you see me in this bed.

So, I made the choice to keep you out of it. I hated the choice, know that. I hate myself for doing it. But I'm selfish now, apparently. I should have been then, when we were twenty-one. Guess I'm seizing the opportunity to do that now, though.

Don't be mad at everyone else for very long, okay? They hate me for this. Not a single one of them is happy with me. And imagine how that makes them feel—being upset with the dying guy?

Can't say I feel great either.

But I take solace in the fact that you're probably happy right at this very moment that I'm writing this. Your happiness, Briar—that's what I'm doing this all for. Hiding this all for. It's always been for you. I don't mean to put any of this on you. It's all been my choice. My choice for you... Which probably isn't fair... The space and the time apart. I'd take it back now because dying makes you not really care about other people in a way that not dying would, in turn making you care about them in a way you wouldn't otherwise as well. I don't know if that makes sense but I'm writing this in pen, so it's staying. But, I'm not sorry for any of it other than the pain it's all going to cause you.

And I know there will be pain. You feel everything so much. You hide so much of it. But never from me. And I know you won't know where to put it all, what to do with it all. So, I'm sure it's probably well over a year from my death that you're even opening this.

And. I'm. Not. Mad.

Not at you. Never at you. Remember that moving forward.

Catt's calling you tomorrow to bring you home. My dad and I have talked a lot in the last few weeks. He knows you well, like a daughter, he said. And he knows that it will be a bit before you can look at any of them again without feeling so much anger. I'm sorry for that, Briar. But no one will blame you. He told me that, I knew that but needed to hear him say it, I think. No one will be upset with you for being mad at us. What we are doing, did, by keeping this from you...

We understand and we love you. We love you today. We will love you tomorrow. And we will love you when you want us to show you that again.

I wish I could change it all. I wish I could go back in time and just be with you. I wish I didn't get sick.

And I wish that when I see you next, when I tell you I love you for the last time, ask you to marry me, hold you as tightly as I can...

I wish that all of what will make my final moments full of love and life... weren't the same moments that will break your heart and ruin the next bit of yours.

I love you, my sweet Briar. Every second of every day, I love you.

Forever yours, eternally sorry, always in love,

A.L.B.

I picture his heart-shaped face, tan and forever young. His dirty blonde hair, longer than his mom ever preferred it but just how I always loved it. His eyes—like my favorite storm. Gray and always waiting for me. And his smile... bright and wide and warm.

"You are my sun," I whisper to him. "And I will love you like I believe the moon loves the sun—irrevocably and until the end of time."

I reach for a tissue, remembering I put some in my pocket. My fingers grab onto a piece of paper I didn't know was in there.

YOU ARE SO LOVED, BRIAR.

—M.

"He's good," I tell Aster. "How lucky am I to love two great suns in my lifetime."

I press my fingers to my lips, kissing them, and then pressing those to the bouquet of flowers on Aster's stone.

"Forever would have been wonderful. Save me a dance up there, yeah? I love you."

thirty-seven

"Give yourself grace as you grow through grief. Be patient with your pain." —Alex Elle

One Year Later

"CLIFFS OF MOHER." *He swallows hard and looks to where his hand now rests on mine before bringing his eyes back to mine. "He tells her, his best friend and favorite person in the world, his other half... that he doesn't want to be* just *her best friend anymore."*

I feel time stop. Like this moment will be suspended, frozen, put on paper and forever remembered.

"He doesn't?"

"No, he doesn't. He can't. Not anymore. Not after he realized just how special she is."

"And what caused that realization?"

"Her laugh." He says it so simply. So factually.

"Her laugh?" I ask with a giggle of my own.

I have zero idea of where this is going at this point. All I do know is that if his hand leaves mine any time soon, I might very well die. Right here, in this Jeep.

"A kid in class told a joke that wasn't at all funny. This kid is bad at jokes, he doesn't tell them well. But he tries and he's nice. A little weird, and the other kids make fun of him. But she doesn't. She smiles at him and talks to him and asks about his bearded dragon and she laughs at his bad jokes every day. She sees him and notices him. And when she laughed at this particularly poorly executed joke..." His eyes go wide like he just realized what he did. What he said.

Henry... He is talking about Henry. And me. Aster is talking about my odd, little pal Henry and how bad his jokes are and how I like him anyways because he's a goober and he's nice and the kids in our school aren't.

"So, what does he do after he tells her how special he thinks she is?" I whisper.

I don't know how I am still breathing but here I am, inhaling his words and everything that he is.

"I don't want to just be your friend anymore." Aster's voice is soft but sure, this hypothetical vacationing couple no longer existing. "I like you. A lot. I like your laugh and how you give it freely to those that you love, those that have earned that part of you. I like your smile and how it's constant but also not. I like how smart you are and how you always help me figure shit out without making me feel stupid. I like you, Briar. A lot. And I'll stay just your friend, if you want. But I... I'd like to be way more than that. If you want."

"I want." It comes out immediately, on the very last letter of his declaration.

His whole face lights up at my rushed admission.

"You do?"

"Badly, Aster. I love being your friend. But more *sounds like it could be really fun too."*

"The Cliffs of Moher," I whisper to myself, to *him*, as I look out over them.

It's wet and cold here, in Ireland. Especially in April. Did you know?

I did. I researched this trip at least once a year since the day Aster and I became *Aster and I.* So, when Miles asked if I wanted to go with him on a family trip to his grandparents' old home... I practically jumped at the opportunity.

"What was that, my love?"

I look over to the man I love. The same man I get to see every morning and night at home now.

Our home. Miles moved in at the end of the first year we were together. We love our house, no plans to leave it. We want one kid eventually and our house has one spare room. So really, we're quite set there.

"I love you," I tell him as he wraps his arms around me from behind.

He's so handsome, my Miles. His dark hair is a bit shaggy right now, his beard hanging a couple inches off his face. His dark gray pullover has little spots of darker gray from the mist, his dark jeans wet at the cuffs over his boots.

I look down at my feet next to his. My laced-up boots, tall white socks, black leggings, white hoodie. It's all very much giving "tourist" I am sure. But what probably gives me away is the absolutely frizzy disaster of hair pulled back in a bright green claw-clip.

"Is tú mo ghrá." He kisses the back of my head, a pro at dodging clips by now, before backing away.

I'm sure he's making his way to where his family is waiting. We got here an hour or so ago and are set to leave soon. I take a few more minutes to soak in the site.

"Made it to Ireland," I say in my mind. "Only took over fifteen years. But I'm here. I miss you."

Home life has been good. I see Mark once a week now. Lately we've been discussing how well things are going with my siblings, all four of them, and myself. I haven't spoken to Jack since last year—zero regrets there from either party, so it seems. I see my brother and sisters on Jack's side as often as we can all make it happen. My little niece is perfection incarnate and I think I was made to be an auntie. Quinn comes with sometimes, everyone getting along well.

We have Sunday Suppers at my parents' house every other week now instead of every Thursday at *The Blue's*. And it no longer is just the Davies family. Aster's parents come every Sunday. Adelaide and Quinn are going strong, so she joins us as well. It's become my favorite two or three days of the month. Which is saying something because this time last year, I dreaded Thursdays.

Miles and I have supper with his parents once a week, our house or theirs, every Friday. Which I also love. There is something so comforting about Freya. Being near her is always so cozy and easy. And Declan is the funniest guy I have ever met—next to his son, of course.

I go visit Aster's gravesite once or twice a month. Sometimes I go and sit and tell him about my day, or Miles. Occasionally I cry to him about how much I miss him. Every now and then I'll have a day where I feel so mad at him that I could just scream. So, I do. I stand in front of his headstone, and I yell at him. I wave my hands around the maniac I am sure to look like and I tell him how angry I am still that he left the way he did.

A few times Miles has come with me. He'll sit down next to me, holding my hand. He'll talk to Aster, telling him stories about me from that day or sometime recently that Aster would probably find funny. Every time, I fall in love with him more and more.

I smile at the thought of the last time Miles went with me, a week or so ago. He told Aster all about how I burned a batch of chocolate chip cookies which I have most certainly never done before. I was so mortified and upset with myself. Almost decades of making the best chocolate chip cookies in my family and I burn the first batch I make for Freya?

And Freya and Declan were already at our house. So I couldn't even play it off and whip up another batch.

I wanted to hide in my room and pout.

But no. Miles wouldn't allow it. He ate half a dozen of my burnt cookies just to prove that they were edible—*they weren't.*

Aster would have really loved Miles.

I take a deep breath and turn around to find Miles and his family.

My hands go to my mouth, my knees almost go to the wet earth.

"Mo chroí." Miles smiles at me. He looks a little nervous and a lot excited. "Could you take a couple steps closer, babe?" He whispers it, gesturing to the distance between us. I laugh, obliging him. "Thank you."

He clears his throat. "We are in no rush, you and me. Never have been. It's one of my favorite things about us. We just exist with each other and live as we go, no rules or timeline or frame. You're my favorite person on this planet. Everything about you is my favorite way it's done. How you brush your teeth—no one does it better. The way you sing in the shower—best concerts I'll ever go to. Your lasagna—still better than my mom's. And honestly, with how much she loves you... she might not hate knowing that."

I laugh and so does Freya from somewhere in my peripheral.

"Briar, you once told me that you think you're the moon and we are the sun... I say *we* here because I think it's important that you know we probably both feel this way... There is no moon without the sun, my love. I cannot shine without you. I uh," he rubs a hand over the back of his neck. "I went to visit Levi and Fiona a few weeks ago, asking them their thoughts about all of this. Fiona cried, as she does. Levi and I, we uh... well, we took a drive. We went to see Aster."

"What?" My eyes are big, and my heart is bursting at its seams.

"It's never been a secret that your heart holds space for the both of us. I've never found it to be daunting or tiresome. Not everyone will understand how you can love the boy you loved first and also love me... But I do. And that's all that matters. I don't doubt your love for me. I don't doubt the amount and weight it holds. I don't doubt my importance to you."

I track a tear as it makes its way down his cheek. "You show me every day where I sit in your life—where you hold me in your heart. I'm so lucky to be loved so well by you. And after talking with Levi, hearing that he gets it too, I think Aster would as well. And while that isn't the driving factor here, I won't lie when I tell you that it does make me feel less guilty for getting to keep you knowing that he's probably here, right now, cheering us on."

It's in the wind, the mist, the way the sound of the waves below sing a bit through the air—he's here. It's him. I can feel it. In my bones, in my heart, in my soul. I can feel the happiness he has for us, for me.

"How lucky I am to be loved so well."

He flashes me my favorite smile in the world.

"Marry me, mo chroí."

"Oh, mo mhuirnín. In a literal heartbeat."

He jumps up, his one knee soaked through, and lunges at me. We fall to the ground in a heap, not caring about the moisture at all. Soaking it all in, really.

I take it all in, then. I stare up at my fiancé, his bright eyes and wide smile. I hear his family cheer and laugh, then soon I hear my family, all of them, over someone's cell phone whooping and hollering for us.

Joy.

That's what this is. It's joy. It's something I never thought I would feel again. Not truly.

"Feeling alright?" Miles asks me, still on top of me on the soft ground of Ireland.

"Feeling everything," I say, happy and loved, smiling.

<h1 style="text-align:center">epilogue</h1>

"And now that you don't have to be perfect, you can be good."
—John Steinbeck

Ten Years Later

I PIPE ORANGE FROSTING, the finishing touches, onto this white cake, smiling down at it.

"Beautiful job, mo chroí," Miles says, wrapping his arms around my waist and kissing my cheek.

"Think he'll like it?"

"Oh, he'll love it." Miles swipes his finger through some of the frosting in the bowl next to the cake. "Everyone's outside ready to sing when you're ready."

I step back, wiping my hands off on a towel. We've been in this house for six years now and it's still one of my favorite parts of it—the backyard parties we can have. Everyone is here. My parents, Aster's parents, Miles's parents. Quinn, her wife Lina, their twin daughters. Catt and Garrett, their nine-year-old daughter. Kyle and Nicole and all five of their kids. Christine and her husband, along with Mad's the forever and happy-to-be third-wheel. Aside from the Nebraska clan, we have the rest over here weekly for Sunday Suppers. My siblings and their families drive up from Chadron for birthdays and big games for the boys. We go that way too for what we can for their kids.

A lot of give and take. All of us are happy to do it.

I feel Aster's absence still. Especially on days like today when we are all together, when his dad is here laughing their laugh. Not as prominently as I used to, no. But sometimes I'll watch my kids eat their Skittles from Halloween, or we'll watch *Big Daddy*, and I'll miss him a little extra in those moments.

Today we're celebrating our oldest son, Declan. It's his eighth birthday.

"Can you believe our first baby is eight, Miles?"

He looks at me from the sliding glass door to the backyard. "Not at all. It's wild. Let's go sing to him, yeah?"

And so we do. Everyone does it loudly and proudly, making my sweet boy blush and smile. Declan looks just like his dad. All tall, long legs, broad frame. Thick, dark hair. The brightest, bluest, eyes. He's got his mama's pale skin, poor kid. The handsomest boy.

Neck and neck with my sweet baby Miles, of course. Six and a perfect mix of both his mom and dad. Dark hair, tan skin, tall and broad, brown eyes.

"We made good looking kids, eh?" I say to Miles, his arm around my shoulders as we watch our kids play with their cousins on a bouncy water slide.

"Hell yes, we did." He kisses the top of my head. "Should have made a whole football team of them. Missed our chance."

I laugh and roll my eyes, sitting down next to Catt and Fiona.

"Sweet Briar, great party. How are the boys liking school?"

"Thanks, Fi. Good I think, only the second week back."

"Mom!"

I turn as Declan rushes up to us. "Yeah, bud?"

"School," he pants like he doesn't run everywhere he goes. "Project."

"More words, please."

"Okay," he holds up a finger. "Okay. School project." Declan sits down next to his dad and grandad Declan on the other side of the table. "We're doing this family tree project at school. There's a question about if we're named after someone."

Everyone within hearing distance pauses what they're doing.

"Granny Fi always gets kind of, what do you call it? Mushy?"

We all laugh, I nod and put my arm around Fiona.

"Anyways. Granny gets kind of mushy when she says my full name and I was wondering if that's what that question means. 'Cause I'm named after her son."

I smile at my son—*Declan Aster Davies O'Brien.*

It was Miles's idea. I was about twenty weeks pregnant with Dec. We were lying in bed—all of my most favorite conversations have happened while lying in bed with my husband.

"Question," Miles says.

"Answer," I reply sarcastically.

He flicks my nose before going back to rubbing circles on my growing bump.

"A boy."

"Correct."

"Do we have a name picked out?"

I laugh at his question. "Like you wouldn't know if we did. No. We don't. I was thinking after our dads somehow, though."

He nods his head. After a moment of thought he says, kind of quietly, "Declan Aster Davies."

I sit up, far slower than I would like to be able to, and face him. "What?"

"I just feel like it would be cool."

He shrugs his shoulders like he didn't just suggest naming our son after my deceased first love.

As though that isn't incredibly kind and gracious and wonderfully thoughtful.

"Are you-"

"The Briggs are important to both of us, Briar. Hell, Levi might be one of my best friends, honestly. It's as much for me as it is for you. Well, maybe not as much. But-"

And then I was on him like I couldn't last another second without him on me.

And that was how we ended up with Declan Aster Davies. We also have a Miles Quinn Levi.

I smile and nod at Declan, answering his question. "Yes, my very best friend for a really long time. His name was Aster." My eyes burn slightly.

"Will you tell me about him?" Declan's eyes are lit up with excitement.

Miles reaches over the table, his hand taking one of mine. Fiona has the other.

I nod my head, one tear falling down my cheek.

"I would love to tell you about Aster."

Acknowledgements

Always first... To my husband. You never make me feel like a weirdo for this whole "writing a book, or three" thing. Thank you. I know it's not your schtick... But you love it for me anyways. And I love you.

My babies, the reasons I try every day to work through the shit I need to work through. Every day I want to be better for you. How lucky am I to get to be your mom... I love you both endlessly.

To Bailey the barista at Starbucks for asking me if I was writing another book when I started this one. That made me feel fucking cool and I honestly won't ever forget that.

To Rachael at the 'Bees. Even if you don't go to Seattle and meet some man with a little hat named Marco or whatever name we came up with, that reads poetry and loves espresso... I'll forgive you. I'll miss seeing you when you do leave and follow your dreams. I'm damn proud of you though. Thanks for all of the hype these last few weeks.

To Matthew Vaughn. I like adjectives, dude—deal.

To my friends and family, including the bookish family I've made through all of this, that hyped me up over another book... I know, I know. It seems very cool. And it is. But also, I don't have much else going on so... Do with that what you will.

To ABH for being the busiest person I know but still making time to tell me to "pull it together" and check out my cover ideas and throw input in on blurbs and things. I'd still be lost without you, please don't think otherwise.

Jenah... My alpha, the alpha. Thank you for telling me this book didn't suck when I was halfway through. I was shaking in my Birks while I waited on your thoughts and even though you're fairly easy to please... I appreciate you and your time and your opinions, and most importantly... you.

My betas—Emily, Cassie, Jenn, Samantha, Dora, Steph, Chelsea, Lena, and Amber... I love you. Truly and genuinely. Thank you for your time and effort and thoughts.

To my ARC readers—I appreciate you and your time and opinions and taking a chance on Briar and her story. You're so valuable to me.

And to you, the reader—If you found any single sentence in here anywhere near relatable... That was the goal. I see you. You're good. You're worthy. You're loved. Keep on keepin' on, babe.

xoxo,

A. L. Fox

About The Author

A. L. Fox is an indie author, though she feels weird calling herself the "a" word. She spends her days with her two small children and her farmer husband. She enjoys 70 degree weather and rain, Starbucks and Target, and laughing. A. L. Fox was born and raised in the Midwest and likes to think her writing will reach who it needs to. She plans to continue to create but has no real, big goals while doing so. She's thankful everyday for the chance to do this whole *thing*.

Her main goal: *bring joy to others.*

I WISH.

Though... I suppose this one was more to make you—*me*, feel seen... So...

Also by

I'll Never Be.
And Then I Saw You.

www.ingramcontent.com/pod-product-compliance
Lightning Source LLC
Chambersburg PA
CBHW031443160726
47994CB00005B/1846